Sea

Sea

HEIDI R. KLING

G. P. Putnam's Sons
An Imprint of Penguin Group (USA) Inc.

G. P. PUTNAM'S SONS A division of Penguin Young Readers Group. Published by The Penguin Group. Penguin Group (USA) Inc., 375 Hudson Street, New York, NY 10014, U.S.A. Penguin Group (Canada), 90 Eglinton Avenue East, Suite 700, Toronto, Ontario M4P 2Y3, Canada (a division of Pearson Penguin Canada Inc.). Penguin Books Ltd, 80 Strand, London WC2R 0RL, England. Penguin Ireland, 25 St. Stephen's Green, Dublin 2, Ireland (a division of Penguin Books Ltd.). Penguin Group (Australia), 250 Camberwell Road, Camberwell, Victoria 3124, Australia (a division of Pearson Australia Group Pty Ltd). Penguin Books India Pvt Ltd, 11 Community Centre, Panchsheel Park, New Delhi –110 017, India. Penguin Group (NZ), 67 Apollo Drive, Rosedale, North Shore 0632, New Zealand (a division of Pearson New Zealand Ltd). Penguin Books (South Africa) (Pty) Ltd, 24 Sturdee Avenue, Rosebank, Johannesburg 2196, South Africa.

Penguin Books Ltd, Registered Offices: 80 Strand, London WC2R 0RL, England.

Published simultaneously in Canada.

Printed in the United States of America.

Design by Richard Amari.

Text set in Legacy Serif.

Library of Congress Cataloging-in-Publication Data

Kling, Heidi R. Sea / Heidi R. Kling. p. cm. Summary: Despite recurring nightmares about her mother's death and her own fear of flying, fifteen-year-old Sienna accepts her father's birthday gift to fly to Indonesia with his team of disaster relief workers to help victims of a recent tsunami, never suspecting that this experience will change her life forever. [1. Coming of age—Fiction. 2. Emotional problems—Fiction. 3. Tsunamis—Fiction. 4. Disaster relief—Fiction. 5. Orphanages—Fiction. 6. Aceh (Indonesia)—Fiction. 7. Indonesia—Fiction.] I. Title. PZ7.K679758Se 2010 [Fic]—dc22

2009028321

ISBN 978-0-399-25163-4

1 3 5 7 9 10 8 6 4 2

For the survivors and victims of the tragic 2004 tsunami disaster; D, E, and A, the sweetest Orange Popsicle Haze of my life; and to everyone who has loved, lost and dared to try again.

FOUR WEEKS AFTER

I'm sitting alone on the other side of the world talking to a sea turtle that might be my mom. The boy I love is with the girl he loves, and the girl he loves may not be me. If I was halfway to Crazy before, I've fully arrived now. Fire ants swim over soggy debris and snake across the beach like tiny demons; I'm too hot to move out of their way.

Squinting through the sun, I watch the turtle as the sapphire sea froths into a thickening brown. I don't trust my ears, but I swear, in the lapping waves, I hear echoes of drowning cries. Some sort of flying dragon buzzes around my neck; too late I slap it away, knowing full well it left a swollen bite. Flash on his smile instead. On the way his veins stick out of his arms, on the haunted look in his eyes when he says my name.

How long am I supposed to wait for him?

I'm dizzy. Dizzy from the tropical heat, dizzy from the spice-wet air, dizzy from everything. When the sea turtle stares me right in the eye, I cringe at the sound of my own voice.

"What am I supposed to do now?"

It's always the same dream. But it's not her plane; it's mine. The downward spiral of the airplane thundering toward the sea like the death-drop roller coaster at the beach boardwalk but worse, because there's no happy ending to the ride—no cotton candy waiting once the scary part is over. Just a deafening crash and seaweed. Freezing water and foreseeable death. I sink down, down, down and then land with a silent thud on the ocean's murky floor. My eyes are open, but I can't see. Drowning in darkness, I scream bubbles until someone shakes me awake.

"Sienna, can you hear me? Wake up."

I jerked upright, grasping my dad's arm hard. "Did I scream?"

Dad nodded, his glasses framing worried eyes.

"It was just a bad dream. No harm done," he said, patting my arm. "When you get dressed, come on downstairs. I have a surprise for you."

My fifteenth birthday and I still woke up in a cold sweat. "I'll be right down," I said.

Yanking on sweatpants, I twisted my blond hair into a ponytail. Under my tank top I pulled on the bra that was dangling over my chair and made my way down the stairs. My fingertips skimmed along the chipped banister as I carefully skipped the uneven bottom step that Dad swore he'd fix years ago.

"Here she comes, Siennnnnaaaamerica!" a familiar voice boomed as I rounded the corner into the breakfast nook.

Imagine Hagrid from *Harry Potter* with red hair. Now add an MD and faded Hawaiian clothes and you get my dad's best friend, Big Doctor Tom.

My groans turned into awkward giggles as my godfather pulled me into a bear hug. "Stop. Please. Can't. Breathe."

"Fifteen years old. *Mamma mia!*" Tom rubbed my hair like he was trying to start a fire. I slapped his giant hand away and plopped into my usual seat at the farm table, retying my ponytail. "All grown up." Tom shook his head. "Can't believe how fast the time goes."

"Where's Oma?" I asked. Tom *couldn't* be my birthday surprise.

As if on cue, the sliding glass door opened and my grandmother slipped into the house, bringing morning fog with her. Oma moved into our granny unit three years ago to help Dad with me, or, like she insists, "To keep us company."

My grandmother smelled like pink jasmine when her silver hair grazed my cheek. "Happy birthday, sweet Sienna," she said, giving me a kiss.

"Thanks, Oma." I eyed the door for my surprise. What could it be? I was too young for a car.

On the edge of my seat, I nibbled a warm croissant. Then I noticed my grandmother eyeing Tom suspiciously.

"I'm surprised to see you here, Thomas. I thought you were in Africa," she said, something deeper than curiosity stretching across her brow.

Tom shifted in his seat. He was still scared of Oma from when he and Dad were fourteen and he crashed his mom's station wagon into her garage door.

Glancing at Dad, Tom said quickly, "I was in Africa, Mrs. Jones. I just got back last night."

Then everything got quiet.

I looked from Dad, to Oma, back to Tom. Talking about Tom's continuing international mental health relief work was sort of like talking about Mom. You could do it, but you'd regret the silence that followed.

I tapped on my juice glass, looking around the room. No decorations. Nothing to remotely hint that it was my birthday celebration. Just silverware and plates stacked on the counter buffet-style. Obviously this wasn't a real surprise party at eight a.m., when my friends were still sleeping, enjoying their first day of summer vacation. I knew nobody else would come this early but my best friend, Bev. She was always up at dawn, jogging or studying or something. She would come if she were invited. So where was she?

Dad cleared his throat and asked Tom, "Jet lag bad, old man?" His voice had a lilt of joke to it, but I could tell he just wanted to change the subject.

Tom thumped his chest. "Nah. I'm made of steel." Then his voice lowered a tad. "Just like falling off a horse, Andy. Gotta jump back in the saddle if you're going to learn to ride again."

I rolled my eyes. It was way too early in the morning for clichéd horse metaphors.

Oma frowned, stirring a mint tea bag into her mug. I watched it swirl around and around as the lines on my grandmother's face deepened. I guessed what she was thinking.

After Mom disappeared, Dad stopped working abroad completely to stay home with me. With us. He joined a private psychiatric practice here in El Angel Miguel, our little beach town south of San Francisco. I guessed he thought I couldn't handle the chance of him vanishing too. But I was fine now . . . or at least sort of. I spent a lot of time pretending I was, anyway.

"How was the beach, Mom?" Dad asked, his eyes dodgy.

"Lovely," she said. Her voice was crisp and curt as she wiped her hands on her jeans. "The fog's starting to break," she added. "And I found many new birthday shells for my favorite girl."

Oma set a bowl filled with sandy seashells in front of me. I thanked her and grabbed a bunch, inspecting them for flaws. I've collected sand dollars since I was a little kid. Whole ones were hard to find.

I eyed the stairs, considering dashing back to bed. No offense to Oma, but this was my surprise? Shells?

Then *she* knocked on the door.

The insides of my stomach stretched like a rubber band about to snap.

What was *Vera* doing here?

"G'morning, everyone, sorry I'm late; I stopped for bagels!" Vera, dressed from head to toe in a hot pink gym suit, held up a white bag as she let herself in. "Please tell me you have coffee, Andy! I have the worst headache coming on."

"You addict," Dad deadpanned, but his eyes were smiling. "Let me put on a fresh pot."

"My hero," Vera cooed before turning to me. "Happy birthday, Sienna." Vera was my former therapist. Key word: *former*. I quit after five sessions and didn't know how Dad could stand working with her. Never mind bumbling over himself to fetch her coffee.

"Thanks," I mumbled into my juice.

Why in the world would Dad invite *her* to my birthday "celebration"?

Leaning over me in her typically intrusive fashion, she grabbed a handful of blueberries off the table and popped them into her mouth. I tried not to stare at the white skunk stripe running down the middle of her frizzy brown hair.

"How are you *doing*, Sienna?" she asked, laying a manicured hand on my shoulder.

Vera's words transported me back to after Mom's plane went missing: Me sitting across from her in her office. That same practiced, compassionate voice asking me the same. Exact. Thing. *How are you doing, Sienna?*

I remembered my twelve-year-old self staring at the banana tree in the corner, counting its waxy leaves, trying not to cry.

"I'm fine," I said, after a beat.

I'm fine, I repeated in my head. The same lie I told her then.

It wasn't until Dad handed her a steaming cup of coffee in the JOY mug I gave him last Christmas that she smiled. And then it was an overly grateful display— bleached white teeth and all. I mean, it was just *coffee*. Then she took an unnecessarily long sip to prove how much she appreciated it.

"Great blend, Andy. Ethiopian?" *Slurp.*

"Fair trade *Indonesian*, actually," Dad said with a wink. Icky chills ran down my spine.

I cursed under my breath, but no one seemed to hear.

"Ahhh, to mark the occasion," Vera singsonged back.

"Marking *what* occasion with fair trade coffee?" Oma asked. "What are you two talking about?"

"Haven't gotten there *quite* yet, V," Tom said, elbowing Vera.

"Oh. Oops." Vera threw her hand over her mouth like: Did I just do something wrong?

Dad didn't say anything. Instead, he set a plate of fresh pancakes on the table. They were sprinkled with powdered sugar just how I liked them, but I wasn't hungry anymore. Something strange was going on, and I didn't like it.

"Birthday girl gets first pick," Dad said, but his face was all twisty and weird. Then I looked at him more closely. I should have suspected foul play when he woke me up sporting a dress shirt tucked into ironed pants, looking more like a young prepster than the ancient hippie that he was. He usually wandered around on Saturday mornings in Mom's old robe clutching a cup of coffee, looking sort of lost.

"What's going on?" I asked, patience running out. "Haven't gotten *where* yet?"

"I was going to wait until after breakfast, but . . ." He smiled broadly. "Happy birthday, sweetie." Dad reached inside a drawer and handed me a white envelope with a big red bow on the top. "It's really from the whole team. We're so happy to invite you aboard."

Aboard?

I slowly opened the envelope, my heart racing.

An airplane ticket.

I scanned the type in disbelief:

PASSENGER: Ms. Sienna Hope Jones
Flight 13003 depart San Francisco International Airport

(SFO) to Yogyakarta (JOG) June 10, 12:00 a.m. Arrives 5:00 p.m.

CHINA AIR connect in Taipei, Jakarta

Returns . . .

But my eyes weren't reading anymore. The words blurred together.

"This must be a mistake. Dad?" I asked.

Silence. Everyone staring at me.

"No. No mistake, kiddo. It's for you," Dad said. He rubbed his temple, watching me with a little bit of fear. Like I was teetering on the edge of a cliff and he wasn't sure which way I'd fall.

Oma pushed her chair back from the table and stood up to read the ticket over my shoulder. "What is this about, Andrew?"

Dad cleared his throat again. "We'd like Sienna to join us for about two weeks at an Indonesian orphanage, a *pesantren*." He turned back to me. "We think you could really help us with the kids who survived the tsunami, honey. Many of them suffer nightmares and other symptoms of post-traumatic stress disorder, PTSD, and our goal, well, one of our goals, is to restructure the dormitories into a family-style system, with an older girl acting as a 'mother' or 'big sister' figure for the younger trauma survivors to improve their well-being. . . ."

His words spun into gibberish.

He wanted me to go on a plane?

A plane over the ocean.

This was my big birthday surprise?

I dropped the ticket like it was aflame.

"You should have talked to me about this first," Oma said, slicing through the silence. "Isn't there a war still raging in Aceh? Never mind the whole place is a disaster zone full of disease. How long have you been planning this?" Oma's usually calm face flushed, her eyes angrier than I'd ever seen them. "You know how afraid she is of flying. I'm shocked you would do this. Especially after the way Hope was killed."

Hope.

Mom.

Dad slammed his coffee mug on the table so hard, hot liquid spilled over the top. Vera quickly grabbed her own napkin and wiped up the mess. "Sienna's *my* daughter, Mother," Dad said. "I know what's best for her. And Banda Aceh was the epicenter of the tsunami; we aren't going there. We're traveling to Java. We'll be perfectly safe."

Safe?

How could Dad promise we'd be safe? He said the same thing three years ago.

He came home and Mom didn't.

Safe.

How could he ever make that promise again?

"Sienna, are you okay?" Oma asked. "Andrew, get her some water! She looks like she's going to faint."

Their voices drifted into echoes, like they were arguing from opposite ends of a tunnel. A horrible knot grew in my throat that I couldn't swallow away. My hands shook. My heart raced faster than I knew it could. I could barely breathe.

"I . . . I'm not thirsty, I'm . . ." The bright kitchen morphed into black and then dotted with flashes of white spots like a psychedelic planetarium show. Alternating shocks of heat and chills coursed through my body. I had to get out of there.

Stumbling up the broken stairs, I headed toward the only thing I needed to see.

THE POSTCARD

Behind my locked bathroom door, my hands shook as I held the worn postcard, watching the sea turtles swim carefree in blue-green water. Gently outlining their hard shells, I dared to flip the card over and read the familiar handwriting, faded and streaked from my old tears.

Dear Sweet Sienna,

I hope you and Spider are having a great time at surf camp! We can't wait to see your new moves when we get home. Daddy and I miss you so much. We spotted two giant sea turtles today that looked just like the ones on this card. They are two of the ancient ones that live to be a hundred. We swam together, the four of us, wishing you were with us. See you soon to celebrate your birthday!

xoxo, Mom (and Daddy)

I swallowed back tears. The postcard arrived three years ago on my twelfth birthday in a mix of other cards and junk mail. A week after Dad came home from Thailand without her.

I never even told my dad I got it, because it was ours. The last secret I shared with my mom.

Carefully, I tucked the card back into my old journal

and splashed cold water on my face. I stared at myself in the mirror, the counter cool marble on my palms.

The glass was clear. But three years later, I still didn't look like me.

SPIDER

My bedroom felt dusky in that walking-out-of-a-matinee-movie way when the pinging started.

Ting bing.

I got up off my bed and moved aside my window curtain.

Spider?

I blinked to make sure my eyes weren't teasing.

With his free hand, the one not wrapped around his surfboard, he waved up to me, his sandy blond hair still wet from the sea. I cracked open my window and a cool foggy breeze rushed in.

"Are you throwing rocks at my window?" I asked.

"Shells. Guilty as charged. I heard you locked yourself in your bedroom."

"Really? Who told you that?"

"Bev told me you called her, freaking out. I figured it wasn't a good time for me to knock on your door, but I figured you might let me harass you from down here." He grinned confidently. Everyone was always happy to see Spider, and he knew it.

I couldn't help but smile back. It *was* good to see him.

When his head cocked to the side, his eyes weren't joking anymore. "So I found something of yours the other day. And since it's your birthday I figured it was the perfect time to give it to you."

He remembered my birthday? I hadn't talked with Spider one-on-one in forever. Whenever I saw him, it was in passing at his and Bev's house or at the beach surrounded by his posse of surf rats and girl groupies. He barely even looked at me at school when we walked by each other in the halls, and now he showed up at my house all nonchalant, remembering my birthday?

"Really? What is it?" I asked.

He scrunched his eyebrows, teasing. "Not telling. You have to come over and find out. It's in my closet, waiting for you."

I felt my face flush imagining being in Spider's house not because it was Bev who had invited me. About being in Spider's room alone with him after all this time.

I had to think of something to say.

Tugging on the back of my hair, I asked the obvious. "You were surfing?"

His eyes lit up. "The waves were shoulder high," he said. "Must be a storm coming in. You should have been there."

I should have been there? *Yeah, right.*

Speaking of giant waves. "So Bev told you about my birthday 'surprise.'"

Spider nodded. I nibbled on the rough skin next to my

index finger and startled myself when I blurted out, "You know I don't fly."

"I know," he said without missing a beat. Of course he knew. He was there when it all happened: Sienna doesn't fly anymore. Sienna doesn't surf anymore. Sienna doesn't do anything anymore. Sienna just *doesn't*.

"But if things were . . . different, it would be kind of cool helping the tsunami survivors and all that," he said encouragingly.

Then I grew suspicious. "Hey, did my dad ask you to try and talk me into going with him?"

Spider frowned. "No. Why would you think that?"

"I don't know. It's just . . . I'm kinda surprised to see you."

Spider bobbed back and forth from one bare foot to the other on the sidewalk, the same sidewalk we used to skate race when we were kids. Once white and smooth, the concrete was now chipped and cracked, bits of scraggly grass growing between the spaces.

"Look," he called up, scratching his salty hair, "I better jam. Just wanted to stop by and wish you a happy birthday. Come over when you've bailed yourself out of your self-imposed isolation cell," he joked.

"Okay," I said.

He looked up at me for a second like he might want to say something else. But then he just shrugged. "See ya," he said, with a little wave over his shoulder.

"Spider?"

"Yeah?"

I wanted to ask if he was here because he wanted to be friends again and if so, why after all this time? But that sounded lame, so no words came.

He cupped his ear like a conch shell. "I can't hear you, Sea," he yelled up.

I winced at the sound of my old nickname.

"What'd I say?"

He must have noticed my expression. I wondered how to explain it. That we weren't little kids anymore, that instead of being the skinny hyper kid I used to know, Spider was one of the hottest guys on the cove, his body filling out his chin-to-toe wet suit in all the right places, his lean surfer body six feet tall.

He was Mr. Cool and I just . . . wasn't anymore. I wasn't Sea anymore. And I got over him a long time ago.

"It's Sienna now," I corrected him.

He blinked. "Oh, right." He sounded disappointed. "I forgot."

Shrugging, I tore my eyes away from Spider's, stared past him, down the long street of our neighborhood, toward the peek of silver-blue ocean.

If there were ever a tsunami here, it would hit Spider's house first.

I imagined the tall windows shattering into razors of glass. Spider, Bev and their perfect tennis-playing parents running from the giant wave as the water thrashed over their expensive furniture, flooding their polished wooden floors and overflowing their granite countertops.

Spider wouldn't be so happy-go-lucky after that happened.

Cringing, I looked back at his uncomfortable face and felt horrible. What was wrong with me?

"See ya, then, Sienna," he called up from below.

"See ya," I echoed back.

A half smile crept up his mouth before he turned to go. Why wouldn't it? It wasn't like he could hear my awful thoughts. Spider had that easy way about him that people who have never had anything bad happen to them seem to possess.

Lucky him. Lucky Spider.

I took another deep breath of salty air, let it tingle down my throat. Even after all the grief it had given me, the ocean still smelled good.

I watched Spider walk away until he disappeared up his driveway ten houses down, leaving nothing but watery-gray footprints on the sidewalk.

TSUNAMI

Dad was reading a thick book about child soldiers when I peeked into the den. The African boy on the cover was staring straight ahead, his eyes angry but empty somehow. He looked about ten years old and was bare-chested, pointing a gun toward a broad blue sky; the gun was obviously not a toy. A dim fluorescent light bent over Dad's book, illuminating the unsettled look on his face.

Dad's office smelled like stale coffee and lavender; lavender from Oma's garden, dried and hanging on the wall. The scent still reminded me of Mom, and I wondered why Dad kept it in here, when it seemed like most of the time he didn't want to be reminded, or talk about her, anyway. About what happened.

"Oma said you wanted to talk," I said, standing in the doorway.

My birthday was several days ago and we'd pretty much been avoiding each other since.

Worked for me, but apparently it wasn't working for Dad.

Jazz music blasted from two old speakers on opposite ends of the mahogany desk where Dad sat. When I was little, he used to spin me around and around in that worn black office chair. Now I didn't come in here much; we all have our corners in this house. This den was Dad's.

"Hey, kiddo. I need to talk to you about the trip."

My insides twisted into a sticky web. "That looks like light reading," I said, trying to stall him.

"The book isn't light reading; that's the point," he said defensively, his face half shadowed in the light. "These ugly things are really happening in the world, and if I can, I'm going to do something to help. If I can't help stop it, I'll do something to help heal the wounds. That's what Team Hope was . . . *is* . . . all about."

"Team Hope? That's what you're calling your group now?"

"Yes. We changed it . . . in honor of your mom."

I didn't know what to say. His international work was the reason she was gone.

My stomach clenched as I connected the dots.

That was what my birthday morning was all about: Dad? *Check*. Tom? *Check*. And . . . they needed a third person now.

Vera.

It was obvious who Vera was replacing.

My stomach seized. "Whatever." I spit out the word, spun around to flee.

"Sienna, stop."

"What!" I snapped. The circles under his eyes were

darker than usual, but this time I didn't feel bad. I was tired too. We were all tired.

He moved toward me, setting his hand on my shoulder in his robo-Dad way. But I shrugged it off.

"Listen, I know you're still mad about your birthday and I want to apologize. I thought if I surprised you with the ticket, you might not be as adverse to coming along— okay, that's a lie." He chuckled a little, making me want to scream. "I knew you'd say no and I really wanted you to say yes."

I didn't answer. He was supposed to know better than to act like this. He was supposed to be an expert! My eyes stung with frustration.

"I'm sorry, honey. Being a dad of a teenage girl doesn't come with instructions," he said.

Neither does being a daughter of a widowed psychiatrist, I wanted to retort, but instead I said the worst thing I could think of. "How could you even think of bringing her in place of Mom?" My words cracked like a whip. As soon as they were out, I wanted to suck them back in. Wanted to take back the whole stupid week. The whole last three years.

Dad just stared at me.

He scratched his beard, avoiding my eyes. "That's not . . . ," he started to say but let his words trail off. "Wait. Just wait."

As I stood in the doorway fuming, Dad reached under his desk and held up a DVD. "I have a proposition for you."

The cover of the box was a faded photograph of three little girls standing in front of a massive gray wave. "What's that?"

"A documentary shot at the orphanage we'll be volunteering at. Look, I know you're angry, but I want this trip to be your choice. I'm not going to force you to go. Watch this DVD and decide for yourself."

I didn't trust him a bit. "What's the catch?"

Dad's face relaxed. "No catch. I'm sincerely sorry for how I acted." He raked his fingers through his thinning hair. "How this all seems. I've been a mess, and I can't apologize enough. You're fifteen years old now, so I might as well be honest with you." He sighed. "I hate my practice. I hate listening to spoiled women whine about their rich husbands spending too much time on the golf course. I can't even bring myself to fix the stairs, Sienna. I'm sure you've noticed."

I grunted in agreement.

"See? The house is a wreck. It's falling apart. And as dear as she is, your grandmother drives me crazy. I'm just . . . I'm just lost." He sighed again. "Do you know what I mean?"

I nodded. I knew exactly what he meant.

His voice picked up, as if energized by my understanding. "I need to feel useful again, kiddo. I need to help people with real problems who actually need my help. This trip is something I have to do. And I really want you to come along. If you would just think about it? Please?"

When I squinted, the broken pieces of Dad's face blurred and he looked like the dad who taught me to surf, to ride my bike. He looked like the man I used to believe could fix anything.

"Okay, Dad," I said.

THE BACKPACK

Spider's room still smelled like crusty salt water and cheese puffs. But now there was a musky scent, some cologne mixed in, that made it even nicer to hang out in.

Surf posters still covered the walls like ocean-themed wallpaper, and I could barely see the floor, it was so covered in crap. Maybe that's why we used to get along so well—we both enjoyed lounging around in our own chaos.

A surf movie was on his flat-screen TV, but I was paying more attention to the fact that we were sitting next to each other on his bed. "Want some more?" Spider asked, dangling a half-empty bag of chips in front of me.

"No, thanks."

Spider shrugged and continued to munch.

So.

When are you going to show me the thing you found for me?

Like he could read my mind, he rolled up the empty bag, shot it easily into the basketball hoop beside his door and watched it swoosh into the trash can underneath.

"Nice shot," I said.

"Some things never change," he said ironically. "Did you decide about Indo yet?" he asked, facing me.

I could have told him about the DVD.

How I watched half of it before with Bev in her room. That I didn't finish it. Not because I didn't want to, but because I couldn't. It was too scary hearing the kids' stories mixed in with news camera footage: the massive wave rushing through villages, destroying everything in its wake. The screams as the people ran and swam and struggled for safety. How one little girl, with a white flower in her hair, hid from the camera's questions the whole time. She wouldn't speak at all, like she was hiding from her own story. The whole time I watched, I couldn't stop thinking: Maybe she'd speak to me.

"Can we talk about something else?" I asked Spider. I didn't want to admit I was actually considering going. That even though Bev and Oma both thought it was a terrible idea, I might do this.

I might really go.

I noticed the summer freckles sprinkled across his nose when he asked, "Come on, you don't want to go to Indo even a little bit? Because I remember, we used to . . . Well, you used to always say you wanted to travel with your parents one day."

I narrowed my eyes. "Do you *swear* my dad isn't bribing you to persuade me to go? I mean, I know Bev would never succumb to that kind of pressure, but you," I said with a grin, "are an entirely different story."

"Swear." He held up his pinky—our old ritual. "And I take offense at the suggestion," he said, but he was grinning too.

I stared at his tanned hand.

Did he want me to twist mine into his? I didn't dare reach out and touch him. From the corner of my eye I watched him pause for a beat before folding his hand back into a fist and reaching over the side of the bed.

"What's that?" I asked.

He set a kid-size backpack on my lap. "Remember when we were eight, your parents were leaving for Vietnam and we thought we'd stow away in your dad's Jeep? Well, I found yours."

"No way!" I held up the Scooby-Doo pack. *Sea* was written on top in bright pink cursive. "I can't believe you still have this!"

"They almost missed their plane when they found us hiding in the back. Your dad was so pissed, but your mom just laughed . . . ," he said, and then stopped when his words stuck to the air like flypaper. I tried to swallow them away, but my throat was a desert.

I carefully unzipped the top. The inside was still stuffed with the little kid clothes I'd packed all those years ago.

"I think this is a sign, Sea," Spider said, his voice low, cautious. "This time you really get to go."

Was it a sign?

I didn't believe much in signs, not anymore. But this was pretty coincidental. I stared at the bag but didn't dare look at Spider, who was leaning so close I could feel his breath on my cheek.

I leaned back, staring at the backpack while I talked.

"If I decide to go, I have to get a ton of shots. They have serious diseases over there, you know," I mumbled.

"We'll just have to put you in a bubble when you get back so you don't contaminate us with your cooties." I felt him leaning closer.

"Would you visit me in the bubble?"

"Of course," Spider said. "I'd bring you Popsicles and cheesy celebrity magazines."

"In that case, it might be worth going. I think a bubble house life would appeal to me."

Then Spider started tickling me. I feigned protest, hugging the backpack to my chest. "Spider, stop!"

Then we kind of rolled around laughing.

It felt good to laugh. Strange. Like I didn't recognize the sound of my own laughter.

Spider started tickling me again and I laughed some more until suddenly Spider's face was too close. He stopped laughing. His eyes looked different.

Something clicked. He was right. The little girl on the documentary. The backpack. Him.

I jumped up. "I need to go, Spider. You're right!"

"You mean go home? What's wrong?" Spider stood up from the bed, concerned.

"I'm fine," I said. "I just need to tell my dad I'm going."

He held on to my shoulders and I froze.

Was he trying to kiss me?

No. That couldn't happen.

"So you're going to go?" he asked, puzzled. "And you decided that *just now*?"

I kept the backpack firmly between us. "Yeah," I said. It was the truth.

Ducking out of his arms, I headed for the door so he couldn't see the confusion on my face. "I think . . . I think it's the right thing to do."

Even if I wanted him to, I couldn't let Spider kiss me.

I remembered the last time as clear as if it were yesterday. His curious eyes and his cherry soda lips.

And then the horrible thing that happened after.

I wasn't sure about a lot of things, but I was sure about this.

I would never be brave enough to try again.

I ran out of Spider's house the same way I had that terrible day.

Maybe an ocean between us wouldn't be such a bad thing.

SHARKS

"So you're really going tonight?" Bev asked.

A week later, we were lying side by side on matching striped towels down at the cove, waiting for the rest of the group to arrive for our fare-thee-well bonfire.

"Looks like . . ." My stomach churned when I even thought about the midnight flight.

"You're going to be okay, dude."

I looked at her sideways. Then I took a swig out of my water bottle. "I hope so."

"The person you should be worried about is me," Bev joked, smoothing down her straight black bob. "I mean, two whole weeks without you? I'm going to be so bored."

"You have your brother," I said, uneasiness creeping into my voice. I hadn't seen him since that awkward day in his room.

"Yeah, right." Bev rolled her eyes. "I'm completely ir-relevant to him. As is anyone who doesn't surf."

That stung, but I let it pass. Bev was right on, as usual. I didn't want to think about Spider anyway. All I wanted to do was soak up the sun and watch powder-puff clouds float in the sky. I didn't want to think about the trip or how sore my arms were because of all the needle-poking shots.

I sighed, leaned back, basked in the heat of the day.

Sunny Cove's golden beach was packed, dotted with

families, zigzagging Frisbees and seagulls grazing the sand for PB&J crusts. The teal waves were breaking perfectly. Dozens of surfers were out waiting for that perfect ride.

"Why don't you surf again, Bev?" I asked, forgetting her reason.

"Three words: great white sharks," she said with a snort, pulling a vintage T-shirt over her head. "You know that."

Sharks. Now I was thinking about Spider and everything else dangerous and lurking underwater. "Do you see your brother?"

"No, but I'm not exactly looking for him."

I scanned the waves and stopped. I knew his surfboard like I used to know him. A short, red-and-white board with a black spiderweb painted on the nose. On his belly, bobbing on the board up and over the smooth water, waiting for the next set of ride-worthy waves, I found Spider.

And he wasn't alone.

Someone was bobbing next to him, and that someone had thin shoulders, long red hair and a curvy wet suit.

"Who is *that girl* with your brother?" I asked, surprised at how jealous I felt.

Bev, now busy rubbing white Bullfrog on her nose, didn't answer.

I shielded my eyes with my hand. "In the water? Some surfer girl. Can't you see them?"

"Not really."

"I'm pretty sure it's a girl. Look at her hair: it's not hippie-boy long; it's girl long. And I see boobs. Can't you see her boobs? It's definitely a girl."

"Um. Sienna. News flash. I don't exactly sit on the beach in order to stare at girl boobs. That'd be my brother's department."

I tilted my head so she couldn't see me grimace.

"And so what if he's surfing with a girl; what else is new? Why do you suddenly care what my stupid brother does, anyway? Because you guys hung out together last week in his room?"

She glanced at me suspiciously before flipping open the front page of the *New York Times*. She scanned down the newsprint with her pinky finger, humming and nodding to herself. "Status update: all clear. No new terrorist attacks in Indonesia or Bali, so you should be g-to-g for the whole trip. Good to go."

I snorted. "Oh, right, and that means the whole two weeks will be threat level what? Yellow for low risk of terrorist acts?"

"Something like that."

I leaned in closer. "Sure you don't want to come with me, Bev? You could be my personal bodyguard."

"Ha. I'll pass. But don't you worry. You can be your own bodyguard armed with my info." She tapped the side of her skull. "Knowledge is power."

I laughed. Right. Those warning levels worked about as well as Dad predicting a plane crash. No one knew anything, so why warn at all?

I watched Spider and that girl bob around in the water some more. I could almost feel it in my stomach, the sense of rising and falling, as I watched them go up and over the waves.

I doubted that girl would give Spider the cold shoulder if he tried to kiss her. And I doubted that Spider worried for even a second about the possibility of sharks lurking under inky blue waters or plane crashes or terrorist attacks as he paddled hard into the building curve of water. All he cared about was catching this one perfect wave.

I studied his form as he rose up on the board.

Knees bent, arms out, he braced himself for the foam-topped thrill ride and, as always, cruised effortlessly toward the shore.

THE HAZE

That evening, Spider and I walked barefoot, together, in the sand.

Away from Team Hope. Away from Spider's family. Away from Oma. Away from the crackling bonfire and roasted marshmallows and veggie dogs.

He had said he wanted to talk to me.

Alone.

Sitting cross-legged in the sand, Bev raised her eyebrow, and so did Dad. And so did I, frankly, but I shrugged and followed Spider toward the cliffs anyway. My stomach tied up in the same twisted knot of seaweed that hadn't managed to untangle itself since my birthday.

"What's going on?" I asked once we were out of earshot.

"Nothing." Spider glanced over at me, sunset washing over his face.

"Nothing?" I asked. *Then why* . . .

He ran his fingers through his hair, tugged on a handful like he was trying to remember what he wanted to say. "So, you all set for the trip? Didn't forget your toothbrush or anything?"

"I probably have three extras," I said, playing along. "Vera made sure the car was totally packed before she agreed to the farewell bonfire. If you haven't noticed, she is nothing if not organized."

Spider laughed, angling in closer. "So, are you nervous? I mean last week—you were acting sort of weird."

I shrugged away. To ensure an even safer distance between our swinging hands, I tucked mine in my hoodie pocket. "Kinda," I said. *But this instant, I'm more afraid of being alone with you.*

He squeezed my shoulder and then let go, probably worried that I'd freak out if he lingered. "Here, I found this for you earlier." He dug into the pocket of his sweatshirt and pulled out a perfect-circle sand dollar. Not one crack. Not one flaw. "It's for good luck," he said.

He set the ivory disk in my palm.

"Where'd you find this? The ones I've found lately have all been cracked."

"I have my sources." He grinned.

Violent waves pushed clay-colored foam toward the shore. "Isn't it weird how the ocean changes so fast?" I said. "This afternoon the waves were so clear and blue. Now look at them." I nudged a snake of slimy sea rope out of my way to prove my point.

"Yeah, they're supposed to be head-high tomorrow." He looked at me from the corners of his eyes and mumbled, "Too bad you won't be around."

Right.

I wouldn't even get my toes wet, never mind go surfing. Again, Spider knew that.

I countered with a teasing voice. "You could always meet up with that surfer girl, what's her name . . ."

Spider frowned. "Who?"

I tripped over a piece of driftwood. "That girl you were surfing with earlier," I said, steadying myself.

"Lia? I doubt she'd go out on a big-wave day. She's just sort of learning."

"Oh, and you're her teacher?"

He looked at me like I just told him the earth was flat and I had definitive proof.

I shoved my hands deeper in my pocket. Spider must be so confused. He wasn't the only one.

We were both quiet for a minute, watching the waves whirl into more murky muck. "Why do you want to know about Lia?"

I shrugged.

The corner of his mouth rose like he was testing a smile. "You jealous?"

"No."

Spider kicked a clump of sand into the air. "Oh."

I wasn't jealous. Not really. If I were jealous of all the girls Spider hung out with over the years, my blood would run green. Spider wasn't my boyfriend; he was barely even my friend—he could surf with whomever he wanted. Right?

I tucked a piece of loose hair behind my ear. *Right?*

Then I noticed he wasn't smiling anymore. And then we both stopped walking.

I wasn't sure if he stopped first or I did, but there we were, standing awkwardly watching the waves. I sat down first and dug two small ditches into the wet sand with my heels. Cool wind picked up as Spider plopped down next to me, hugging his knees to his chest. I noticed how light the hairs on his legs were, how the fool's gold stood out in the flecks of sand dusting his skin.

Why did everything have to be so complicated?

I fingered cracked shells partially buried in the dark sand, the shattered pieces sharp as cut glass.

"The sailboats are heading in," Spider said finally, breaking the long silence. "Hey, look"—he pointed—"the *Jolly Roger*'s back."

"That old pirate ship," I responded with a nonchalant eye roll like I wasn't excited to see it at all. "Tourists." But the smirk that crossed his face let me know he didn't buy my attitude one bit.

"You were always a sucker for pirates, Sienna." His smirk turned into a curious grin. "Hey, do you remember that story your mom used to tell us?"

Mom told us lots of stories. "Which one?" I asked.

"Our favorite one. The one about the ship lost at sea."

"Not really."

If I said yes, he might not tell it, and for some reason I needed to hear it.

Spider narrowed his eyes. "I can't believe you don't remember it! Let's see if I can get this right." He cleared his throat and spoke in a fake British accent. "A long, long time ago, sometime in the 1800s, there lived a sea captain whose great and only love died very young. He was so heartbroken that he vowed to never step foot on land again. He'd sail the seas forever and never return to the homeland that stole his true love."

"You can use your regular voice, you know."

"No interrupting!" His fingers waved away my comment, but he changed his voice back to normal. "The captain was a man of his word, and for five years he stayed at sea, not even walking into the port towns for supplies—he had his crew do that; he always stayed on his ship. Then he received a letter—let's say it was in a bottle just for fun—proclaiming his mother's dying wish: for her son to return home and kiss her one last time. How could he deny her this last request? He was a righteous man, a good man. So, with great sadness about abandoning his personal quest, he pointed his ship toward home."

Spider pantomimed steering the wheel of a great ship and headed straight at me. "Onward, Miguel!" I couldn't help laughing. "Day and night he traveled the high seas, the rough and wild seas. When he was just moments away from his destination, a tremendous storm hit and his ship nearly capsized. But now the captain was determined to get home.

"The storm was so dark and violent that he lost sight of land and was drifting off to sea again when he saw a light. An orange pinkish glow hovering over what appeared to be land. It was the light of a star, or the light of an angel. He followed the bright glow all the way to shore, and when his ship crashed on the rocks, the light disappeared. At last, by the bedside of his beloved mother, he swore the light was his lost love bringing him home to the shores of our town, which they eventually named El Angel Miguel after the sea captain and his angel."

I listened to the rhythm of the waves crash. Wiggled my fingers deeper into the damp sand. "Then what happened?"

"The sea captain ended up marrying the most beautiful girl in the village. And they had like ten kids. All of them brilliant surfers, of course," Spider said. "And of course, they lived happily ever after."

I wrinkled my nose. "Of course."

"So how'd I do?" he asked, his voice softening.

"Awesome," I said. And I really meant it. "Hey, do the surfers still call the light the Orange Popsicle Haze?"

"We just call it the Haze. It was *you* who made up the Orange Popsicle part 'cause you were so obsessed with those sticky things." He laughed. "Seriously, though, some of the guys swear they've seen the Haze after a bad wipeout. Or when it gets too dark, a little darker than it is now. They watch for the orange light hanging over the sand, lighting their way home."

I watched the sun set deeper and deeper into the sea until it disappeared into the horizon. I remembered Mom telling us that story when we were kids. And like everything she told me, I believed it. We used to watch for it a lot. The Haze. But I hadn't searched in a long time.

"Have you ever seen it? The orange light?" I asked quietly.

"I'm not sure. Maybe. Then again, I always know my way back to shore." Spider looked at me pointedly, telling me something more. "And you do too. You just don't know it yet."

He wasn't talking about geography anymore.

He was talking about me.

Doesn't he get that the girl he knew before is gone? If Spider didn't like me the way I was now, maybe it was time for him to really let me go.

"Spider . . ."

He looked at me like he did back in his room. Like he was trying to get closer to me.

"Yeah?" he asked, his eyes silently asking why I wouldn't let him.

I looked down. "Never mind," I said.

"*What?* Sea?" He scratched his head, frustrated. "I mean Sienna, just tell me. I can handle it, you know."

I shook my head, wishing I could. Wishing we could go back to how we were. Before. When I used to tell him everything and he used to understand. Before the taste of orange Popsicles soured, when I used to chase after him into the sea.

THE PLANE

"Flight attendants, prepare for takeoff."

"This is it. You okay, kiddo?" Dad asked.

I'm paralyzed with fear, actually; thanks for asking.

I gripped the two armrests like they were safety handles. "Is my seat belt tight enough?" I hardly recognized my squeaky, high-pitched voice as Dad reached over and tugged on the blue strap.

"Looks good to me," he said, pulling even tighter as he said it.

I yanked on it again just to make sure.

The Chinese flight attendant walked through the aisle glancing at our laps, talking to the many Asian passengers in words I didn't understand. Another attendant was demonstrating the safety vests we were supposed to stick over our heads and blow up in case we crashed into the ocean. My mental image of Team Hope floating in a lone yellow raft in the middle of the sea surrounded by sharks while our plane sank into the dark abyss was not a joyous one.

My stomach nearly flew out of my mouth when the plane's engine roared to life and we started to move down the runway.

Dad patted my white-knuckled hand. "It's going to be just fine, kiddo. You've flown lots of times. Always been fine." The way he said it made it sound like he was comforting himself as well. And maybe he was. He hadn't flown since Mom's plane disappeared over the ocean either.

Tom flashed me the thumbs-up sign. I was shocked to see Vera leaning back on her seat, her blackout mask tight on her face like a supervillain.

Was she *seriously* already asleep?

More engines buzzed and hummed. Lights flashed overhead.

Please don't crash, please don't crash, please don't crash.

I repeated the mantra, leaning back, squeezing my eyes as tight as I could until I finally felt the plane go up at an incredibly unnatural angle that was both terrifying and familiar.

My silent begging got more specific as we started to level off: *Please, God, Buddha, Mom, whoever is listening. Please don't let us crash.*

"You can open your eyes now," Dad said as I felt the plane balance itself in the sky. "Piece of cake."

Not convinced it was safe to look, I heard Tom's voice. "You know what they say, kid, takeoffs and landings are the only trouble spots to flying. Smooth sailing for the next twelve hours or so."

Twelve hours on a plane.

I fought off a yawn, my eyelids weighted. That little blue pill Dad gave me at the airport must have started working. There was really no point in opening my eyes at all, even if I could.

"Your Indonesian guidebook is in your backpack. That will explain everything you need to know about the local culture in Yogyakarta. In the back there are key Bahasa Indonesia phrases you should learn too before we arrive. . . ." Dad's voice rambled on and on.

But I fell asleep before I had a chance to respond.

CRASH

The flight attendants scream in Chinese. Suitcases tumble out of overhead bins, and somewhere in the back of the plane a baby cries the worst cry I've ever heard, like a desperate animal caught in a trap. Yellow life raft tucked under my arm, I run down the aisle. "Here it is!" I scream, spotting the door marked Exit. "I found it!" That's when I notice nobody else is moving. The other passengers are reading quietly or listening to their headphones, totally oblivious to the fact that our plane is barreling toward the sea. "We're going to crash!" I screech to deaf ears. "Did you HEAR me? What is the matter with you? We're GOING TO CRASH!"

"Sienna! Sienna! Wake up!" Dad was shaking me.

"Dad?" I clawed at his shirt. My face was wet with tears. "The plane was crashing!"

"It's okay, sweetie, the plane is fine. You had a night terror. Just a bad dream."

"Oh my God. I hope I didn't scare everybody."

"It wasn't *that* loud," Dad said. "I don't think you woke anybody up. Except me." He laughed, but his eyes didn't look like he thought anything about it was funny.

"It wasn't the same dream. It was the plane crash like always, but there were Chinese flight attendants."

"Reflecting your current reality. Dreams are fascinating, aren't they? Portholes into the subconscious."

"I guess," I said. Clearly I suffered from a pretty wacky subconscious.

Dad pulled a cinnamon-raisin bagel out of his leather backpack and handed it to me. "You might feel better if you ate something. And remember, we're perfectly safe up here."

The perfectly safe line again. But I didn't say anything. Biting my lip hard, I checked it out for myself.

Outside my circle window the sky was death black. I couldn't see the ocean, but knew it was down there lurking. Waiting. Ready to swallow us up if it had the chance. I slammed the window shade down and turned my back to it, then choked down a few bites of dry bagel.

"See? Everything's fine," Dad said, squeezing my arm more meaningfully than he did back home. "Try and get some more sleep."

I curled into the seat the best I could, but I couldn't get comfy. The AC drifted through the cracks where my flimsy blanket was too small to keep me covered, freezing only parts of me. After squirming around in the dark for what felt like hours, I finally rested my head against the plane's cool vibration and closed my eyes.

Dawn Over the Ocean

I woke up to Dad and Vera talking about me in hushed voices. I kept my eyes closed so I could listen.

"So I'm thinking Sienna can work with you," Dad said.

"She's good at art. Maybe she could do some art therapy with the younger kids in the morning and attend therapy groups in the afternoons?"

"The art part is fine, Andy, but I'm not sure about the therapy. She was pretty resistant the last time we worked together, if you recall." Her voice changed cadence like she was making sure he got her point. "I don't want to cause a bigger strain."

"Yes, but she's older now . . . ," Dad said.

Vera's voice reduced to a whisper. "Don't you think that would be too much for her? Listening to those trauma stories?"

"I can handle it," I said, leaning forward.

Dad's and Vera's eyes were wide like I'd caught them making out in their car. Their shoulders were touching, their faces nestled in close together. Ew.

At the sound of my voice, Dad faced me, his tone guilty. "I thought you were asleep, kiddo." He leaned away from her and sat straight up in his seat. I don't think I made up the flare of disappointment shooting across Vera's face. "If you're sure, that would be a big help," Dad said. "Also, we're going to place you in a dorm with a group of the younger kids, to try out the family group approach."

Vera's blackout mask pulled back her wild hair like a headband. She asked the flight attendant for coffee; Dad and I ordered orange juice.

"Don't the little kids already have older kids rooming with them? Or an adult?" I asked.

"Strangely, no," Dad said. "But we've persuaded the *pesantren* owner to try out our theory. We'll mix the teens with the younger kids and observe the pros and cons of doing so during our two weeks there."

"Two weeks doesn't seem like long enough to do something like that," I said.

Dad shrugged. "We couldn't close the practice for longer than two weeks this time around. Two weeks will make a difference. You'll see."

"I don't see how changing the bunking arrangements is going to help a six-year-old deal with the fact that her entire family was killed in a tidal wave," I said.

He studied me for a beat. "A tsunami isn't a tidal wave," he said, totally ignoring the meat of my comment.

"It's not?" I asked.

"No. There was an underwater earthquake. It hit about a 9.0 on the Richter scale and changed the level of the water, so instead of a single wave, like you might imagine, the entire ocean rose a hundred feet higher than it had been for centuries, if that makes sense."

"Not really," I said.

"Apparently, you had to see it to believe it. The entire ocean rose and poured through the city." He glanced at Vera. "And, well, you know the rest."

"But the kids on the video. Most of them looked so happy? I can't imagine that."

I couldn't imagine losing your parents and still being okay.

Vera leaned forward and peered at me over her reading glasses. "Remember the children were being filmed. My guess is they're not happy all the time."

Dad turned back to Vera. "Good point," he said. "Here comes the breakfast cart."

I ordered eggs, which turned out to be some sort of noodle dish. While I picked at it, I wondered about Mom and Dad. What they were like on their trips back when it was just Tom, Dad and Mom instead of Tom, Dad, Vera and me. What did they talk about on long trips over the sea?

I pushed the tray aside, the smell making me queasy.

The sky outside the plane broke into the full colors of day: swirls of orange, red and yellow. The glaring sun warmed my forehead as I thought about the Orange Popsicle Haze and daydreamed of Mom sitting next to me on the plane. Of her laughter instead of Vera's as Dad told a joke. I closed my eyes again but didn't bother trying to sleep.

Even Later

"Are we almost theeeere?" I whined. My butt was killing me. The too-small blanket was driving me so crazy, I chucked it onto the floor. Dad's hair was starting to look all oily—the shadows under his eyes darker. We'd been flying nearly eight hours.

"Easy, tiger. We still have a long way to go. How much of the guidebook have you read? If you're bored, this would be the perfect time to crack it open."

I grumbled and, needing to stretch my legs, I excused myself to the bathroom.

"Hey, kid, if you want to switch places with Vera later, we can watch this game show together," Tom said as I passed him. "It's hilarious!"

A spiky-haired male host wearing a plaid suit was jumping around on a circus stage, screaming into a microphone. "How can you understand what's going on? You aren't even wearing headphones."

"I can't." He laughed. "That's the fun of it."

Okay.

The line outside the bathroom was three deep. Nasty poop smells were leaking from the crack under the door. Great. I thought the one in the front of the plane might be better, so I headed up the aisle, passing ten rows of young Chinese men wearing matching red uniforms. A soccer team, maybe? One of the guys smiled at me and I smiled back. The door to this toilet was unlocked and it didn't smell as bad as the first one. I pulled down my pants and sat on the pot. Before I even had a chance to go, the tiny bathroom started rattling. The plane jerked, and

I fell forward, grasping onto the wet sink. Another big bump followed by a bunch of smaller ones; my hands were slipping around on the slick metal basin. Even the mirror and the soap and the paper towel dispensers were jiggling around. My heart was racing like crazy. It was just like my nightmare. I knew we were going down.

The flight attendant said something frantically over the loudspeaker in Chinese. The flashing light above the door read:

RETURN TO YOUR SEAT
FASTEN YOUR SEAT BELT
系紧安全带

What was I supposed to do?

If I got up, I'd fall. But I had no choice. I had to get back to my seat and prepare for whatever would happen next. My chest pounding, I pulled up my pants and flung open the door. I ran back as fast as I could, bumping against the aisle chairs. Like in my nightmare. I was expecting the other passengers to be in turmoil too, shoving dangling oxygen masks onto their faces like in the instructional video, but no one seemed to notice. Or care. And no oxygen masks were in sight.

When I reached our section of the plane, Vera and Dad were blabbing away and Tom was still hypnotized by the game show.

"Dad!" I yelled. "Didn't you feel those bumps? Buckle your seat belt!"

"It's okay. It was a bit of turbulence; it's already stopped."

I plopped down into my seat as fast as I could and buckled up, tugging the belt tight across my lap. "I was stuck in the bathroom!" I said accusingly. "Weren't you going to come look for me?"

I blinked away anxious tears, hating how my fear got the best of me.

Dad squeezed my arm reassuringly. "It's okay, sweetie," he said, his green eyes calm. "Turbulence happens from time to time. It doesn't mean there's anything wrong with the plane. Take a deep breath and relax."

I knew he was right. Turbulence happened. But as Dad knew well enough: *planes did crash.*

"Just forget it," I said. Feeling stupid, I stared back out the window.

Over Taipei, Taiwan. Didn't know the time. Didn't care.

Dad held my hand as we prepared for landing.

As the plane started to descend, I lost my stomach. Literally. A death drop, yes, but this time, no death. Just pools of barf all over my pants that dripped down my knees onto and *into* my favorite pair of yellow Converse.

Blech. Dad mopped up the nasty throw-up with the blue blanket. Vera and Tom wore masks of sympathy. My face was greasy, my hair disgusting and oily, and now my mouth was filled with cream-cheesy puke. You'd think with two world-adventuring relief-worker parents that some sort of recessive tough gene would have kicked in with me by now, but nope. No such luck.

I'd never felt so revolting in all my life.

Our plane bounced to the ground, pinning me to my seat as it screeched to a halt. I squeezed Dad's hand so hard, his knuckles turned white. The flight attendant spoke over the loudspeaker in Mandarin. Part one of our flight was over.

I was covered in barf, but at least I was alive.

LANDING

The airport was crowded. And broiling. And so humid it was like walking through a vaporizer on full blast.

"Great, now I will reek even more like rotten milk," I moaned, imagining curds popping up all over my clothes. Me. A human quart of cottage cheese. When you start grossing *yourself* out? That's when you have a problem.

"You can change in the bathroom," Dad said. "Hang in there. And make sure you stay right next to me. I don't want to lose you in here."

"Aye, aye, Captain," I said. As our group was pushed along by a huge wave of Asian people swarming the terminal, I clung to Dad like a stinky little kid.

In Taipei, we boarded another plane, swapping Chinese passengers for Indonesians, and again, we were the only Caucasian people on the flight. I'd never felt like such a fish out of water in my life, and I tried not to stare. In California, I'd seen Muslim women before dressed in traditional robes with silky scarves covering their hair. But I'd never seen so many all at once.

I felt out of place. Like I should go change into something more, I don't know, formal. "Do all the women in Indonesia wear those wraps on their heads?" I whispered to Dad.

"The Muslim women usually do. In Indonesia they are called *jilbabs*."

"For religious reasons, right?"

"Yes," Vera said. "The more devout they are, the more their skin is covered. See that woman over there?" She gestured across the aisle subtly and lowered her voice. "Hers is wrapped loosely, showing some of her neck and hair, but more-conservative Muslim women show only the front of their faces."

"Will all the girls at the orphanage be dressed like that?"

"Most likely, since it's a *pesantren*, a formal Muslim or-phanage," Dad explained.

"Will I have to wear one too?"

"You won't have to at the *pesantren*. Just keep your hair back in a ponytail and it should be fine."

I wasn't sure which way would be worse. Standing out because I was the only girl *not* wearing one or awkwardly trying to fit in by trying it. I guessed the ponytail route would be a happy medium. "Okay," I said.

The dot to dot of islands below my window was lush and green. Normally I wouldn't dare look down, but I felt ten times better than I had on the last leg of the flight. I de-barfed the best I could at the last airport, changing into a clean long-sleeved T-shirt and dark tan cotton pants, which I would never wear at home.

It probably sounds gross that I ate so soon after puking,

but when I spotted the Golden Arches at the Taipei airport, I was suddenly *starving*. I almost hugged the Chinese boy taking my order when Big Doctor Tom, my new personal hero, ordered my meal in Mandarin.

After dipping them in my vanilla milk shake, licking the salty fries was the best moment I'd had since listening to Spider's story on the sand. I ate until I was stuffed and when it was time, I boarded this plane without complaint.

I had a fresh blue blanket, a fresh white pillow, and an Ashton Kutcher movie dubbed in Indonesian playing on the wide screen a few aisles away. I sat back and savored. Not because I liked him, I didn't really, but because outside of Team Hope nobody on the plane was even slightly familiar to me and it made Ashton feel like home.

Yogyakarta, Indonesia

De-boarding the plane at the Yogyakarta airport, my eyes darted this way and that, taking in the flood of different faces.

The airport was sort of like the ones in Hawaii: all open and bathed in moist hot air like a sauna with too many people piled inside. My new shirt was already sticky with sweat. Women draped in colorful robes and head coverings walked by, carrying bundles of packages or full baskets of food. Some men were wearing turbans, and some women's faces were covered with veils, with only their dark eyes peering out. Most of the veiled women walked straight ahead without looking around.

"Man, it's hot." I paused, shifting my backpack from one shoulder to the other. "Don't they have air-conditioning here either?" I asked Dad. Dumb question. If they had it, why wouldn't they turn it on?

He didn't humor me with a response because he was reading a sign posted above us that froze me to my spot in line.

Azab untuk penyelundupan narkoba adalah Kematian
THE PENALTY FOR DRUG SMUGGLING
IS DEATH.

Oh, great.

Finally something written in English and that was it? *Death.* A scene from that scary movie where the girls end up in a Thai prison because some jerk at a beach resort planted drugs in one of their bags played in my mind. I patted my pockets and prayed that the customs officer didn't find anything on me. Where did I put that extra Tylenol PM? Was that considered an illegal drug here?

Sweat poured from places I didn't even know had sweat glands.

Then Dad pulled out some American money and paid the armed Indonesian officer. "What are you paying him for?" I whispered through clenched teeth. Was he paying him off to let us in? A bribe?

"Visiting visas," Dad said.

I gulped with relief as the officer waved me through after I handed him my passport. Spending the rest of my life in an Indonesian prison? Not part of my plan.

"Our host should be waiting for us outside. The hard part is over," Dad said, resting a palm on my head and ruffling my hair like he had when I was a kid. The relief in his smile matched mine. We made it over the ocean in one piece.

The closer we got to baggage claim, the more the open-air terminal filled with spices. Whiffs of cinnamon and cloves wafted through the heat. Locals were selling wraps weaved in all colors of the rainbow. Flowing skirts and elegantly carved wall hangings were displayed in small wooden booths. Masks, marionettes and large orange spiky fruits I'd never seen before were for sale by eager shop owners who called out to us, "Lady, lady!" holding up their wares.

"Can we buy stuff?" I asked Dad as a gap-toothed man dressed in a deep purple tunic pedaled by right through the center of the airport driving a meat-on-a-stick cart. My eyes darted from him to another booth. "Hey, are those puppets made out of paper?"

"They're shadow puppets," Tom said, sweat trickling down his hairline. "Pretty cool, huh?"

Vera scooted between me and Dad. "We'll have plenty of time to shop later," she said, as if I were asking her. "We have to get our bags."

We did and then, near the airport's exit, a group of men stood holding signs with various names written on them. I scanned for ours. Not one read TEAM HOPE.

Vera's high forehead glistened with sweat as she poked at her BlackBerry with her pen. "We have a message. The driver went to the wrong airport." She looked apologetically at Dad. "I'm not sure what happened."

Dad touched her elbow. "No problem. We'll just take a cab."

Keeping Vera at ease was apparently a top priority.

"Hey," Dad said, "did everyone remember to take their malaria pills this morning?"

Everyone nodded except for me. "Oh, sorry. I forgot. Is there a drinking fountain?" I asked.

Tom burst out laughing. "Yeah, if you want to get malaria! Bottled water, sweetheart. Remembering that will save you a lot of time in the *mandi*." He handed me a fresh bottle of water out of his backpack.

"What's a *mon-dee*?" I asked.

Vera's eyes widened. "You didn't tell her, Andy?"

Tell me what?

"She read the Indonesian handbook," he said. "Didn't you, Sienna?" He raised his eyebrows expectantly.

Uh.

"I read some of it," I exaggerated. I did flip through it, but I was looking mainly at the pictures. But I couldn't exactly admit that now and look totally unreliable. "I don't remember anything about a *mandi*."

Tom snickered. "Then *clearly* you didn't read the handbook."

"You only had umpteen hours to read it." Dad sighed. "Never mind. Let's just get our bags and hail a cab. They'll be expecting us at the *pesantren*. You can catch up on your reading there."

Feeling guilty, I looked down at my ratty orange Converse.

"Hey, cheer up, kid," Tom said. "Now you'll get to find out about the *mandi* the fun way."

I slugged him on the shoulder. Whatever this *mon-dee* thing was, how bad could it be?

CRACKERS

As we waited at the curb for an empty cab, motorcycles whizzed down the busy street in front of the airport, weaving through taxis and tiny square cars that were screeching along way too fast.

"Look at that lady," I said, pointing out a woman dressed in a traditional black robe and head covering. She rode a motor scooter sidesaddle. "Oh my God," I cried, "is that a *baby* on that thing?"

Sure enough, a toddler was balancing on the driver's hip as she zoomed past us.

"They all drive *motors* here," Tom explained. "Women, men . . . even babies."

I was shocked. "Do they crash a lot?"

"They crash all the time," Tom said. "See those helmets? They call them crackers because your head cracks open if you crash while wearing one."

"Don't they work?"

"They're cheap plastic helmets. Not like the ones at home. In fact, a volunteer I knew crashed while riding here. Split in half when he hit the pavement."

"His *head*?" I was appalled.

"No, silly, the helmet," Tom said.

"So he lived?"

Tom shrugged. "No. He died."

Fabulous. I looked to Dad for help.

"Tom, that's enough," Dad said.

"Yes, lovely, Tom. Thank you," Vera chastised him.

I was shocked out of my gourd. "This place is nuts," I said.

"Just stay off *motors*, kid, and you'll be fine," Tom said, picking something out of his teeth with his fingernail.

"I would NEVER go near one of those crazy things. Why do they even sell helmets if they don't work?"

Vera stroked the skunk stripe in her moist hair. "Careful about making rash cultural judgments, Sienna. Remember, they might think our customs were odd if they came to America."

Like what? Helmets that worked?

I stepped farther back from the curb as a female driver wearing a chic black pantsuit cruised by. The sun was bright, the tropical air too hot and too wet. I pulled my sunglasses out of my bag and slipped them on.

Vera, now adorned in a dorky floppy white hat, squinted into the light. Horns blared, and I noticed the skyline was brown, like Los Angeles on a high-alert-no-playing-outside kind of day. It also smelled like smoke.

"It's pollution, and from burning garbage and rice fields," Dad said when I asked him why. "They don't have air pollution laws like we do in California," he explained.

An empty cab finally pulled up, and an enthusiastic driver hopped out, a cigarette hanging from his mouth.

Dad spoke to him in Indonesian and we all squeezed into the backseat, which reeked like melting plastic and BO. Dad sat next to him, shotgun. He pulled out the address and gave it to him. I was impressed by Dad's grip on the language. Though I didn't understand a word of what they were saying, I listened to them talk as the driver lit up another cigarette and blasted off into traffic.

At first I didn't think about the immediate danger as I rolled down my window to avoid the secondhand smoke. The hot air felt good on my face. I could have called it wind, but the air wasn't moving enough to earn that definition. Then I realized how fast we were zipping through traffic. And the fact that there was nothing strapping me into my seat.

"Remember that scene in *Star Wars* where Han is zigzagging his ship through the asteroid field?" I said in a shaky voice. "This is just like that." I was trying to be cool and breezy like Tom. Trying not to think about our heads splitting open on hot black asphalt.

"Arrrr." Tom pounded on his chest, a terrible Chewbacca imitation. Everyone did it except me and the driver. The driver probably thought we were insane.

"Don't distract him! He needs to concentrate on the road!"

"Live a little, kid," Tom said with an obnoxious grin.

I rolled my eyes as the driver jerked the car to the right and then a sharp left to avoid crashing into rows of outdoor market stalls. I imagined the baskets of fish and fruit and brains splattered all over the streets.

Live a little. Okay, fine.

"I'll give him some credit. He must be very good at video games," I mumbled.

Tom cracked up and then pointed past me. "Check that out!" We whizzed past a booth selling funky wooden clocks in every shape and size you could think of veiled by a kaleidoscope of blankets blowing in the breeze. "I'm going Christmas shopping while we're here for sure. Look at those bamboo cooking supplies!" Tom said.

While I was worried about our body parts being splayed all over the road, Tom was dreaming about playing Santa.

What had I gotten myself into?

A short, shoeless man stood beside a booth at the top of a driveway, a cigarette dangling out of his mouth.

"Are you sure this is the right place, Dad? Where are all the kids?" I asked.

I stepped cautiously out of the cab, and noticed the thick air had turned into drizzle.

This was the orphanage?

The man said something to Dad in Indonesian and then held open a decrepit white gate for us as the taxi driver unloaded our bags.

I hung back by the cab, clutching my backpack to my chest.

"Vera? You *sure* you guys gave him the right address?"

Cats were everywhere. Skinny feral cats: on the cracked tile porches of the dying square buildings I saw through the gate, on the mostly dead lawn and now, rubbing against my pant leg.

I was more of a dog person.

"Sienna, come on," Dad said, coaxing me away from the cab. "We're here."

When the taxi skidded off, shooting wet dirt into the air, I resisted the urge to run after it.

And then boisterous yelling rang through the silence.

Some boys about my age were messing around across the way. Dressed in grungy T-shirts that looked more like dishrags than clothes, they were pulling aluminum cans out of a filthy river.

"Are those the orphans?" I asked, wincing a little as I said the *o* word. "I mean, are those the kids that live at the *pesantren*?"

"Street kids, probably. Collecting cans to sell," Tom said.

"The street kids don't live here?"

"No," Dad said. "Some might be runaways, some orphans."

"If they don't have a home, then why don't they live here?"

"Come on, sweetie. We have to find the owner."

I should have moved, but I couldn't take my eyes off the kids.

"This school is capped for the number of kids they could take," Dad explained. "In fact, the *pesantren* owner was able to take only one-third of the tsunami orphans who wanted to come here from the refugee camps in Aceh."

I cringed as another black cat, this one carrying a dried-up bone in his teeth, slinked against my leg. His body was so thin and scrawny. Didn't anyone feed him?

Dumb question that I didn't even bother asking out loud.

If nobody was feeding the street kids, why wouldn't the cats be on their own too?

That's when a man about Dad's age, but shorter and wearing a black cap on the crown of his head, walked down the path to greet us.

"Welcome!" he said, arms outstretched. "Thank you for coming, doctors." He spoke in thick-accented English. "How were the logistics of your trip?"

"Excellent, thank you," Dad said, extending his hand for a shake. *Excellent* was a bit of an exaggeration, I thought as they exchanged pleasantries and introductions.

And then the owner said, "Now we go meet the orphans. They have prepared a special evening ceremony to greet our welcomed guests."

"What time is it?" I asked Dad.

"We landed around five p.m. It's about seven p.m.," he said. "That reminds me." He fiddled with his watch, resetting it to Indonesian time.

I followed Team Hope and the *pesantren* owner down a muddy path past dozens of white-paint-chipped outbuildings decorated with blue accents. Peeking through many open windows, I saw empty rooms, with kids' clothes draped over scrappy-looking bunk beds.

On the overgrown lawn, a lone goat was tied to a palm tree with a fraying rope. The same tree held one end of a ripped volleyball net. Besides the mews of the starving cats, the place was silent. Ghost town silent. Like a summer camp might feel like if you stumbled on it years after it was shut down.

The owner walked with purpose, his feet solidly pounding the ground, speaking to my father in a polite but assertive tone until we came to a long rectangular building, also white with blue trim but with double doors etched in elaborate Indonesian designs.

It was the center of the door that caught my attention. Two carvings shaped like the flower bulbs Oma planted in the winter and waited patiently for spring to bloom.

"You ready, kid?" Tom asked quietly.

I had no idea what I was supposed to be ready for, but when the *pesantren* owner opened the creaky door, it became clear what he meant.

A sea of faces stared back at me. At us. Dressed in black and white, some of the younger children squirmed on the tile floor until they noticed the *pesantren* owner. Then they sat immediately at attention: backs straight with legs tucked underneath.

I flashed on a school assembly at home in El Angel Miguel. Principal Sanchez couldn't get us to shut up for ten seconds. But this tiny, stern-faced man in wire-rimmed glasses could quiet them with one look? That's power.

Scanning the crowd more carefully, I noticed the boys were wearing white long-sleeved dress shirts tucked into black pants with small black hats, like the one the owner wore, on the crowns of their dark heads. The girls dressed in the same colors but with flowing *jilbabs* covering their heads, necks and shoulders. Most of the girls wore skirts instead of pants.

I was really glad I hadn't shown up in a tank top and shorts.

"All the orphans are gathered for our honored guests," the owner explained.

The room looked split by gender, with the girls on the left and the boys on the right, the younger kids kneeling in front.

"The two hundred children of the tsunami from Aceh are in the center of the room," he said in a not-so-subtle voice.

My eyes darted to the group he was talking about; I recognized some of the kids from the DVD. When I saw their faces, I heard their voices, heard their stories. Saw the wave rising up and over . . .

The owner addressed them in Indonesian, and suddenly the kids started clapping and cheering. A tall older student, a boy, translated his words to English as we stood in front of the room. "These are visiting doctors from America who have come to meet you," he said. "Orphans from Aceh, please stand."

A huge group, more than half the room, stood up; some of them stared down at their feet uncomfortably. I caught the eye of one little girl. She was standing in the front row of tsunami kids, a curtain of black hair falling out of her *jilbab,* veiling an eye.

She looked just like the shy girl in the video! The one I wanted to meet. I smiled at her, hoping she'd notice me, but she didn't.

"Orphans from Papua, please stand."

The Aceh kids sat down and about fifty other kids stood up. Tom whispered to me that many of those kids suffered from post-traumatic stress disorder too, because many witnessed their parents' deaths in street riots.

His words hit me like an anvil to my chest. If you bottled up all the trauma in this room . . . I couldn't even imagine. And these kids were my age and *younger.* Suddenly I was very glad we were here. Like Dad said—these were people who really needed his help.

"Thank you, children," the *pesantren* owner said, and then he turned to Team Hope. "The Acehnese orphans have prepared a special welcome ceremony for you. Children?" He nodded to the crowd and led us against the wall, where we were apparently supposed to watch.

A dozen mixed-age boys stood up off the floor and carried gold and red drums entwined with dark leather straps to the front of the room.

One of the boys stood out immediately.

He and his drum were the tallest, broadest, most striking. The other boys' eyes were only on him, silently asking him where to sit, what to do next. He told them with gestures of his head, his hands. His lanky body moved with a sort of shrug, like he was almost annoyed to be there but had committed to going through the motions anyway.

I totally got that.

Once situated in a circle on the floor, the instruments splayed across their laps, the boys began lightly slapping both ends of the drums with their palms. The tone was soft at first, then elevated until the beat came harder and faster, their music creating a rich sound that vibrated through the flat-roofed room so frenetically that my pulse raced along with it.

I couldn't stop staring at the tallest boy, the one pounding his drum like he was out for vengeance. I didn't know how he did it, but his music throttled its way through me, straight to my core. He glanced up. Once. Caught me staring. His eyes electric, but steady. I still didn't break his gaze. Instead I sucked in a breath. Blinked. Took in the sight of him. The sweat trickling down his temple, his square-boned jaw, his rippling arm muscles as he beat the crap out of that drum.

When his strong hands slowed to a quiet rhythm, when the thumping finally faded to a slow, easy pulse, applause erupted around me. Almost as an afterthought, I clapped along too but couldn't stop looking. Couldn't unlock my eyes from the drummer wiping his forehead with his sleeve.

I hadn't expected to find anything like *him* behind those carved doors.

"The Aceh orphans are talented," the owner said to my dad. Then he lowered his voice. "Talented, but problematic."

Did he mean their nightmares and anxiety were problematic? That they screamed out in the night like I did? That he wasn't sure how to help them? But something about his tone told me that he meant something else. Something less kind than all of that.

As the applause died down, as the boys packed up their drums and wandered back to their seats, I wondered why the owner referred to the kids as the Aceh orphans anyway.

Just because they survived the tsunami, why should they be defined by it?

I'd be beating the hell out of a drum if someone kept referring to me that way too. What if Dad had been with Mom on that small plane? What if I had lost both of them to the sea?

Orphaned by a plane crash, Sienna Jones, please stand.

Then a chorus of little girls approached the front, taking the place of the drum circle. They stood side by side, facing their peers and four American strangers.

"The song is about a fragrant *jeumpa* flower that grows

only in Aceh," the translating boy explained in a throaty voice.

Of course, I didn't understand a word of what I assumed was now Acehnese, but I could tell by the far-off looks on their faces that the girls were singing about their home.

When the song ended, the girls bowed and we all clapped.

I was already glancing at the back door, ready to bolt. The hot, stale air was suffocating, and my shirt and pants were both stuck to my skin with glue-like sweat.

Just when I was about to flee, a line of older boys began to form, winding their way toward us.

"What's going on?" I whispered to Dad.

"They're coming to meet us. The boys first, then the girls."

He had to be kidding. "All five hundred?" I eyed the door.

"I think so. Are you okay? I know this is an awful long time to stand."

I fanned my face. "It's just so hot in here . . ."

Too late.

One by one, the boys approached us like we were a receiving line at a wedding reception. When I realized the leader of the drum circle was first, my heart sped up. I stopped worrying about the heat. Wished I were wearing something clean. Something nice.

Out of the corner of my eye, I watched the drummer take Tom's right hand, hold it to his forehead and then let it fall as he touched his own heart, bowing as he did.

Closer now, I noticed the boy's thick sideburns, his full, serious lips, the stubble of goatee peppered across his chin like it wasn't sure if it should keep growing or fade away.

I swallowed. I was next.

Quickly, I wiped my sweaty hands on the sides of my pants.

"What is that?" I whispered to Dad, suddenly wishing like heck I'd read that handbook.

"It's their welcoming handshake," Dad whispered back.

And then he was standing in front of me.

He looked about sixteen or seventeen. When his eyes met mine, they were so intense and dark. Bottom-of-the-ocean dark, the darkest eyes I'd ever seen. Up close his eyes were even more piercing, like he was trying to peer right into my soul.

Before I had time to wipe the new nervous sweat off my palms, he reached out, took my hand in his and lifted my fingers gently to his forehead. His skin, the color of driftwood, was soft, smooth, hot to the touch. When he let go, when he let my fingers fall gently by my side, his penetrating look dove even deeper. When he touched his heart with his palm and shyly bowed his head, then, only then, did he lower his gaze.

Whoa.

My brain was swimming, and I had to focus to remember the one Indonesian phrase I overheard Dad say to the taxi driver.

"Terima kasih," I whispered. Thank you.

At that the boy raised his eyebrows, mischievous, teasing.

What? Had I pronounced it wrong?

I hoped he couldn't hear my heart pound. I tried to calm down, but it was hard to do. Practically impossible, in fact. When he finally walked away, I watched the hard muscles in his back ripple under his white shirt, shadowed with sweat. He walked with a slight limp, which only added to his allure. I wanted to find out why.

But he didn't turn around again.

When he opened the back door and slipped into the daylight, I had to fight the urge to run after him.

"Sienna?" Dad's voice slowly pulled me back to reality. "This young man is trying to get your attention," he said.

"What? Oh. Sorry."

Standing in front of me waiting to greet me was another boy. A new boy. I gave him my hand, but I knew his welcome would feel nothing like the one that came before him.

ELLI

Even after the hundredth greeting, I started to eye the door again, distracted, wondering about the drummer. Then the little girl from the DVD wound her way up in line to greet me. I smiled at her, and when she grinned back, the space where her two front teeth should be were tiny pearls budding from her gums.

"Hello," I said.

"Hello!" she mimicked, her voice sweet as maple syrup.

She repeated the traditional gesture, my hand to her forehead, and gave another shy grin, like she was inviting me into a game only she knew how to play. Her energy dazzled me. Both of her parents were dead? How could she seem so alive?

At the end of the greeting, she didn't let go. Instead she tugged on my hand, led me out of the crowded room and into the drizzle. I glanced back at Team Hope, who were standing around chatting. The little girl was the end of the line, so it probably didn't matter if I took off. I almost called out, letting Dad know that I was going, but instead I held on tight to her hand because it was pretty obvious that she knew more about life here than I did.

"Hello!" she said again once we were outside.

"Hello!" I said back, trying to match her enthusiasm.

"*Nama saya* Elli," she said, touching her chest.

Oh. My name is Elli.

"*Nama saya* Sienna."

"Sienna!" she said. "Sienna!"

Shyness evaporated, she dragged me by the hand down the same muddy path we walked to the meeting room. Past the decrepit dorms and into one of the white buildings with open blue-trimmed windows that I had been peeking into before.

The room was in worse shape than I had imagined.

Metal bunk beds lined the floor. Articles of clothing flopped awkwardly over rusted frames. The air smelled like moldy bread and stagnant pond water. Two small rattan dressers on the far wall held overstuffed drawers. The open window had no glass and no screen, just chipped blue folding shutters that I doubted could even keep the big bugs out.

I focused on keeping my expression neutral so Elli didn't feel my honest reaction to the place that was now her home.

"You," she said happily, pointing to the top bunk by the window. "Me."

Then she pointed to the bottom bunk under the one she said would be mine. My reaction probably wasn't what she wanted, so she repeated louder and clearer, "Sienna." Point. "Elli." Point. She tilted her face expectantly.

I got that she wanted me to sleep above her; I just didn't want to imagine actually sleeping on that stained mattress. I forced a grin. "Okay." I pointed to the top bunk. "Sienna. Thank you, Elli. *Terima kasih.*"

She giggled and clapped. We were communicating.

Glancing out the open window, I watched early-evening light cast shadows across the moldy walls. I thought about the boy with the limp and wondered if he was thinking about me too.

I found Dad a few minutes later passing out newly inflated soccer balls with his trusty sidekick Vera. A group of boys were crowded around Tom, listening to him eagerly as if he was the coach in a huddle.

"Hey," I greeted Dad.

"There you are! I lost you after the ceremony."

"Oh, sorry. This is Elli. She sort of dragged me out and then showed me around her room. She wants me to sleep in there with her. Is that okay, or am I assigned a different dorm?"

"That sounds great! We were going to put you in with the youngest girls anyway."

While Dad and I started talking about the logistics of bunking with the kids, what to look out for as far as PTSD signs, Vera approached a group of teenage girls.

"What's she doing?" I asked.

"Gathering interest in her group therapy session. We hope all the survivors with PTSD symptoms will participate, but we're definitely not going to force them to."

Dressed in various pastel-colored *jilbabs,* the girls listened to Vera intently. Some nodded, intrigued, while others looked away as if they didn't want to hear her words at all.

I would definitely fall into category B.

Past them, I noticed a group of older boys I recognized from the ceremony but who were now dressed in T-shirts and long pants, sauntering along the edge of the lawn. I scanned their faces, but the drummer boy wasn't among them.

"Are you okay, kiddo?" Dad pulled a bottle out of his backpack. "When is the last time you drank water?"

I shrugged off a bit of disappointment, wondering where the drummer was. "The airport."

"Sienna! You're dehydrated. I need to take better care of you. Sorry, sweetie. Here, sit down, sit down."

I sat down. I drank. But I still didn't feel much better.

"It's the jet lag," Dad said. "You'll feel better after a good night's rest."

Vera flagged Dad over, and I couldn't help but notice the bounce in his step when he answered her call. If they weren't working together, I'd swear they were interested in each other. Thank goodness Dad didn't date. He still wore his wedding ring. Even if she was gone, he was still married to my mom.

It was one of the things that made me admire him. Even if it was totally irrational—Oma said that over and over again—Dad hadn't given up on her either.

Dad spoke with Vera for a moment before tossing one of the fluorescent yellow soccer balls we brought as gifts to a grinning boy about eight or so. He was wearing a ripped-up X-Men T-shirt and too-small shorts. All the kids were now dressed in play clothes. I guessed they changed after the ceremony. The Wolverine fan caught the ball easily and kicked it to a friend.

"You like soccer?" I asked.

He nodded and chatted to me in his language. I didn't understand a word of what he and his friends were saying, but their excitement, like Elli's, was contagious.

"Is he speaking Acehnese or Indonesian?" I asked Dad when he wandered back over.

Dad said something to the boy and then turned to me. "He's from Aceh, so he speaks both languages. He was speaking Indonesian to you. Most of the younger children don't speak English. Many of the older kids do, though. They've been studying longer."

Tom, from across the field, kicked a soccer ball at me. I caught it as he jogged up, red-faced and panting. "You guys talking about how I'm the next Beckham?" he huffed.

"Yes, what else would we be talking about?" Dad said, and I laughed.

"Dad's explaining who speaks English, who doesn't," I said, throwing the ball to a kid.

"Ah," Tom said, collapsing onto the grass. "I know *one* English speaker who will be getting plenty of attention. Especially from the boys. I'll give you a clue. It rhymes with Vienna. And has long blond hair. Anyone?"

Tom's chest heaved as he tormented me. But I couldn't help flashing on my drummer boy, hoping, in this one instant, Tom was right.

"Leave my girl alone," Dad said, handing Tom a fresh bottle of water. "Sienna has more important things to concentrate on than boys. Besides, she's too young for all of that."

With a burst of energy, I grabbed another ball and kicked it high into the air and watched the little guys run after it.

Dad was smiling at me so wide I thought his face might rip.

"What?"

"I knew it," he said.

"What?"

"Bringing you here was a great idea. You're already bonding with the kids." He shot friendly daggers at his best friend. "And I don't mean those *teenage boys,* Tom."

One *teenage boy,* I thought. *Specifically, one.*

I caught the ball. "The art stuff sounds good. When do I start?"

"Tomorrow morning. Use the markers and chalk we've brought and do free art. Let us know if their drawings are about the disaster or about their time here at the *pesantren.* It really helps us gauge where they are mentally."

"Where are you two going to sleep?" I asked.

I kicked the ball back to the boys.

"Tom and I are sharing a private room near the Aceh boys' dorm . . ."

When he said "Aceh boys," I wondered if Dad would be sleeping anywhere near the drummer boy.

". . . then once you're settled into the art, you can start working with Vera's therapy group in the afternoons, like we talked about on the plane."

Ugh. "Why can't I work with you and Tom?"

"I'm afraid not, kiddo. It would be inappropriate to have a young woman in the boys' group. Besides, Vera's an expert in talk therapy," he said, a note of pride in his voice. "You'll be learning from the best. Remember you already agreed."

"Yeah, but why is it inappropriate?" I asked, ignoring the inane Vera praise. If I got into Dad's or Tom's group I might run into the drummer again. And besides, I'd experienced Vera's version of therapy, making her patient feel totally inferior to her. Yeah, good times. If she was the "best," I couldn't imagine what the worst was like.

"It's a cultural thing," Dad said. "The boys could feel uncomfortable having you there and may not speak as freely around you."

Getting tongue-tied around the opposite sex—I got that completely, but how was I supposed to get to know this awesome guy if I couldn't be around him? "What am I supposed to do to help Vera?"

"You could be her assistant in group. Since you understand"—Dad cleared his throat: uncomfortable subject warning alert—"some of what these girls are going through, Vera and I thought that perhaps you could be an extra ear. Having a peer who understands how they're feeling, some of their symptoms, the nightmares, the anxiety, might help them feel more comfortable—I'll be right back." Dad wandered across the field toward Vera while I imagined afternoon after afternoon sweating in the stifling heat listening to her.

Coincidentally, a rogue soccer ball slammed into my ankle at the exact time I felt like smashing something into oblivion.

I tossed it into the air, watched it spin and then launched it super-hard, as hard as I could, straight drive down the field.

I wasn't trying to hit her.

I just had bad aim, you see. But lucky for her, Dad dove into the air Superman-style, swooping in seconds before the ball smacked her upside the head.

"Sienna!" he yelled across the field. "You almost hit her!"

"Good thing you were there to save the day," I muttered under my breath. They both walked up to me, faces masked with disappointment.

"You need to apologize," Dad said. "Sienna. I'm waiting."

"Sorry."

"Not to me! To Vera!"

Um.

Thankfully, at the very moment, Tom started doing belly-baring handstands and lopsided cartwheels. His audience grew larger as more kids gathered around. Some of the kids yelled, *"Gemuk! Gemuk!"* as they danced around him. I was relieved the apologizing-to-Vera moment had passed as we all turned to look at the commotion. I asked Tom what the kids were saying.

"They're impressed with my girth," he said, not at all embarrassed. *"Gemuk* means 'fat,' and in Indonesia to say someone is fat is a compliment."

"I'll have to let Bev know. Maybe that will change her mind about carbs."

"They also like big noses, which is probably why your dad is so popular," Vera said.

"Very funny," Dad retorted, matching her playful tone.

Do they love skunk stripes too? Because if they do, you're bound to be a hit.

"Sienna, don't you have something to say to Vera?"

Oh God.

Suddenly I was five, had just stolen a cherry snack pie from the mini-mart and Dad was making me confess.

"Sorry I almost hit you with the soccer ball," I said.

Vera rubbed her head like she felt invisible pain. *Please.*

"That's okay," she said in a saccharine voice. "Accidents happen."

"So I hear," I muttered.

"Sienna, your tone, please."

"It's fine, Andy." Vera held up her hand. "It's been a long day. Sienna must be exhausted. Not to mention jet-lagged and probably dehydrated. Lay off her."

Yeah, lay off me. Wait. Did Vera just stick up for me?

And then my dad, instead of announcing, I AM HER FATHER. I KNOW WHAT'S BEST, like he does when Oma intervenes, said, "You're right, V. We're all tired. It's okay, sweetie." But he wasn't looking at me when he said it. He was looking at *her*.

"I'm heading back to the dorm for a bit. I'll see you in the morning?" Vera said, her eyes lingering on my dad's.

"See you," Dad said softly.

What?

Should I say something? Confront them?

No. It was just my imagination playing tricks on me. Dad. Dad loved Mom. Vera probably loved . . . furry nocturnal animals. She was the classic crazy cat lady—destined to be found by neighbors dead from natural causes on the floor of her studio apartment at age one hundred and something with her only companions, twenty beloved cats, eating her bony remains.

Nothing was going on between them, I convinced myself. Nothing at all.

PRETENDING

After Vera left, Dad and I sat quietly on the grass, just the two of us, watching the kids play with Tom.

I was amazed how happy they seemed. The kids. I expected something . . . different. I thought they'd be wandering around homesick or depressed or something. Maybe they were like me. Maybe they were pretending.

"I want to talk to you about something," Dad said suddenly.

I closed my eyes and leaned back on the moist lawn. "Dad, I already apologized for the soccer ball incident."

"No, no, not that. Listen. I need your help with something."

I sat back up, slowly. "What is it?"

Dad lowered his voice. "After the welcoming ceremony, the *pesantren* owner spoke with me privately about a boy named Deni. He's popular with the Aceh boys, their leader, it seems, and I don't want to ask the other kids for him because it will get back to him that the owner mentioned him specifically. Information here spreads like wildfire. Everybody knows everybody else's business. Nothing is private."

"Why didn't he just point him out?"

"He said Deni was one of the boys in the drum circle,

but he was gone by the time I spoke with the owner. He said if I couldn't find him by tomorrow, he'd quietly point him out."

The leader of the Aceh boys? In the drum circle? I wondered if it could be the same boy.

My boy.

"They like to gossip?" I knew all about gossip. The queen bee of my freshman class, Sandra Bizmark, was also the queen of gossip. You could tell her something in the morning and the whole school knew by lunchtime.

I learned not to tell her *anything*.

Dad rubbed his beard. "Gossip has more-malicious implications. Their talk-talk doesn't have ill intent; they just don't have the same sense of autonomy that some Westerners do. If something happens to one person, it affects the whole."

"So what's the problem with this Deni guy?"

"Apparently, he has issues with the way this place is run, argues with the owner . . . I don't know much more than that—but I do know that we're here to help the kids from Aceh assimilate into this *pesantren* with the rest of the kids. . . ."

"Why aren't they assimilating?"

"In Aceh things were different. They had more freedom, fewer rules. This is a very conservative institution: strict bedtimes, school schedules, mealtimes. It's like, imagine transferring to a strict Catholic boarding school after living at home and going to El Angel Miguel High, where you have an open campus and wear shorts to school."

"And worse, if I was going because my entire family was dead," I blurted out.

My words looked like they caused Dad physical pain. "Yes. You can imagine how hard it would be to adjust after you've lived with so much freedom."

"I get it."

"So if Deni has a problem with how this place is run, I don't want him to get the idea that I'm on the pesantren's of the conflict," Dad explained.

My eyes popped open. "So you want me to be a spy?"

He tilted his head. "Not a spy, per se . . . I just want you to find out who he is if you can."

I matched his sly tone. "Ah . . . I see, and what will I get for said *information*?"

"You will be forgiven for past crimes with soccer balls?" He eyed me knowingly. He knew full well that wasn't a complete accident.

"Fine," I said. "Game on."

"I knew I could count on you, kiddo. Just ask around, see if one of the kids will point him out to you. The *pesantren* owner has to leave town for the next few days, and before he gets back, I'd like to make some headway with Deni. I really want to help smooth over their conflict before we go back home."

"Why is it so important to bond with Deni? I mean, he's just one kid," I said.

"If I want the Aceh kids to be honest about what's going on with them and their emotions during group, it needs to start with their leader. Acehnese are a very patriarchal society. These kids don't have a father anymore, so they look to this boy Deni as their father figure. If I'm going to help with their healing process, it's going to need to start with Deni, and then the rest will follow."

I thought about the drummer boy subtly letting the younger kids know what to do during their performance. How they looked at him, emulating his every move.

What Dad said made sense.

Dad put his arm around me and squeezed. "I hope I won't disappoint," I said.

The beginnings of sunset bounced off the plain gold band that he wore on his left finger. The steadiness of Dad's wedding ring soothed me.

"You won't," Dad said in a tone I believed.

I yawned, sucking in a bit of burnt air.

We watched silently as the sun slipped into the sludgy river. The haze was pink and brown and reminded me of Mom's story about the ship captain.

"Remember the story Mom used to tell about the ship captain?" Dad asked.

Seriously?

"I was just thinking the same exact thing."

"Really? How funny. I was thinking about it on the plane over too—especially the bit about the sailor hurrying home. The sky's like the light the captain was looking for, isn't it?"

"Yeah, except it's not pink and orange like at home; it's brownish—Fudge Popsicle Haze." I started laughing.

But Dad didn't laugh. "You look so much like her now, you know. . . ." His voice cracked, and the lines in his face deepened.

"Huh?"

"Like your mom. And here . . . for some reason, you remind me of her so much. It's hard to put a finger on exactly what it is . . . but it's something."

He used to tell me that a lot when I was little: *You lovelies are two pearls cut from the same oyster,* he'd say with pride.

"Thanks," I said.

Dad looked at me cautiously before he asked, "Is it . . . hard for you to be here, knowing we are so close to where we lost her?"

The Indian Ocean.

"Yeah," I admitted. "I know it sounds stupid, but I'm still always hoping she'll turn up."

Dad looked at me sadly and then gently spun his ring around and around his left finger.

"It's been three years, sweetie. They combed the ocean, the land. I didn't come home until they were sure . . ."

". . . But they never found the wreckage," I said.

Dad sighed. "I know. But if she was . . . if she were alive, sweetie, don't you think she'd have come home? She loved us too."

"Maybe. But maybe she . . . I mean hypothetically, she . . ." I let the words trail off.

I ran out of Maybes and Hypotheticals and Buts a long time ago.

Yet here I was trying the same exact thing again.

"Perhaps while we're here," Dad said, in a cautious voice, "I was thinking of maybe doing a little ceremony; we could drive out to the Indian Ocean, say a few words. . . ."

My eyes stung with tears. "No."

"Sienna, I think maybe it would be good . . ."

"No. No way."

I dug my fingernails into my palm.

"Just think about it?"

"NO."

He breathed out a long, slow sigh as my heart raced in my chest.

"Okay." Dad stared at his ring. Tapped on it. Pulled it halfway off, then stuck it back on.

I felt a little better.

He loved Mom and would never stop loving her. Just because he couldn't see her didn't mean she wasn't there. Their marriage was a constant. Forever.

I swallowed away the painful moment and breathed.

Too bad Vera hadn't heard our conversation, so she could give up hope that my mom's husband would ever be her man.

"There's nothing quite like being on the other side of the world," he said.

Dad patted my knee, and together we watched the Fudge Popsicle Haze disappear into the horizon, sure we were both thinking about the same person.

CONNECTION

My favorite little girl didn't walk; she bounced.

"Hello!" she said, skipping up to us, the last glow of sunset painting her white *jilbab* pink.

"Hello, Elli. This is my dad."

"*Nama saya* Andy," he said, shaking Elli's hand.

"Doctor Andy," Elli said proudly.

"Yes," I said. Then to Dad. "Shouldn't it be almost her bedtime?" I asked.

Dad checked his watch. "It's almost nine."

The sky was getting dark, and I remembered I hadn't gone to the bathroom or brushed my teeth since the airport. I confessed to Dad.

"Seriously?" He groaned. "Okay, let's find the girls' *mandi* and then get you some more water. *Aku mau mandi?*" he asked Elli.

"*Kamar kecil! Waay saay!*" She grabbed my hand and skipped down the path.

"Way say?" I asked.

"WC," Dad said, walking fast to keep up with us. "Water closet, like they say in England."

Dad followed us partway down the path and then stopped short as if a force field had stopped him in his tracks.

"What?" I asked.

"I can't go any farther. This is the girls' section, and men aren't allowed."

"But you're my dad!"

"Doesn't matter, kiddo. No boys in the girls' area."

Dad dug into his backpack and handed me two energy bars and two bottles of water. Then, almost as an afterthought, he handed me a package of baby wipes.

"What are these for?"

"The *mandi*. It's sort of like camping. You'll see."

Oh yes, Tom's *mandi* joke. I guessed I was about to find out the "fun way."

"You need to use the bottled water to wash your face and brush your teeth. Remember when you wash your hair to spit the water out the whole time you're pouring the bucket over your head. If you get even the slightest amount of water in your mouth, you could get sick from the microorganisms living in it."

"Microorganisms? Why didn't you tell me this before? What bucket? There aren't any showers? Dad, I haven't showered since we left home. I need to clean up."

"Honey. Calm down. Don't forget to take your malaria pill tomorrow, and remember to wear flip-flops in the *mandi*. You don't want to get a fungal infection."

This was getting more fun by the second.

He looked at me wearily before he said, "Okay. Well, I guess I'll see you at breakfast."

Butterflies fluttered in my stomach. "Wait! Where is breakfast? How will I find you?"

No cell phones. No landlines. He wasn't even allowed in my room! I didn't even know my way around, and he was just ditching me?

He spoke to Elli in Indonesian. "Elli promises to take excellent care of you," he said with a wink in her direction. Then his tone changed to more protective. "If you need anything, you can ask Vera. She'll be bunking in the girls' area too. I'm not sure which dorm, but you should be able to find her easily enough."

No, thanks. I'd rather tough it out alone.

Dad kissed my cheek quickly. "You'll be fine. *Sweet* dreams." The way he said it wasn't the same way most dads said it. I heard him loud and clear: *Think good thoughts; try not to have a nightmare. I can't help you here.*

"Okay." My throat clogged with homesickness. "I'll be fine." I tried to convince myself.

You're fifteen. You're not a baby. Pull it together.

"I know you will," he said, his face showing confidence that mine lacked.

And just like that he was gone.

Pulling open the creaking door for me, Elli pointed inside. *"Mandi!"*

In the middle of a wet, moldy floor was a hole cut into once-white tile. Next to the hole sat a dirty blue bucket, a metal pitcher, and a rusty drain in the ground. In the corner of the furry green floor was a squatting bug-eyed creature. I jumped back behind Elli. "Is that a *frog*?"

Elli erupted into a fit of giggles when I shrieked. Then she skipped into the filthy room and scooped the frog into her hands, presenting the bumpy amphibian to me as if it were a rare gift.

"Kodak," she said. *"Kodak."*

When the frog croaked, I flinched and she collapsed into more giggles.

"Okay, here goes nothing."

I closed the *mandi*'s rickety door after Elli stepped out. There was no clean place to set my backpack, so I balanced it on my lap, after pulling down my pants and squatting over the hole. Dad's warnings haunted me: *fungal infections, microorganisms.* My scalp itched, and for a second I considered attempting to wash my hair but then gagged when I glanced down into the blue bucket, the one I was (per Dad's instructions) supposed to pour over my now-greasy hair. There, in mucky water, bobbed two wiggling brown worms. You've got to be kidding.

I was going to *kill* Dad in the morning for leaving me here.

Then I noticed there was no toilet paper. Could it get any worse? Then I remembered the wipes! Careful not to fall on the slippery floor, I dug into my bag and grabbed a couple. But there was no trash can. Should I toss them in the hole? I didn't think that looked right, so I opened one of the energy bars. I set the chocolate chip bar loose in my pack to salvage for later and stuck the used wipes into the wrapper.

And I thought barfing on the plane was bad.

Cursing under my breath, I got the hell out of there.

THE PICTURE

The first thing I noticed was that they weren't wearing their head coverings anymore. Dressed in nightgowns, with long dark hair flowing down their backs, a crowd of little girls was gathered around something in the center of the room.

The second thing I noticed was that thing was my opened suitcase.

T-shirts, pants, bras, flip-flops, my digital camera, even my journal were strewn out all over the dirty floor. "Girls!" I called out. "That's my stuff!"

I started shoving everything back into the suitcase; some of the girls helped, but most backed off nervously.

One girl, taller with a thinner face than Elli's, was wearing my blue polo shirt backward; another kid was opening and shutting my compact powder case. Then I zoomed in on Elli, who had opened my journal and was flipping through the few pictures I had stuck inside before the trip.

"Hello!" she said to me. She waved around the one picture I had of me, Bev and Spider, taken when we were about twelve, laughing, and then she flung it into the air like a baton. Before she could launch it again, I snatched it out of her hands and the whole upper corner, half of Spider's surfboard and part of his head, ripped off and fell onto the floor.

Elli looked mortified as she picked up the ripped piece and handed it to me.

She didn't know. She was just a kid.

I glanced up. A ceiling fan sat broken and still; two of the four blades had been snapped in half, leaving splintered edges.

I retrieved my journal from Elli, my camera from another girl, and set them up on my bed.

"Go ahead and play with the rest. I don't care," I said, swallowing away a gnawing feeling of regret for the greater good of keeping the peace.

The kids looked up at me expectantly, not understanding my words, so I gestured with my hands and forced a grin. "It's okay! You can look!"

Elli spoke to them in Indonesian and then went back to giggling and digging through the only things that reminded me of home. I knelt down next to them, showing them my stuff. When they started yawning, I knew that no grown-up was coming to tuck them in. There were a few other staff, the teachers, Dad said, but they slept in their own rooms at night. The kids were without evening supervision, which was part of the problem. I said, "Time for bed, girls," and pointed to their bunks. Elli reached out cautiously, threw her arms around my neck and gave me a squeeze. I hugged her back and tucked her into her bed.

Then I pulled the lightbulb string and veiled the room in darkness.

When I hopped onto my top bunk, I felt the rock of motion, which reminded me of the plane, which reminded me of my night terrors.

"Oh no," I said out loud. I forgot to ask Dad for a sleeping pill! How would I fall asleep? My body clock was upside down and backward.

But if I didn't fall asleep, I wouldn't have the nightmare.

Maybe I'd just stay up all night and think about stuff.

Once the room was filled with the gentle breaths of sleeping girls, I sat up cross-legged, mindful not to hit my head on the water-damaged ceiling, and opened my journal, slipping out the other pictures from home.

I saw Spider in the slit of moonlight coming through my window, leaning against his surfboard, a lopsided smile on his sunburned lips.

Oma leaning over her flower garden, digging in the fresh earth with a wooden spoon instead of a real tool, with her gray hair pulled up into a loose bun. She was dressed in her favorite butterfly-patched jeans and white beaded tunic. She was frowning at the camera. She didn't like to be photographed, and Dad caught her off guard.

My picture of Bev is from the school debates last year. Wearing a brown suit with a white button-down shirt not unlike the shirts the kids wore here, her mouth was open; she was talking when I took the picture for the yearbook, her eyes fierce with passion. She looked like a young Hillary Clinton.

But the best picture of all was of Mom. She was grinning at the camera, holding the dimpled hand of a fluffy-haired baby wrapped to her chest in a red sling. Dad said she used to call me dandelion girl because of all that blond fluff. The picture was slightly out of focus because Dad said Mom was laughing when he snapped the photo.

It was my favorite picture of the two of us. Mom's crinkly, blue-eyed smile was what home really meant. Before. Now. Still.

I shut the book and leaned over my bunk to check on the little girl sleeping beneath me, her eyes shut tightly. She looked so tiny and alone, I had to resist the urge to curl up next to her like my mom used to do with me. But because I wasn't her mom, because I wasn't even her sister, I whispered instead, "Good night, Elli."

'Cause I was the only one there to say it.

I'm on the plane nosediving toward the sea. A boy, tall and shirtless, limps down the cabin aisle. I follow him. Stumbling. Clutching on to blue headrests so I don't fall. The other seats are empty. We are alone on the plane. I run after him, yelling, "Wait! Wait for me!" But he doesn't turn around. Instead he flings open the cockpit door. No one. The steering wheel rotates by itself as if the plunging plane is being flown by a ghost. The boy sits down in the captain's seat. I rest a hand on his shoulder, and his skin is like quicksand sucking me inside him all the way to his chalk white bones. He spins around, startled, haunted eyes digging into mine—telling me a horror he thinks I'll understand. And then, as quickly as the wound opened, his shoulder heals around my hand.

Screaming, I jerked upright, smacking my head on the corner of something hard.

Cursing under my breath, I blinked.

Someone was there.

Fractioned by the slits of the shutter, I saw a boy peering back at me. Soulful eyes, a scar etched across his forehead. Our eyes met for a second.

What the heck? Getting up on my knees, I pushed the shutter all the way open, leaned out into the pink-dawn light, but he was gone.

Was I still dreaming?

My head throbbed with pain and confusion. Then I noticed my miniature roommates scurrying around the dorm fitting their *jilbabs* onto their heads and carrying rolled-up carpets under their arms like they were late for peewee yoga class.

"What is that noise?" I asked, covering my ears. Loud chanting swarmed our dorm room like camp reveille on speed.

Elli glanced up at me and said, "*Azan!* Allah!" Then she ran out, a swarm of other girls nipping at her heels.

That noise was Allah? I must have still been dreaming.

Then I remembered Dad mentioning "call to prayer" on the plane. Every morning at five a.m.

Which meant I'd never sleep past then.

I groaned and buried my head under the pile of wrinkled clothes I was using for a pillow. I tossed and turned for a while, but it was no use.

I couldn't sleep and the call to prayer was not going to stop.

But then it dawned on me that I was alone. Privacy! I got up and dressed, then braved the *mandi* quickly, brushing my teeth with bottled water and spitting the toothpaste into the drain on the floor. I did the same thing with washing my face. The worms, now dead and turning a ghastly shade of white, were still floating in the bucket.

I didn't have enough bottled water to wash my hair, so

I twisted it back into a bun and put on a wide crocheted headband to conceal the two (three?) days-with-no-shower ick factor.

Maybe I'd brave the bucket wash tomorrow.

In a fresh white polo shirt, cotton pants and with sunscreen on my face, I felt a whole lot better than I had last night.

I knew I had one mission for the day: to find my mysterious drummer and to look for Deni. If what I guessed was true, if the rebellious leader of the Aceh boys and the drummer guy with the haunted eyes were one and the same boy, I might have a good day.

With my tiny tour guide gone, I followed the trail alone toward the chanting. The call to prayer blasted from rusty speakers along the path, but I was already getting used to the chanting. I walked across the soccer field and over toward the edge of the grounds where a low wall faced the river. The street kids weren't hanging out on the dirty shore. Just a few stray cats and scrawny-looking dogs lurking around the rocks, sniffing at trash, so I sat down on the wall, back to the *pesantren*, and waited in the morning sunshine, thinking about those eyes staring at me in my dream state, that scar. That boy.

When the prayer ended, I heard happy yelling and turned to see a flood of children pour out of the meeting room and toward another long blue-roofed building. The air smelled like ripe bananas and cooked rice. I guessed that was the dining hall and walked over to find Team Hope.

"Good morning, Sienna!" Dad cried from the end of a very long table. "Come, we saved you a seat." He patted the empty spot on the wooden bench next to him.

"I see you survived the night," Tom teased. "And the *mandi?*"

Microorganisms, buckets of worms, dawn wake-up.

"Barely."

"It will all take some getting used to," Dad said. Then he lowered his voice and leaned in toward my ear. "Did you have the nightmare? I was thinking about you. I could barely sleep."

That was nice. "Sort of," I said. "Just like on the plane, the dream was a little different."

"How so?" Dad asked.

"I'll tell you later. It was no big deal," I said, playing tough. The last thing I wanted was to act out a play-by-play in front of Team Hope.

Dad cocked his head. "Okay, we'll find some time later to talk. About the other thing we talked about too," he said. I knew what he meant. Deni.

Breakfast turned out to be plain sticky rice. A short, smiling woman who Dad explained was the cook carried a giant pot up and down the rows of tables, scooping one white lump into each of our wooden bowls. The kids, in turn, dug in with their fingers, scooping the rice into their mouths.

"There isn't any silverware?" I asked.

"Nope," Tom said, a grain of rice in his beard. "Isn't it great? I love Indonesia."

I noticed the cook kept her left hand tucked behind her as she scooped with her right.

"Why is she holding her hand behind her back?" I asked.

"Should we tell her?" Tom said, his eyes sparkling.

"Um. Yes, that's why I asked."

"Guess," Tom said.

"It's a custom?"

"You could say that." Tom grinned. Oh no. Tom grinning like that was never a good thing.

Vera, rolling her eyes at Tom, lowered her voice and leaned in toward me. "They do everything here with their right hand: greeting people, eating, serving, everything. You *never* use your left hand in public."

"Why not?"

"Because you use the left hand for cleaning yourself," she said matter-of-factly.

"*Cleaning* yourself? Like a washcloth in the shower?"

"No, cleaning yourself like your hand is toilet paper," Tom said, and burst into rumbling chuckles.

"Ha, ha," I said. "Good one." Even though I loved him, sometimes I could hardly believe Dad's friend functioned in the real world, never mind made it through medical school.

Vera flashed him a chastising look. "Thomas, seriously. Sienna needs to understand this. It's not a joke."

"Sorry, sorry." He waved her away and went back to scooping food into his mouth.

With his right hand.

I narrowed my eyes.

"Dad, come clean," I demanded. "Is Vera telling the truth?"

When he heard "come clean," Tom laughed out loud again.

"Shush, Tom," Vera said. "You don't want to embarrass the kids. To them it's perfectly normal."

"I know it is! I think it's a great custom. It's hygienic, and it saves money on TP."

Dad lowered his voice too, bending his head toward me. "It's really no big deal, but I'm sure you noticed there was no toilet paper in the *mandi*?"

"Uh. Yeah. They obviously just ran out, right?"

"Can't run out of something that was never there," Tom said. "And people have to wipe with something."

Wipe with something? "They wipe themselves with their hands?" I said a bit too loudly. "Seriously?"

Dad nodded, trying to act serious, but the corners of his lips were raised. "You pour the water over your bottom and then—well, you wash your hands very well afterward. It's quite sanitary once you get the hang of it."

The pitcher in the bathroom. That's what it was for.

I screeched a whisper. "Do you all do that? Do you wipe your butts with your hands?" I looked from face to face. All three members of Team Hope shrugged. Guilty as charged!

"When you work abroad, you adjust to local customs," Vera said.

I shook my head in disbelief. I couldn't imagine wiping my butt with my own hand. I mean, seriously, if the kids at school found out about that, I'd be shunned forever. "So because they don't think it's sanitary? That's why they don't use toilet paper?"

"It's also a waste of resources," Tom said with a mouthful of rice. "They can't afford to waste paper like we do. We shouldn't do it either, but we do. Ask your social studies teacher when you get home. We're the most wasteful country in the world." Watching Big Doctor Tom shovel piles of food into his already two-ton belly didn't just prove his argument; it won the case.

"Yeah, well. I'm not doing it!"

Dad nodded. "You don't have to. That's why I brought the baby wipes."

Subject change. Someone? Anyone? "Let's talk about something else," I said. "So after art, do I have a break before therapy?" I wanted to start asking around for Deni.

"We'll break for lunch," Dad said. "And yes, then group therapy with Vera in the afternoon."

"Is there anything else to eat?" I was still hungry after my small bowl was empty.

"I'm afraid not, honey. They don't have much, and to share with us is very generous. Maybe we can go out to lunch later in town," Dad said.

Glancing down the rows of kids, I thought about how they must still be hungry too. Rice wasn't much for a whole meal. Besides, no protein, dairy or vegetables? That wasn't good for growing kids like Elli. I thought about our kitchen at home with the big bowls of fresh fruit I took for granted; the endless boxes of pasta and cereals in the cabinet and organic milk and yogurt in our fridge.

"Can we do something to help them get more food? Talk to the *pesantren* owner or something?"

"The thing is, they rely on donations to keep the place going. If they have a donor come, they have a better variety of food; if they don't, it's a lean month for the kids."

"Oh. It just seems like, maybe we could think of something? Maybe donate something?"

"We are. We're donating our time. It might seem odd to you, but it's all we can do, sweetie . . . ," Dad explained. "Our specialty is mental health, so that's what we're giving them. They aren't starving; look at them." I looked around at their mostly happy faces. They were thin, but definitely not skinny.

"Compared to most developing countries, believe me, these kids have it good," Tom added.

It didn't seem like enough.

And then a loud ruckus broke out at the other end of the table.

Some older boys were roughhousing around, but they seemed kind of angry. A big scrappy boy pushed a scrawnier, shorter kid, and I couldn't really tell what was going on, but the energy in the dining hall changed. Chatter quieted; everyone stopped eating to watch. The kid that got pushed started whaling on the bully, and then a group of maybe three or four older boys took sides and got all up in each other's faces.

My stomach squeezed like it did at school when the rare fight broke out, usually among the football players. I hated fighting. The cook yelled at them in Indonesian. She grabbed the scrappy boy by the back of his T-shirt and threw him out the door. Scrappy's friends protested, standing up with their arms raised, talking fast in Indonesian, but one of their voices was louder than the others.

He spoke slowly and firmly, his feet steady on the ground like he wasn't moving until she heard what he had to say. His friends stopped yelling, so he lowered his voice too but kept his tone serious. I had no idea what he was saying, but there was fiery passion behind his eyes, and I could see that the woman was listening to him. He was gesturing, and I guessed explaining what had happened. Then he looked at her expectantly, but she was already grinning like she was his friend too. He nodded once gratefully as she walked away.

Impressive.

The other boys sat back down at the table and reluctantly continued eating, looking at the boy like he was some kind of hero.

But he wasn't looking back at them.

As he cast his eyes down the table, they stopped on mine just for a moment, a flash of something in them. Some sort of question. Was he checking to see if I was watching? I raised my eyebrows once, a tiny smile on my lips. He nodded back quickly, but his eyes danced. I knew it.

"That's him," I heard my voice whisper to Dad. "The leader of the drum circle. He's the leader of the Aceh boys. I know it. That's Deni."

"Hmm. Maybe you're right," Dad agreed.

Tom asked incredulously, "How do you know for sure?"

My heart skipped a beat when I said with utter authority, "I just do."

He stayed only a few seconds longer before he disappeared out the same door his friend was ejected from.

"I'll see you at art!" I said, darting for the exit.

It was sprinkling now. I looked around but didn't see him at first. Then I noticed an older boy heading down the path away from me. From this distance I wasn't sure it was him, so I sped up. As I got closer, I could see he was walking with the same slight limp as the drummer. Bingo.

The rain fell harder and I walked faster. I didn't have a plan other than to ask him his name, and for now, that was enough. But then thunder cracked once above me and the rain seemed thicker and hotter and was falling faster. I jumped and ducked behind a building, watching as a younger boy about six or seven cried out at the sky's snap too. I wasn't sure what he was doing out here alone while everyone else was eating.

The older boy whipped around and without a second thought scooped him up onto his shoulders. Lightning zipped through silver clouds and lit up the path. The older boy glanced up at the sky as if daring it to do it again. I was close enough to see water dropping against his clenched jaw, pouring down his sinewy arms.

And then he was looking at me too.

I felt like I was caught spying, but he wasn't mad. He was just staring, and so was I.

I couldn't look away; my eyes fused to his. Finally, lamely, I waved.

He didn't wave back, but he didn't turn away. What should I do? Calling out through the brewing storm, "What's your name?" suddenly didn't sound like the greatest idea.

Streaks of electricity shot against the sky as the-boy-I-guessed-was-Deni grabbed hold of the younger boy's ankles, dangling from his shoulders. Then he furrowed his brow and yelled, "The storm comes, *rambut kuning*. Go."

Rambut kuning? What did that mean?

And he spoke English?

I flashed on my nightmare. The boy stumbling down the aisle of the crashing plane.

I grounded my feet in place to keep from running after him as he took off into the storm as fast as he could manage with a limp and a kid on his shoulders.

Finally, with thunder cracking over my head, I ran too, toward safety.

It was pouring rain. *Pouring*. Like gallons of water being dumped on the dorm's roof.

My little roommates were hanging out waiting for instructions when Vera finally knocked.

Her mascara was smeared and running down her cheeks. *Mascara?* Seriously, in this weather?

"Sienna? We've decided to relocate art to this room."

"Okay."

She nodded as if surprised I was being so cooperative. "Great. Well, the children's regular classes were canceled because of a major leak in their classroom's roof. Andy, I mean, your father, said that room is already starting to flood."

Vera set down a wet box of art supplies: crayons, markers, pencils, paper, that we brought from home.

"So what should I do?" I asked.

"I will gather the girls and you can pass out the supplies?"

Easy enough.

We all sat in a big circle on the floor. The girls sat on their knees, so I did too.

Vera cleared her throat and sat up tall. "I'd like you all to draw home. The first image that comes to your mind when you hear the word *home*." I think Vera said it in English for my sake, because the kids looked blankly at her until she repeated it in their language.

The kids all started coloring, so I did too.

I colored a house with Dad, Mom and me standing in the front yard throwing around a Frisbee. I drew myself with short yellow hair and red overalls. I was about six. I don't know why. Maybe because that's how old I guessed Elli was? Maybe because that's the first image I thought of when I thought of home.

I peeked over at Elli's drawing. A few green palm trees, a small brown house. A purple airplane flying in the bright blue sky between two puffy pink clouds.

Half of the piece of paper had a red background. The rest was white.

"Home?" I asked her quietly, not wanting to disturb the other kids who were busy working.

She didn't say anything. Kept scribbling more and more and more red.

"My home," I said, pointing to my picture.

She looked over at the family with the young child. She narrowed her eyes, confused.

She said something to Vera.

"Elli wants to know why you aren't in the picture with your little sister," Vera said.

I felt sheepish. "Tell her that is me when I was a kid. That I don't have a sister."

She did.

Now Vera must have thought I was even nuttier than she did before.

Crayon-art evidence of me being stuck in the past.

But Vera didn't look judgmental at all. "We all think of home in different ways" was all she said.

Then we went around the circle discussing our pictures. Some of the kids drew big waves. Some drew rainbows. Some drew the *pesantren*.

"Why did she draw an airplane?" I asked Vera, referring to Elli's art.

Vera asked her in a smooth, patient tone.

Elli looked at her lap while she explained. My gut told me it was some awful reason.

"Because she wished an airplane would have flown in to rescue her mother from the sea. The day the wave came."

How ironic, I thought. One kid's nightmare is another kid's hope.

"What is the red about?" I pressed.

Vera asked Elli.

"She thinks of the tsunami as death and she said the color of death is red."

My voice caught in my throat. "Like blood," I said.

"Yes," Vera said sadly, "like blood."

I cleared my throat and felt hot. Listened to the pounding rain on the roof. Poor Elli.

Vera asked me to hand out a fresh piece of paper to all the girls. I did.

The rain outside was getting louder.

"This time I'd like you to draw yourself. Any way you'd like. Just make sure you are in the picture." She said it in English, then translated to the group.

Elli scribbled quickly another palm tree with a tiny stick figure standing below it. This time, thankfully, there was no red.

"You?" I asked, pointing.

"Elli," she said, patting her chest.

"It's good." I smiled. Then I turned and whispered to Vera, "Why did she draw herself so small?"

Vera's eyes widened as she translated Elli's answer. "She said that is how she feels when she wakes up each day without her family. Very small and very alone."

Tears stinging in my eyes, I grabbed a green marker and even though I probably wasn't supposed to, I drew a stick figure on Elli's paper next to the tiny one.

A tall girl with yellow hair and orange shoes.

I pointed to my Converse. "You, me, together," I said.

Elli leaned into my shoulder before beginning to draw again.

This time she drew another figure, then another.

She was drawing her friends here at the *pesantren*.

"You are not alone," I told her. And I think she may have understood what I said. Maybe next time she would draw herself a little bit bigger.

Maybe I would too.

• • •

At lunchtime we ran into the hall to eat more noodles before breaking into afternoon groups.

This time in one of the older girls' dorm rooms.

I noticed the boy with the limp wasn't at lunch and wondered when I would see him again.

Wind slashed against the shingles. Vera spoke loudly above the rain.

We were sitting cross-legged on the floor. The girls were sitting on kaleidoscope-colored prayer mats. One girl offered to share her mat with me, so we were sitting together.

Vera said I could take pictures, so I zoomed my lens on the doe-eyed face of a girl about my age who was wearing a lime green *jilbab*. I listened as she told her story, in English.

"I was home with my mother and my sisters when I heard the sound. The sound of thunder. My father and my brothers were fishermen and were working. I ran out the door and saw people running toward me, away from the ocean. They were crying out: *The sea is coming, the sea is coming.* My mother grabbed my baby sister and the two older girls and they ran. I grabbed my younger sister's hand and we ran as fast as we could away from the water. My sister was seven and couldn't run any more. Even though she was big, I lifted her into my arms, and to-gether we ran until she was too heavy and I stumbled on a fallen man and my sister slipped from my arms. I tried but I couldn't reach her. There were many people running. The water moved so fast behind me and was so thick and tall that . . ."

She stopped talking and crumpled forward onto the carpet.

Vera said something too quietly.

The girl wiped her eyes and continued talking. Her words had frozen me to the floor and I didn't know what I wanted more: for her to stop talking or to finish the story.

"It's okay," Vera told her, gently prodding.

"My sister was swept away."

The knot in my throat swelled up. I leaned in to hear the rest.

"I had no choice but to run. To leave her behind. I climbed up a banana tree and hung on tight as muddy ocean rose around me. Many people go past me. And some already quiet."

She lowered her voice. Her face was broken.

"Finally, when I cannot hang on any longer, the water falls back to the sea. When I climb down, for days and days I look in the camps for my mother and for my sisters. One of my sisters is here at the *pesantren* with me. But not the sister I lost. I never found that sister again."

Vera put her arm around the girl and spoke quietly, letting her talk and cry.

"It's not your fault," Vera said in English before translating. "You were a hero for trying to save your sister. You are a hero for saving yourself."

The girl's eyes widened. I could tell Vera's words really helped her and I believed they were true too.

I set the camera down without taking a picture.

THE TEMPEST

I screamed. But this time not from a nightmare.

Lightning flashed through the pitch-black room like a strobe light, followed by a massive crash of thunder.

It had to be the middle of the night.

After a long first day of the emotional art therapy with Elli and then the super-sad teen therapy group, I was completely drained by bedtime and quietly cried myself to sleep replaying the girl's story in my head to the melancholy beat of the rain pounding on the roof.

And now this.

Rain poured through the narrow slits in the shutters, leaving half my bunk soaked. Elli was so afraid, she jumped up onto my bunk and clung to me.

"It's okay, sweetie. It's just a thunderstorm," I said, but her face was soaked with tears. The sounds of the other girls' cries were drowned out by the heavy thunder. Rain hammered against the window so hard, I was afraid the shutters might blow off their hinges. "We better move," I said.

I slid down, Elli clinging to my neck. I yanked on the string and the light sparked once, pulsed and then fizzled out. Great. Following the whimpers, I stumbled across the floor, finding half of the kids huddled together on a lower bunk, looking scared to death. Meanwhile, the rest of the kids were slowly waking up wondering what all the fuss was about. They didn't seem to be fazed by the storm at all.

Strange.

Then I realized my bare feet were wet. Water was leaking in from somewhere. "Crap," I muttered.

I sat Elli down with the other kids and investigated the leak with my flashlight, which thank goodness was easy to find under my balled-up hoodie pillow. I pointed up at the ceiling, but aside from old water damage and mold it looked okay. Then I shone the light at the front door.

"Get some towels—uh, get some clothes." The girls didn't understand me, so I grabbed a bunch of my stuff— T-shirts, one sweatshirt, an already-damp striped towel— and shoved them into the crack of the front door, hoping to stop more water from pouring in.

There was a loud crash of thunder and the girls shrieked; it sounded like it was right outside the door. Lightning flashed across the dorm room again, the shutters flapping open and then slamming shut with the heavy wind. My barricade wasn't working: the water was soaking right through the material. What was I supposed to do?

I bit my lip and made a decision.

"Okay. Everybody up. Move over and climb onto that

bed; it's farthest from the window and the safest place to wait out the storm."

The huddled girls didn't budge, so one at a time I picked them up and carried them across the room, setting them on the top bunk. Elli wouldn't let go of me, so I was doing double duty, balancing two girls on my hips. The rain beat the roof like hail.

"Okay," I said as I got the last girl on the top bunk. "You guys stay here." I held up my hand for emphasis. "Stay. Here. I'm going to go find some help." My dad said the storm might be bad, but I didn't think he meant this bad.

Elli was still clinging to me, so I carefully unhooked her hands from around my neck and handed her my flashlight and my journal. "Here, you can look at these pictures. I promise I'll be right back."

She smiled a bit and nodded, flicking the light on and off.

Then, I slipped on my sneakers, and grabbing a towel to use as a tarp, I stepped out into the storm.

The lightning was so close, I hugged the side of the building as I went.

The wide path was ankle deep with water. My sneakers were drenched and the rain was hitting my face so hard it was like standing under a faucet on hyper-speed. I ducked my head and ran.

I could have gone looking for Vera, that would have

been the most logical choice, but I wanted to find Dad, to make sure I was doing the right thing with the girls. But mostly I just wanted my dad.

So even though it was totally against the rules, I ran down the central path and then headed down the muddy trail toward the boys' dorms, screaming into the streaking blackness, "Dad! Tom!"

Lightning shot across the sky as I stumbled through the mud—now as deep as a half-filled baby pool. "Dad!"

From outside, the boys' dorms looked just like the girls'. I'm not sure what I was expecting, but I was surprised: white with blue roofs and basically falling apart. I heard terrified shrieks coming from a stocky building with a flapping blue door. Shadowy figures were scurrying in and out of the flap. They were using the sort of scoopers I saw in the buckets in the bathroom to bail the water off the floor. Ick. Then I saw who was doing the scooping.

"Sienna!" Dad yelled when he saw me. "What are you doing here? Are you okay? Are the girls okay?"

"Yeah!" I screamed. "They're scared but okay."

Dad handed his scooper to Tom and gave me a quick wet hug. "Good. Just go back to your dorm. It's on higher ground than this one. Shut the door tight and shove anything you can find under the crack to keep the water out."

"That's what I did."

"Great. And put the girls together on the highest bunk farthest away from the window."

"I did that too."

Dad's answer was a kiss on the cheek. "Well done."

I have to admit it was nice to hear. "What else should I do?"

"I'll walk you back, and you should just keep the girls company and wait it out. If things get rougher, which I don't think they will, go find an older girl to help you entertain the girls or move a few of them into the older girls' dorms a few buildings down."

Peeking inside the dorm, I noticed the youngest boys were huddled together on the top bunk. One of the boys' heads was bleeding and he was holding an X-Men T-shirt to his hurt scalp. My Wolverine boy from the soccer game. Poor guy!

"What happened to him?" I asked.

"When the thunder cracked, he jumped and fell off his bunk and banged his head."

"Ooh. Looks bad. Does he need stitches?"

"We don't think so. Vera's going for the first-aid kit to find a butterfly bandage."

So Vera's breaking rules too?

"Tom, I'll be right back," Dad said. "I'm just going to walk her . . ."

I shook my head and squeezed Dad's wrist. I saw how much work he had to do. I got here by myself. I didn't need an escort back. "No, I'm fine, Dad, seriously. You stay here."

Dad looked surprised, and I didn't blame him. His wimpy fifteen-year-old daughter who usually couldn't spend a night without screaming can handle a *monsoon*?

"If you're sure . . ." He glanced back at the Wolverine boy, who clearly needed more help than I did.

I nodded. I could do this. "Positive."

I felt like I was body boarding through a giant wave. I didn't know rain could be like that. Like the sky had burst. And then there were screams from the neighboring dorm. When I flung open the door, I found that more of the younger soccer boys I was playing with yesterday were standing in three inches of slushy water. Using soggy pieces of cardboard, they attempted to scoop rainwater out of their room.

A couple of the smaller boys were crying. An older one, barely older, maybe ten years old, was yelling commands that I didn't understand.

"You guys need help?" I asked.

He looked up, startled, like his face was a flashing alarm: no girls allowed, but I was older, way older, and this was an emergency situation. If Vera could help Dad's group, I could help this one. I pulled back my wet hair and twisted it into a tight knot before dropping to my hands and knees to start bailing water.

Four of us were crawling along the floor trying to sweep the water back outside the door, but it was useless. More water poured in, and wind whipped the door open and shut. I was about to give up and ask Dad to come over when I heard a voice above me ask, "Would you need help?"

Staring at the piece of cardboard that was falling apart in my hands, I nodded. "Yeah, thanks."

"Do you not mean *terima kasih*?" the voice teased.

My head jerked up.

It was him.

And this time there was no place for him to disappear to. Or me, for that matter. I moved stray hairs out of my face, shivers running down my spine. This was not exactly how I wanted to meet up again, on my hands and knees, soaking wet.

White T-shirt sticking to his chest, water dripping from his hair, he looked HOT.

"You are happy to have come to my country now," he said, a glint of humor in his eyes. "Such a warm Indonesian welcome, yes?"

"Oh, well. It's fine," I managed to squeak out. I struggled to stand but slipped on the soggy cardboard instead. He offered a rain-slick hand to help me up, and suddenly we were face-to-face. My hair tumbled loose, falling around my face. Oh God. My heart sped up and I hoped he didn't think I'd done that on purpose, trying to look all movie star sexy or something. I tucked it behind my ears.

When he licked his bottom lip and smiled, I shivered in the wet heat, trying not to stare at the veins sticking out of his arms.

"Girls are not allowed," he said.

Um. "Yeah, I know. I was looking for my dad, and I heard screams. I'll go."

His eyes rooted me to the flooded ground. "I was not wanting you to leave," he said, holding a scooper like the one my dad had.

"Do you need help?" I asked.

"Thank you, but we do not need your help, *rambut kuning.* I am here now," he said confidently. I was just about to ask what that phrase meant when a burst of wind opened and smacked the door shut again. The little girls were probably freaking out.

I should have left and gone back.

Right then.

But Dad said the worst part of the storm was over, so the girls were probably fine and this was my chance to talk to him. I didn't want to leave just yet.

"Please. Let me help."

He cocked his head. "Do not do this dirty work, then. You can please hold the door shut?"

Holding the door shut was *definitely* something I could do.

I stood with my back to the wood, holding out the wind and the rain. He started shoveling water, and when he was ready, he would signal me with a quick flick of his wrist and I'd open the door so he could sweep it out. Then I'd slam the door shut again.

Wordlessly we worked together, sinking into a comfortable rhythm. I was hyperaware of his every move: his arms shoveling, the slight tilt of his face, the furrow of his brow as he concentrated. When I looked down, I felt his eyes on me.

And then thunder cracked and he jumped. "Are you okay?" I asked, shaking a little too.

He stopped scooping. His fist was clenched so tight around the handle that I thought he might snap the plastic right in half. Knuckles bone white like they might burst through his skin, the veins in his forearm popped out even more than before.

He frowned. "The big wave washing over our village sounded like the thunder. Whenever the thunder comes, it is like the wave is coming again. For the small boys too. This is why they cry." He gestured toward the little boys, who were shivering, huddled together on the upper bunks while a slightly older boy comforted them.

"That must have been so scary," I said.

He nodded. "It was like living a most terrible dream."

The door banged behind my back and I shoved my weight harder against it, the wind whistling through the rickety dorm. "How did you escape?"

He stared at me. "I had a *motor*. A scooter, you say? It was faster than the wave."

I imagined him fleeing the tsunami on a motorcycle. Did he look over his shoulder and see the giant wall of water chasing after him? I rubbed the goose bumps on my arms.

"I'm so glad you're okay."

Then he grinned. A small, tender grin, a tiny dimple forming in his tan face. "For this moment, I am glad I am okay too."

The thunder cracked again, and he flinched like someone had punched him. More water poured under the door. "This is not working," he said, frustrated. At first I thought he meant me, talking with me. But then he glanced around the room, grabbed a stained mattress from a bottom bunk and pulled it across the floor. When he shoved it against the crack to keep more water from seeping in, I knew he hadn't meant me.

Awkwardly I stepped back, not sure how to help anymore.

"Now something else can hold the rain out," he said, his voice smiling. "Rather than our guest."

So now we were trapped together.

In the middle of a thunderstorm.

Could be much worse.

He walked over to the little boys and patted their backs, saying something that must have been funny, because they smiled and one boy even laughed. Then they pointed at me and giggled. Not knowing what else to do, I waved at them. A little guy with curly hair and an eager grin waved back. "American!" He laughed.

"Yes, American." I nodded, sort of embarrassed without knowing why.

"He wants to know if you know the SpongeBob with the Square Pants?"

"Sure. He's on TV."

"He wants me to tell you he has a T-shirt of the yellow cartoon. A volunteer gave to him."

"Cool."

"He says to tell you he thinks you are pretty and he likes your yellow hair. *Rambut kuning.* Yellow hair like the Sponge." His eyes twinkled.

Rambut kuning.

Yellow hair.

It means yellow hair.

"Tell him thank you, I guess?"

Then I noticed three other kids goofing around on another top bunk, playing cards and laughing. I watched their faces when thunder cracked. Nothing. They just went on playing.

As if reading my mind, the drummer boy explained, "They are from Jakarta. They were not there for the tsunami, so for them, the thunder, the storm, it is nothing . . . it happens here all the time. The flooding too. But for us, from Aceh, it means everything. It is like the wall of water is coming for us again."

"PTSD . . . ," I said. "From the tsunami."

"Apa?" He walked toward me and stood an inch or two closer to me than someone normally would. I caught my breath.

"PTSD is post-traumatic stress disorder. It's like when something happens that reminds you of something bad that happened before, and you have a physical or psycho-logical reaction to it . . . like . . ." I glanced down at his fist tellingly.

Like your knuckle bones popping through your skin when thunder breaks.

Like the little ones crying, thinking the tsunami is coming back for them.

Like my cold sweats and screams in the night.

"Yes."

He knew what I meant. For the first time in my life I met someone who'd experienced some of the same things that I had. Someone who might understand me. Some-one I could understand back.

He licked his bottom lip again, and I thought I might

go mad if he kept doing that. And then suddenly, a shadow crossed his face and his expression changed. "You go out the window," he said abruptly.

"Huh?" I didn't like the sharp tug back to reality. Or the fact that he wanted to get rid of me so soon. Had I done something wrong?

"You must go back to check on the girls, and we cannot move the mattress to unblock the door." He gestured to the window next to the top bunk. Outside, lightning flashed. That time, we both jerked at the thunder's smash.

"Out *that* window?"

"Yes." He nodded. "It's okay. You are a brave girl."

A brave girl? No one had called me that in a long, long time.

"Okay." I shrugged. What other choice did I have? Besides, he thought I was brave, and I wasn't going to be the one to change his mind.

He helped me onto the bunk and then he pushed hard on the shutters, forcing them open.

I waved good-bye to the SpongeBob fans and flipped one leg outside the window.

The concrete wall scratched my legs as he lowered me down, his hand wet and warm around mine. The water was almost knee high as I sank deep into it, my heart pounding along with the rain.

He landed beside me in the darkness at the same time

a bolt of lightning ripped through the night. I practically dove into his arms.

"Oh, sorry," I said, biting my lip. My hands fell to my sides.

"It is okay to be scared."

My chest felt heavy like my heart had ballooned twice its size in that one moment.

It's okay to be scared.

No one ever told me it was okay. They just told me to stop. Stop being afraid.

The boy looked at me from under long wet lashes. Waiting.

Neither of us stepping away as rain poured down around us. Instead I reached up and gently moved a wet piece of hair off his forehead. I had to find out if I was right, if he was the boy peeking through my window this morning.

Even in the midnight shadows I could faintly make it out. A scar.

He winced a bit at my touch as I traced my fingertip across the deep line on his brow, until his hand moved mine away.

As if I'd already discovered too much.

Water poured down my face. I didn't bother trying to wipe it away.

He waited a beat, a moment that felt like an eternity, before his gaze left mine. I shivered as his eyes, his fingers, his palm, slipped up my forearm, soft as velvet. And then slowly threaded back down as if they were weaving something magical.

I felt electricity. Real electricity. As real as the bolts ripping through the sky. I knew as he twined his fingers through mine that without a doubt, I was fully awake.

My mouth was near his ear, the curled edges of his hair grazing my lips, when I asked, "Why were you watching me sleep?"

"I wanted to see you," he answered quickly, his voice husky and deep. "You were . . . I do not know how to say it in English? Sleep-talking?"

Oh my God. I buried my face in my hands.

"Do not be sad about it. I have bad dreams too."

I let him peel my fingers away from my eyes.

"You aren't allowed in the girls' section. What if you got caught?" I asked.

His whole body shrugged as if that was the most ridiculous question he'd ever heard. "Who could catch me?"

True. He did outrun a tsunami.

"Your name is Deni, isn't it?"

"How do you know?" He raised his eyebrows the same smirky way he had at the welcome ceremony.

"My dad asked me to look for you. He wants to work with you. Get to know you."

Even in the hot rain, his look gave me the chills. "And I want to get to know *you*," he said.

Then lightning struck above us, followed by meddling thunder.

Deni flinched. "But now you must go."

The last thing I wanted to do was leave.

My eyes must have argued too, because he leaned in close and said, "Do not worry. I will find you again."

Then, just like that, he disappeared into sheets of rain and darkness.

BUTTERFLY

Butterflies were everywhere.

Rubbing my eyes, I sat up on my squishy bunk and pushed the shutters all the way open.

The morning heat was intense and moist, the sky blue with not a cloud in sight.

The butterflies flew in close, daring me to touch them as the call to prayer began its morning cries.

And then I looked at the floor.

At least four inches of dirty water flooded our dorm.

"Oh my God, my suitcase!" I hopped off my bunk, splashing onto the floor, whimpering. "No. No. No. No."

How could I be so stupid? My clothes and my random stuff were totally, completely drenched. I reached under my sweatpants/pillow. Thank God. My journal and my camera were safe and dry. A minor miracle. I tucked them into my backpack, which was also safe on my top bunk. I would keep this with me today.

The girls all seemed fine, slowly waking up to the prayers. They were fine when I got back last night too; they'd fallen asleep together on a couple bunks, my pictures spread across their chests.

My clothes were the only casualties of the storm.

Opening the door, I got a panorama of the grounds: the soccer field, the dirt paths; everything was underwater—maybe ankle high now, having receded some during the night.

I wondered what Deni was doing as I recalled his wet hands on my arm, his fingers on mine, his warm breath in my ear. I wondered where he ended up sleeping, where he ran off to in the rain. Mostly, I wondered if he was thinking about me the same way I was thinking about him.

But then Elli came over holding her rolled-up prayer mat and pointing out at the swampy flooded path.

You've got to be kidding me.

"Okay, okay. Just don't put your shoes on. Barefoot, okay? And like this." I pantomimed lifting my skirt even though I was wearing pants. Elli took my hand, and the other ones sloshed through the water behind us.

I tried to keep my facial expression neutral; that is, I didn't moan and groan about wading in possibly bug-, worm-, frog-, dead-cat-infested waters. I focused on the path until Elli started pointing and laughing. "What?"

It was a goat. Standing on top of one of the dorm buildings.

"How in the world did he get up there?"

Elli giggled some more.

"Unbelievably smart goat," I said.

We parted ways at the meeting hall, the chanting flooding the *pesantren* like the water.

I waded alone, looking around for Dad. Looking around for Deni. I didn't find either.

Finally the chanting stopped, prayers ended, and swarms of kids raced outside toward the dining hall, kicking water on each other, laughing, enjoying the morning sunshine. Dad was there too, standing with his arms folded, a big grin on his face.

"Well done, girls! What a brave group of explorers you all are," he said. The girls were wet but happy as they gathered around him.

"I didn't make them wear their shoes. Sorry."

Dad waved off my apology. "You did great, kiddo. I'm proud of you."

"Thanks."

Even though they probably didn't need my help anymore, I followed the kids into the flooded dining hall and made sure they were all situated around the table in front of steaming bowls of noodles before I joined Team Hope.

After a few bites, I glanced down to where the older boys sat, but I didn't see Deni. "Our dorm is a disaster—it's totally underwater. All my stuff is wet—all the girls' stuff is wet. How are we going to wash it?" I asked.

"The same lady that cooks does the wash. . . . Of

course, there's no way she'll be able to wash all the wet clothes. The kids will probably hang them outside to dry. Doesn't look like it will rain again today . . ." Dad glanced out the window. He looked a bit beat-up, his graying beard longer than usual, his eyes tired from the water bailing. "But I could take you shopping—to buy some new T-shirts."

"I can just hang mine up too, if that's what the kids are doing. But man, that water is all kinds of nasty—I can't imagine what might be swimming in there. I keep checking my arms for leeches."

Tom shook his burly head. "Malaria kills all the leeches. You did great last night, kid," he said.

"They were so scared, and I just kept thinking, 'What if I wasn't here? They'd be all alone.' It's such a good idea that you're going to mix the kids up—the older kids living with the little ones. Why didn't the teachers come over to help?"

"It storms here all the time. The dorms flood a lot. The kids that are from here are used to it. That's why so many of them weren't upset. So the teachers don't stress out about it either. They aren't hired to be on night duty."

"I'm just glad we're going to move the older teens in with the younger kids. I bet the older girls will like it too. I know I would if I lived here. Being able to help someone, having someone depend on you, especially a little kid.

Makes you feel sort of . . . important, I guess. I know Deni will think it's a great idea too. . . ."

I stopped myself.

Dad, Big Tom and Vera were all staring at me.

Why was I suddenly a gush of personal information? Too late.

"You found Deni?" Dad asked.

"The boy who made the peace yesterday with the cook *is* Deni. I was right."

"Oh, good," Dad said. "But . . . ?"

I cut him off. "And he said he is happy to meet with you. Whatever the *pesantren* owner told you guys about him is wrong, by the way. You should have seen him last night, bailing the water, making sure the kids were okay, comforting them. . . ."

Dad frowned. "Where did you see him last night? You didn't go into his dorm, did you?"

Uh.

"You know he has PTSD?" I said, ignoring the question. "He freaked out when the thunder crashed."

Confusion spread across Dad's face. "Rewind a minute, please. So you *were* in his dorm?"

"Well, it wasn't intentional. After I left you, I heard cries from little boys, and then he just was . . ." I gulped, remembering looking up from the soggy cardboard and seeing him looking down at me. "Um, sort of."

Vera's mouth dropped open. "Sienna, if the owner finds out, he may ask us to leave. You have no idea what a big offense that is."

"Dad told me you were over there too, Vera. In the off-limit BOYS' area," I snapped. Then felt sort of bad. Especially after how nice she was to Elli and to the teen girls in the therapy session. Still. It was unfair of her to chastise me for doing the same thing.

Vera flushed. Dad noticed her discomfort and turned to me. "Vera's a therapist. It's an entirely different situation, young lady. Besides, you told me you were heading straight back to your dorm to wait out the storm with the little girls. How did you end up with Deni?"

"I was helping! Their dorm was flooding. *Does it really matter?* The point is Deni is great with the little kids. I was just giving you an example of how the family system could work."

Suddenly there was another big ruckus just like yesterday at the other end of the long table. I knew who it was before even turning to follow the noise.

Sure enough, Deni and his friends were walking in late. I sucked in a breath when I saw him dressed in a tight black T-shirt and jeans, making a big production about eating to get the little boys to laugh. The other older kids were mimicking what Deni was doing, sucking up noodles and goofing off. He was helping them forget the thunder, the tsunami, their fears from last night.

"Hmm . . ." Vera twisted a piece of hair around her fingers. "Interesting."

"Why is it interesting?" I asked, annoyed.

"Well, yesterday Deni worked so hard to intervene and keep the peace defending his friend, and today he's causing the same sort of trouble that elevated the problem yesterday. I wonder why the tide turned."

My eyes narrowed. "How is goofing around with food the same thing as pushing another kid?"

"They might not be the same, but both things are breaking the rules of the dining hall," Vera said.

"Maybe he doesn't *always* feel like doing the exact right thing."

Dad looked at me funny; so did Tom. Vera followed suit.

I squirmed in my seat. "I mean, it must be hard to have everyone looking up to you all the time, expecting you to know exactly what to do—"

"So you said Deni exhibited PTSD symptoms—which ones exactly?" Vera prodded.

She was so freaking nosy. I should never have told them anything about him. He shared his stories in confidence.

His weren't my secrets to share.

"I don't know," I mumbled. "Never mind about the PTSD. I was helping him *bail water* out of a flooded dorm room. We didn't talk about religion or politics either. Jeez."

I was exhausted. I was wet. I was not going to sit here and let them give me the third degree. I pushed my empty bowl away.

"If you guys are all so interested in Deni, why don't you just talk to him yourselves?"

GIFT

I stormed onto the slushy path.

"Go straight to art therapy!" Dad called after me.

Yeah, right.

Who did they think they were?

Especially that pain in the ass Vera: flirting with Dad, digging into my business, making judgments about Deni. Where was *she* last night? Certainly not helping out the girls in the storm. Oh no, she was far too busy to help them, because she was helping *Dad.* It made me even more mad that I was actually giving her the benefit of the doubt before. Why was she so cool during therapy and such a witch around Dad?

Just looking at the two of them sitting next to each other during meals made me sick.

How could Dad stomach her?

I stomped harder through the warm puddles. Without the cloud cover, the sun was blazing hot on my skin.

I couldn't imagine Mom acting the way Vera was acting. Mom would be the opposite: giving all the kids the benefit of the doubt, letting them know she was proud of them. Not just the ones she deemed worthy of her attention.

Tears pillowed in my eyes. I wasn't sad. I was frustrated.

And I had nowhere to go to vent.

The field was a swamp, my dorm smelled like mold and my mattress was still drenched.

I cursed, kicking water into the air like a spastic fountain.

"Such terrible words coming from such a pretty girl," a familiar voice teased.

I whipped around and my bad mood vanished.

"Hi, Deni."

"Go on. I don't mean to interrupt you." He grinned right at me.

"It's okay . . . I'm done."

"You are sure? You seem to have a lot to say. And a lot of water to kick."

I sighed. "It's just that woman that travels with us? Vera? I can't stand her."

"Can't stand?" He cocked his head, curious.

"Yeah. It means I don't like her."

"She is not nice?"

"It's not that she's not nice. She just drives me crazy."

"Your father likes her, though?"

He asked it innocently enough, but the words burned my ears.

"Apparently so . . . ," I choked out.

Before he could ask the next obvious question, Where is your mother? I changed the subject. "They think you're a troublemaker. Because the *pesantren* owner said so. It made me mad."

"Why does it make you mad?"

"Because. I don't agree."

"That is kind of you. But I do not care what he thinks of me. Or the American doctors truly. But you, *rambut kuning,* your opinion I do care about."

Raw heat rose to my cheeks. "Thanks," I said.

"The storm is over, and you do not need to be angry anymore," he said cheerfully. Then he looked up at the bright blue sky. "It is a beautiful day. A gift from God."

"So you're not angry about what the owner said?" I was confused. I would be so mad if my principal started a rumor about me and then told a substitute teacher about it.

He narrowed his eyes slightly. "Bapak? He misuses me and my friends, yes. He wants only rich Westerners to come to bring donations to make himself richer. He speaks badly of me because I ask questions. I ask why: Why do we not have better food, more meat, more vegetables for the children? I ask why, if the donors are donating to tsunami victims, why he doesn't share the money with us? He doesn't like my questions, so he calls me a troublemaker."

I had a math teacher at school like that last year. He was happy as long as no one questioned him. But if someone did, *look out.* Dad said that behavior comes from insecurity. An irrational need to have power over someone who isn't in the position to challenge them.

It seemed like this Bapak fell into that same psycho category.

"What does *bapak* mean, anyway?" I asked.

"It means 'father.'" His eyes flashed with emotion. "Though the *pesantren* owner is *not* my father."

Strange that he would call this man he didn't like "father," but before I had time to ask more, he was digging in his pockets.

Then he was dangling keys in the air.

"What are those for?"

"A surprise."

"What?" I raised one eyebrow.

"This is why I left the meal to find you. Come, Sienna."

"How do you know my name?"

"My friend who works in Bapak's office found it on papers your father sent from America," he said, with a slight eyebrow rise like he was so clever. Then he gestured me to follow. Deni approached the gatekeeper, who was busy smoking cigarettes. I didn't have permission from Dad to leave the grounds and knew I'd get the lecture of a lifetime for bailing without telling him, but I didn't care.

At that point, even dressed in crusty-wet clothes, I'd follow Deni anywhere.

Deni said something to the gatekeeper and handed him a box of Djarum cigarettes. The gatekeeper smiled and patted the bottom of the pack. He handed a cigarette back to Deni.

"You know *sepeda motor*?" Deni asked me, taking a long drag and then exhaling.

"Motor? Like a car?"

"Motorcycle."

He exhaled again and I coughed. Deni noticed and threw the cigarette to the ground, grinding out the orange ember with his sneaker.

"Thanks," I said.

"Cigarettes, to my friends," he said, gesturing toward the gatekeeper, "are like gold."

"So you bribed him not to tell the . . . *bapak* we are leaving the gate?"

With a little wink, Deni led me behind the gatekeeper's shack. There, parked in the mud, was a bright orange scooter.

"*Motor.* They are fast," he said like he was trying to impress me. "Come."

"Come?" I asked.

He nodded. "We go. Not as fast as American *laki laki.*" He opened his arms and pantomimed riding a big motorcycle, like a Harley. "*Motor* is fast, but not too fast."

Faster than the great wave of water.

Deni hopped on the front and motioned for me to sit behind him, handing me a thin black plastic helmet. Oh no! Was this one of Tom's "head crackers"?

"Um. Deni. Do you have a thicker helmet?"

He scratched his chin. "Thicker? Not thicker. It is okay. Put it on."

Instead I glanced back through the gate.

I could make up something.

I could change my mind, still go back.

Not risk getting busted by Dad or Team Hope for not showing up to Vera's art group.

Not risk having my head split open.

But then I looked at Deni's smile and I was sick of being afraid.

I had my backpack with me already. And my wallet. And my camera. What else did I really need?

My whole body tingled as Deni snapped the helmet strap under my chin. I looked around for something to hold on to.

"Put your arms around me," he said. "And move closer."

Happily. I scooted forward and wrapped my arms around Deni's waist, pushing my chest as tight as I could into the heat of his back.

"Holding on tight?"

"Yes." I couldn't stop smiling. "Where are we going?" I asked as he turned the key in the ignition and the engine's rattle filled the air.

His eyes sparkled over his shoulder. "Today," he said, "we go everywhere."

THE *MOTOR*

After last night and all the wet, the dry air felt like heaven.

I squeezed my eyes tight as we turned out of the driveway and onto the busy streets. I tried to keep the rest of my body loose to ride out the twists of the congested roads. Cooked meat and spices mixed with the stink of diesel exhaust.

It all smelled divine.

I hung on to Deni's waist for dear life, squishing my face hard into him, breathing in the salty sweat of his back.

"Are your eyes open?"

"No," I yelled over the noise.

"*Ayo*—come on."

"No way."

"You will like what you see if you are brave enough to look. *Buka mata.* Open up your eyes." I forced my eyes open just in time to see Deni narrowly avoid hitting a bright orange mini-bus that blared its horn at us.

"Deni!" I cried. "Watch out!"

He laughed as I squeezed him tighter. "Maybe time to close your eyes."

I couldn't help laughing too, but then we leaned so far

to the left, I thought we were going to tip over. I screamed with exhilaration. Squeezing my thighs around the seat, I leaned into the next turn.

Similar to the rules of body boarding: if my body was tense and I resisted the lucidity of the ocean, I'd wipe out. But if I was loose and fluid and moved with the waves, I'd catch an awesome ride all the way to shore. I used the same logic now, but instead of waves, I was surfing the streets of Yogyakarta.

"Deni! My eyes are open!"

"Good. Now you can truly see. *Do not* let go."

We rode out of town, deeper into the lush jungle, passing men and women wearing triangular woven hats as they worked in fields of rice paddies. The loose ponytail hanging out of the helmet whipped my face in the hot air.

Small mountains peeked through a mist of ashy clouds. The scooter vibrated between my legs as we drove about thirty miles an hour down the straight country road. Suddenly the silver air thickened and it was like we were cruising through a rain cloud.

"Is that an ox?" I yelled as Deni slowed to pass a man driving a wooden-wheeled cart pulled by a sharp-horned bull. The man whipped the animal with what looked like a willow branch.

"Yes. You will see many of them in the country."

Then I saw it.

An ancient temple loomed in the distance on top of a

short hill. Like something out of *The Jungle Book* or *Indiana Jones,* the temple was built of stone into the shape of a pyramid.

"Here is Borobudur," Deni said, pulling the *motor* into a parking lot.

"Borobudur? My dad has talked about this place forever; how did you know I wanted to see it?"

"*Bule* always come here while they are visiting the *pesantren.*"

"What's *bule*?"

"Foreigners. Tourists. Like you," he said.

Even though we were stopped, I still hugged his waist. "Have *you* been here before?"

"No," he said matter-of-factly. "I am not *bule.*"

I laughed. "Good point."

"Now we must get off," he teased.

I peeled my arms from his body.

When I hopped off and tried to stand, I felt like I'd just gotten off a horse. Wobbling, I rose up on my tippy toes to stretch out my legs as he laughed.

"You aren't used to it yet, the *motor,*" he said.

"No. But at least I didn't fall off!"

"I wouldn't let you fall," he said.

I pulled my digital camera out of my backpack to take a shot of the monument.

Deni eyed the camera appreciatively. "Those cameras are much money. Even here."

"I got it for Christmas last year from my *oma,* my grand-mother. I really like it."

"You like taking pictures?" he asked.

I nodded. "Yeah, I do. Sometimes I worry my memories will fade without them."

"My memories never go away."

I stopped. "Really? Because no matter how hard I try to keep them in my mind, some images slip away."

"Like what does slip away?"

He seemed to really want to know. "Well. Like my . . . like my mom. Sometimes I can't remember her the way I used to. I still remember her, but it's like her face in my mind is disappearing or something. It's hard to explain."

He looked like he understood but then asked, "Your mom is in America, no? You will see her soon?"

I bit my lip. "No . . . she's not. . . . She's gone."

He looked at me sadly, but didn't ask me what hap-pened to my mom, probably because he didn't want to talk about what happened to his. We were both quiet for a second before he said, "Take a picture of me?"

"Sure!"

Deni leaned against the *motor* and flashed me a sly look. Just the little image of him on my digital screen sent goose bumps to places I didn't know goose bumps could grow.

I seized the day and took several, just in case I didn't get the chance again.

"Let me look."

I tilted the image toward him. His face lit up when he saw the shots. "Ahhh, not bad. Perhaps I should be one of your American Hollywood-style actors like Arnold Schwarzenegger or Tom Cruise?" He struck a pose on his motorcycle that cracked me up. "America is ready for Indonesian celebrity, no?"

"I don't think America could handle you, Deni. You're way too real for that scene. Besides, you're *much* cuter than either of those guys."

"Cute?" He wrinkled his nose. "Like a baby goat?"

He leaned in close to me, his dimple deepening in his smooth cheek.

"Um. No. Not like a baby goat at all." I stumbled over my words.

Looking into his eyes, I saw he knew exactly what I meant.

"So." Shivers ran down my spine. "Ready to go in?"

THE TEMPLE

Vendors cruised up and down the main dirt road leading to the temple selling touristy things like Borobudur T-shirts, statues of the monument and postcards. They flashed their wares in our faces and used cheesy car salesmen voices to persuade us to buy. One young boy wouldn't take no for an answer, so I bought a couple of T-shirts, a bunch of postcards and two miniature statues of the temple and stuck the loot in my backpack.

"So how much does it cost to go in?" I asked Deni when we were standing under the entrance sign.

"Tourist price one hundred thousand rupiah. For Indonesians only five thousand rupiah. About ten dollars of American money for you. About fifty cents for me."

"You translate the money really well."

"If I'm going to be a big star of movies one day, I must know all about America," he joked.

"That's true," I said, handing the man sitting in the ticket booth some pink paper money. Deni ordered the tickets, and I was happy he let me treat without the money thing becoming an issue.

I followed him as we wound our way up a set of steep stone stairs into the ancient Buddhist temple. I remembered Dad talking about this place a long time ago, that each level told the story of the Buddha—as you curved around, you read more of the picture story carved into the stones.

I told Deni what Dad had told me. "I always wanted to see this in real life; now here I am," I said.

"What is the story of the Buddha?" Deni asked.

"You don't know it?"

"Why would I know it? We are Muslim. We study Islam. I'd like to hear it, this story," he said.

My face flushed. I wasn't a natural storyteller like Mom or like Spider. . . .

"Um. I'll give it my best shot. Just for you." I walked up a few stairs to an elaborately carved piece of stone. "This must be baby Buddha being born out of his mother's side. Kind of weird, right? The story is that Buddha was a virgin birth, like Christ's."

Deni shrugged, like *I've heard weirder,* encouraging me to keep talking. "So . . . the Buddha was a prince, bound to be the next Hindu king. They were Indian and lived at the base of the Himalaya mountains. The Buddha's parents wanted to keep him sheltered, so he stayed in the palace and was pampered. His parents didn't want him to see any of the bad things in life like poverty, pain or . . . death. Hold on a second, I want to take a picture of this one," I said, snapping a few shots. "You get in there too, if you want?" I said, hoping he would, which he did.

He posed, a serious look on his face, which made me laugh. Then we moved on. "When he was older, about our age, the Buddha wanted to go outside. His parents forced him to stay in, though. Then one night his curiosity got the best of him and he snuck out of the palace." I leaned in closer to Deni. "When he snuck out, he took a few servants with him. But what Buddha didn't know was that they were really angels in disguise."

I walked a few steps to the next imprint, the next story. "As he rode his horse out of the palace gates, the angels held their hands under the horses' hooves so that Buddha could sneak out in silence. Cool, right?"

"Like we did today," he said, with a sly look. "Only it was the gatekeeper who held our hooves, no?"

"Uh, yeah, sort of." I nicked into him with my elbow playfully, not wanting to think about how busted I was going to be when Dad realized I was gone. "Anyway, once he got outside the palace walls into the real world, the angels pointed out three things Buddha had never seen before: an old person, a sick person and a dead person being prepared for a funeral. He had no experience with death before." I lowered my voice, knowing a tough part in the story was coming up. "In fact, he didn't know people died at all. He thought everyone lived forever."

Deni and I were standing so close our shoulders touched. Our eyes met as he prodded me on. I swallowed and kept talking.

"Which, of course, we know isn't true. So finally

Buddha figured out he must transcend mortals' fate—pain, et cetera—through enlightenment."

I watched Deni as he examined the relief. "Enlightenment?"

"It means, like, reason over blind faith, the ability to think for yourself."

"I like that."

"Yeah, me too. So Buddha set off on his own path, deciding he should suffer because others did."

"Do you think he was right?" he asked me seriously.

"I don't know. I guess the human experience is to suffer at least some."

His face shadowed. "It has been my experience, yes."

We stood there staring at each other. Other tourists passed by us, but we didn't move.

He cocked his head, looked down at his feet. Then he met my eye. "I think you are a good storyteller, Sienna. No one has told me a story in a very long time. And it is interesting about the boy named Buddha. He has not seen what I have seen, but he wants to. He wants to live and see the bad things instead of to not know."

"Right." I hoped Deni would tell me a story too—his story—how he ended up at the *pesantren,* how he got his scar, his limp. Something about his life before. But Deni didn't offer anything else, and I didn't want to pry. Something about the way we were together told me when he was ready, he would. And it was okay. I could wait.

The sun broke through the clouds and beat straight down on us. I wiped sweat off my forehead with the back of my hand.

"I wonder what is up here?" Deni said, suddenly taking the lead.

I followed him up another flight of stairs. At the top, I pulled out a new bottle of water, which we shared.

As I tucked the empty bottle back into my pack, I watched Deni as he peered inside a gray-stone cutout shaped like a diamond. "Look." He pointed. A beautiful stone Buddha sat in the lotus position and stared back at us. I reached my camera through the cutout and took some pictures. "Sienna . . . ?" Deni said suddenly, his voice throaty like it was last night in the rain.

"Yeah?" I asked, meeting his eyes.

Our chests inches apart, he licked his lips as my heart pounded.

Suddenly a group of loud, chatting Indonesian girls approached us, pointing to their cameras. They spoke to Deni in speedy Indonesian, I assumed. I heard them say "America" a couple of times.

"They wish to take their picture with the beautiful American girl," Deni said mischievously, like he found it very entertaining.

"What? Really?"

"Yes. They are from the countryside and have rarely

seen girls with SpongeBob yellow hair. That's what they said."

"They *did not* say 'SpongeBob,' did they?"

"No." He smiled, touching my elbow quickly. "Just beautiful *rambut kuning,* yellow-haired girl."

"But how could they? I'm so sweaty and gross."

"*Gross? Apa?* What is *gross?* Another word for 'beautiful'?"

He was serious. Seriously adorable.

So I stood in the middle of the group of excited girls, who put their long-sleeved arms around me. They must have been so hot in their *jilbabs* and long dresses, but they weren't even breaking a sweat. We all smiled at Deni, who took our picture with the girls' cameras and then with mine.

"Thank you. Thank you," the girls said as they moved away.

Deni leaned over and said quietly into my ear, "They asked if you were married."

"*Married?* What did you say?"

"I said *belum*" —he grinned slyly—"which in English is 'not yet.'"

My eyes flew open. Did the girls ask if *we* were married? Deni and me to each other?

"In Indonesia we don't say no," he explained. "We say 'not yet.' Everyone hopes to be married one day." His face clouded over when he said that. I wasn't sure why.

"Isn't that a good thing? Getting married?"

He looked like he might tell me a secret. "Another day," he said finally. "I can tell you a story of that another day."

But I did get one story then.

As we silently weaved our way back down the curved stairwell, the shadow lifted from his face, and his eyes lit up. "You know the story of Islam, Sienna? The story of Muhammad?"

"Sort of. We studied it in my social studies class, but I'd like to hear you tell it."

"Then I will. Muhammad was an orphan boy, a prophet, but he does not know at the first. Then an angel visits to him. He receives the word that there is one God and that God is Allah. That is what we say when we say our prayers. The angels tell him to spread the word and he does. Then many, many tribes are spread out across the desert. They're fighting. Muhammad unites them together. Allah tells the words of the Koran to Muhammad. Muhammad writes them down, even though he could not read. He says to the people, 'This is our book. This is our religion.'"

"I like that. Especially how he unites the tribes together."

"Yes. Apart we are nothing, together we are whole. And you are *Christian*."

I shrugged. "I guess. Sort of."

He looked surprised. "But you are from America? What do you believe, then?"

What do I believe?

"Good question." I shrugged again. "I used to believe in God, but now . . . I don't know."

He looked at me strangely, and I remembered what Dad told me on the plane: Indonesians assume everyone has a proper religion; if they don't, then there is something wrong with them.

I didn't want him to think there was something wrong with me, so I quickly changed the subject.

"Do you speak Arabic too?" I asked. I was already so impressed that Deni spoke three languages: Indonesian, Acehnese *and* English.

I knew English and two bits of conversational Spanish.

"Our prayers you hear at the *pesantren* are Arabic," Deni explained. "We study Arabic at school, but most children do not know it to speak other than their prayers and the Koran."

Then, as if on cue, we heard the faint chanting of the call to prayer. I couldn't tell where it was coming from.

"You see the mosque?" Deni said, pointing out into the far distance.

I squinted into the sun. Sure enough, there was a mosque peeking out of the thick green vines miles away.

His forearm glistened with sweat next to mine as we leaned over the railing to watch, to listen. "When the wave came to Aceh and took everything away from us, it did not take the great mosque. Great and proud. Flooded but not destroyed."

We stood silently for a moment, moist air melting into my skin.

"So Muhammad lost his parents too?" I asked softly.

"Yes." Deni nodded, staring out at the white tip of the mosque floating above the trees. "He did."

MAGIC

Outside the temple, we stopped at a food booth and Deni asked the clerk for a *minte nasi bungkus,* a packed meal to go. I followed him to an emerald patch of grass, Borobudur our picnic's backdrop.

Deni carried plastic bags filled with liquid tied with rubber bands in one hand and something wrapped in brown paper in the other. As he juggled everything, he explained what we would eat: *ayam goring* (fried chicken), *gulai* (coconut curry) and layers of green banana leaves that held small servings of sticky white rice.

He made two plates of banana leaves, one for me, one for him.

"And *tempe,*" he said, handing me some sort of soybean cake. "You like *sambal*?"

It looked like salsa, which I didn't like, but when in Rome. I said yes, and he poured it on my *tempe.*

On the grass, we ate the meal silently, using our right-hand fingers as spoons. For dessert, Deni held a fresh coconut to my lips, its dark green top sliced off with a straw sticking out. "Drink," he said. "It's very sweet."

I wrapped my hands around the coconut, thinking he would let go once I took it, but he didn't, and so my hands were on top of his as I drank; milky water dripping down my chin like sugary rain.

Deni wiped the smear of liquid off my skin. "It tastes like candy, no?"

"Yeah," I said. I sighed and lay back on the grass, feeling spinny and dizzy, full and happy.

Deni did the same, resting his head back on entwined hands like his arms were wings.

I watched birds fly over us, heard oxen-driven carts roll slowly by, and the palm fronds that rustled over us in the breeze.

Then I felt his eyes burning into my skin, so I tilted my face toward him. "Hi," I said.

"Hi," he said, a slow smile crawling up his lips.

My stomach flipped.

Then his smile faded; he blinked, sat up quickly. Raked his fingers through his hair.

I sat up too, wondering what had spooked him.

"Do you know *sate kuda*?" he said.

"Um. No. What is *sate kuda*?"

"Horse meat."

My nose crinkled. "Horse?! Seriously?"

He laughed, but it wasn't a real laugh. "I knew not to order it for you."

"Thanks." I fingered moist blades and soil, still curious as to why he sat up so suddenly.

"More to drink?" he asked. "*Es jeruk.* Ice orange. It is my favorite."

"Orange is my favorite flavor too."

The bubbly soda tasted like a Popsicle, which reminded me of Spider, which reminded me of home. Then I felt weird in too many ways at once.

"Can you take a picture of me, Deni? So I can show my friends later?" I asked. I suddenly felt guilty for not thinking about them more.

I handed him the camera and took another long swig of the sweet orange drink. "Try to get the *motor* in the background, okay? Oh, and the temple! And some of the food!"

My enthusiasm cheered me right back up. Deni too.

He smiled and the weirdness from the moment before vanished.

Click.

Outside the *pesantren* gate Deni flipped off the ignition. The high-pitched rattle stopped, but my ears kept ringing.

"You enjoy the *motor* ride?"

I hugged his waist tight. This time I wasn't letting go so easily. "It was just like body boarding back home," I said, pressing my cheek into his back.

"Body boarding is what?"

"Oh. Like surfing—something I did when I was younger, back at home."

"Hang on." Deni stepped off and then stretched his leg back over the seat, facing me.

Beaming from ear to ear, I leaned into him. I couldn't believe we were daring to sit so close hidden only by the gatekeeper's booth.

"I used to body board all the time when I was a kid."

He was looking at me like he wanted to get closer.

"Used to?"

I busied myself with unsnapping my helmet, struggling with the clasp. "Yeah—with a friend of mine . . . but not anymore."

"Let me." I could feel his breath on my neck as his fingers tried to find the snap. "It's easier if you stand."

He offered his hand, helping me off the bike.

And then we were face-to-face again.

He moved in closer to concentrate on the clasp.

"There! You are free." He lifted the helmet off my head, letting my hair fall loose around my shoulders. But he didn't move back; he didn't step away. "You don't body board anymore?"

"No."

"Something to do with your mother?"

"Another day," I said. I closed my eyes as Deni ran a finger tenderly over my hand, shivers running up and down my spine. I rested my forehead against his chest like I'd been dying to do all day. I didn't want to talk about the past. I wanted to hang on to him, to this moment, the smell of sweat and exhaust and coconut—a hint of cigarette smoke still hanging on his clothes.

"Thank you, Deni," I whispered into him. "I had a magical morning."

His hand ran down my hair. "Magical?"

"*Magical* means better than perfect. Almost make-believe. Even without the pictures, I know I will always remember."

He pulled me away from him, tilted my chin up and looked down at me. And then he smiled, dimple and all.

Then laughter and chatter rang out from the other side of the *pesantren* gate.

The sounds of real life. Well, this real life anyway. Which didn't seem very real at all.

"Just one more second," I said. "I have something for you."

I reached into my pocket and pulled out the tiny golden statue of the temple that I had bought earlier. I set it in his open palm. "Cheesy, I know, but I didn't want you to forget."

"Not cheese, *ole-ole*," he said. I looked at him quizzically, so he translated, "When foreigners come, they bring gifts, *ole-ole*. It's just not usually from our own country." He laughed, looking at the little metal temple.

"If you don't want it," I joked, taking it back. He wrestled it back from me and tucked it in his pocket, then he brought me into his arms.

The feeling of his hand cradling the back of my head was the safest I'd felt ever.

"I too will always remember," he said, his voice low. "Especially now that I have your junky tourist toy."

"Hey!" I punched him gently.

Breathing him in, I replayed it all in my mind, a kaleidoscope of snapshots: the temple and then riding through traffic as if our *motor* was being carried by the hands of angels.

And this moment.

I stared up at him. He stared back. Neither one of us was laughing anymore.

His face turned suddenly serious. "Now, if I could, I would like to meet your father."

CLAY

We found my dad easily enough.

He was sitting on the steps of the meeting hall, dressed in the same stiff clothes he was wearing that morning.

"Hi, Dad," I said, prepared for the lecture of a lifetime.

But instead of looking pissed, he shielded his eyes and squinted up like he didn't recognize me at all, like he was seeing a ghost. Dad's wrinkles deepened around his eyes as he inspected me more intently. "Oh my goodness. The way the light is bouncing off your face, you look exactly like your mother."

"Really?" I said, feeling uncomfortable. I glanced at Deni, who was standing there with his hands shoved into his pockets, probably thinking Dad was crazy.

"Wow, the resemblance is uncanny," Dad continued like he was in some daze.

"Well, she is my mom," I said. "Genetics and everything," I added, trying to lighten the moment. Maybe it was my windblown helmet hair . . . or maybe something else. Like the fact I *did* something adventurous and rebellious and romantic and awesome.

Something that Mom might have done.

"Vera missed you at group." He glanced over at Deni and narrowed his eyes questioningly. "Where have you been?"

"Dad, this is Deni. Deni, this is my father, Dr. Jones."

Dad offered his hand to Deni. "I'm pleased to meet you again, Deni. We met at the welcoming ceremony."

"It is nice to meet you too, Doctor." Then Deni was straight to the point. "I hope you can help me and my friends. And that you did not get the wrong idea of me from Bapak."

Dad waved his hand through the air to put Deni at ease. "I trust my own opinion over the opinions of others."

Deni's stiff shoulders relaxed a bit.

"I've heard you are the leader of the Aceh boys," Dad said.

"Leader? I do not know about *leader*," Deni said modestly. "But I am their friend, yes."

"Good. While we are here, we hope to accomplish a few things. One is rearrange your sleeping arrangements so that an older boy, like you, would be in charge of a group of younger boys. What you showed last night was dedication to your friends from Aceh."

Deni shrugged. "They have no one else."

"Right. So we plan on restructuring all the dorms in this way. And we are hoping you can help us motivate the other boys and spread the word that this is a good idea."

"Yes. I will help."

"Great! We could also use your help with translating to

the younger kids. You are obviously fluent in English, and it's paramount in therapy sessions that the younger ones understand."

Deni stood up straighter. "And what do I get in return, Doctor?"

"In return? Like payment?" Dad asked.

I squirmed. What did Deni mean?

He studied Dad hard. "I need to get back home, Dr. Jones. I need to get back to Aceh."

Dad looked at me. I looked at Deni.

"Aceh?" Dad asked. "But it's still underwater. . . . The reconstruction has barely started. . . . You live here now. Your schooling, your housing, everything is taken care of."

"Aceh is my home. Yes, I came here, but now I want to return. If I help you, if I do these things for you, if I get my friends and the little ones to do what you ask, will you help me get back to my home?"

Dad looked torn. I could tell he didn't want to promise Deni something he might not be able to deliver. But he didn't want to lose Deni's help either. "I will be happy to talk with you about it as things progress."

Deni's eyes were intense. He wanted a clear answer. "Then yes?"

Dad paused for a second. "For now, will you take a strong maybe?"

Dad had to run off to a meeting with Vera, so Deni and I walked silently back toward the dorms, my mind spinning from the strange request he made of Dad.

Dad, who normally checked on me every five seconds at home, hardly noticed I was gone for *four hours*? What if something had happened to me? He wouldn't have even known I was gone. Not that I minded not getting grilled about where I was. And I was happy we weren't caught, but still, it was odd.

Dad was so distracted here. And Deni, he wanted to go back to Aceh? The epicenter of the tsunami, where his entire family was killed? And what was he doing with Dad, some sort of blackmail the way he bribed the gatekeeper with cigarettes? It made me feel weird, him talking to my dad that way. Maybe he was using me to get something from him?

I felt sick as I glanced at Deni from the corner of my eye. Was I wrong to feel so close to him?

We walked by a group of older girls who were staring at us suspiciously. "Do you know those girls?" I asked, breaking our silence. Maybe one of them liked Deni. Or was Deni's girlfriend. I hadn't even thought about that before. Did Deni have a girlfriend? And if he did, what was he doing with me?

Deni nodded at the girls and waved. They waved back, and I heard some "Halo"s, Indonesian for "hello."

He lowered his voice when he leaned in toward my ear. "They are talking about us because we are walking alone."

I was glad it was only talk-talk and I was sure glad he was walking with me and not with one of those girls. Talk-talk away.

"Why is your father so surprised I want to return to Aceh? Why would I want to stay here? Does Bapak use rich donor money to buy us meat?" he asked, his hands in the air. "Buy chicken to eat with noodles? Do you know what his house is, Sienna? A palace. A golden palace. Some of the children here are his servants. They say even his water is gold. He eats meat every night off golden plates while sometimes we have so little rice we go to sleep hungry. This is not right. I am better off living on the watery streets of my home."

"I didn't know he was so rich. I don't think my dad knows either."

Deni's fist was clenched. "He is *very* rich. I do believe he did a good thing taking us here after the tsunami. But Bapak can do more for us than he does. The Koran says: *Those who devour the wealth of orphans wrongfully, they do but swallow fire into their bellies, and they will be exposed to burning flame.*"

I didn't talk. I just listened.

Deni shook his head like he was confused. "My plan is

to move back to Aceh, find a job and send for the rest of my Aceh friends . . ." He glanced at me as if he was asking if he could trust me to go on.

"You can tell me," I said.

"Yes," he said. "I think you are a friend, Sienna."

I was suddenly completely aware of Deni's hand swinging by his side. We were walking close to each other again. Closer than I saw any other pair walking together.

"Yes, Deni, I am your friend."

We walked by another set of girls who were whispering and pointing in our direction. "Are they talk-talking too? Why are you laughing? What's so funny?"

"You," he said fondly, "are a funny American."

"Why am I funny?"

"Your America is so different from here. Here, if a boy walks with a girl, people think they will marry. That is why they talk-talk."

"*Marry!* Because we're walking together?" I stopped in the middle of the path.

"Yes, marry." When he repeated *marry,* he looked shy. "We walk with a group if we don't want people to talk-talk. And we never sit in a room together. Especially here at the *pesantren.*"

"*Never sit in a room together?* Sit?"

"If we knew each other from school . . . Pretend this"—he waved his hand through the air—"is not my life. Instead we are in Aceh. If you are a girl I know, you come to my family house for tea, but we sit in the main room of the house with my family. That is the visit."

"And then you'd probably be expected to marry me, right?" I joked.

Deni's eyes were serious. "Yes."

I was shocked. "I just turned fifteen!"

"But I am seventeen. I am a man. And you, in Indonesia, are a woman."

Talking about this must have made Deni upset too, because his right hand clenched tightly into a fist again.

"You must really miss your family," I said quietly.

"I miss my family very much. My mother was very kind."

As if I was on autopilot, I stepped off the main trail and onto a path I didn't know. It wasn't the boys' or the girls' side. Deni followed me.

"What was your mother like?" I asked, slipping behind an outbuilding. I glanced over my shoulder to make sure the coast was clear. Some kids were watching us, but they didn't detour off the main path to follow. Deni didn't seem to worry.

"*Ibu,* that is the word for 'mother,'" he said. "She was tall and proud. She was an artist. She wove beautiful baskets and dyed them all the colors of the rainbow. Ibu was greatly . . . *apa?*"

"Liked? Admired?" I guessed the word he was trying to use to describe his mother.

Deni nodded, leaning against the paint-chipped wall. We were facing the river. The orphanage was behind us. "Some people believe it was meant to be—that the wave came because the Acehnese were fighting a civil war and Allah came to punish us. But I don't believe that. I don't believe Allah would punish my mother. She never harmed anyone. The sea just came." His knuckles were white, his fist clenched tight. It was all I could do not to throw my arms around him.

A salty droplet of sweat slipped off Deni's arm, and that was it.

I reached my fingers out carefully. We were behind the building. No one could see. I lifted his fist up and gently cradled it in my palm.

He glanced down at his hand and then into my eyes and it was happening again. That rush. That buzzy, hot feeling I had when we first met, when he held my hand and touched it to his forehead. That I had last night in the rain and today, again, as I squeezed against him on the back of the *motor,* as we lay side by side on the grass, as he cradled my head in his hands.

His Adam's apple quivered when he swallowed, but he didn't say anything; he didn't try to move away.

Slowly, I uncoiled his long fingers one by one until his hand was flat. I gently raked my fingertips across his palm, like a thin comb sifting through a plate of silky sand. He sighed as I tangled my fingers in his.

"*Rambut pirang,*" Deni said with a raspy choke. He lifted up a piece of my hair. "*Rambut anda cantik.* You are beautiful. Like the sun."

"I thought I looked like SpongeBob?" I grinned.

He smiled. "Him too. Especially when you are all wet from the rain."

Our entwined hands reminded me of a mold I saw once at a flea market, marble fitting perfectly into clay.

The goat was gone.

The old goat who saved his own life by climbing on the roof during the storm. I asked Elli about him as we finished art therapy. It had been a good session. This time we drew family. I included Oma, Bev and Spider and Elli. I wanted to draw Deni but knew that would look awfully conspicuous.

Elli included Vera, Dad, Tom, the cook, her teacher, the *pesantren* owner and me in her drawing.

New morning sun beamed down on the concrete slab we were drawing on.

I pointed to where the goat used to be, tied to the volleyball net. "Goat? *Dimana?*"

With a gray piece of chalk I drew a decent-looking goat on the sidewalk. The girls' eyes opened with recognition. Elli shook her head sadly.

"What?" I asked. "Where is he? Do you know?"

Elli started a new drawing. With orange chalk, she drew a stick figure like I had before. Orange with yellow hair and orange shoes. "Sienna," she said with a smile. Then she drew herself next to me and a bunch of her friends. Then she drew a long table.

"Are you hungry?" I asked, not getting what she was trying to tell me.

Vera, Dad and Tom were meeting to discuss afternoon therapy sessions. Vera had left art a little early, saying that I was doing such a good job with the young girls, I would be fine on my own for the last fifteen minutes or so. She didn't even seem mad that I ditched her group yesterday, but she did eye me suspiciously when I told her I'd had something important to do that kept me from going. Of course I didn't tell her what that important thing was. But felt good that at least it was the truth.

Occasionally, between chalk drawings, I scanned the path for Deni.

I didn't see him.

Eventually, other kids started to wind down the path toward the meeting hall. A European donor was visiting this morning, and the Acehnese kids had to rearrange their schedules to perform the welcome ceremony to greet her.

I thought about what Deni said. Was the *pesantren* owner really getting richer off these donors who thought the money was helping the kids? I thought about his golden plates, his golden life. I wondered how much was true and how much was rumors.

I lay awake for hours last night staring at the broken ceiling fan, urging it to move, wondering what happened at the boys' group meeting after I left Deni behind the outbuilding.

I really wanted to be there, but Dad wouldn't budge. I even resorted to begging—"I'll take notes, I'll run the video camera, I'll help translate." (Dad's eyes lit up at that one.) But it didn't work. He reminded me again how inappropriate it would be for me, *a girl,* to be sitting in on their *boys'* meeting.

Last night after giving up on the fan I squeezed my eyes shut, counted goats, thought about home. I even did the relaxation techniques Dad taught me: first relax your toes, one by one; are they relaxed? Okay, now relax your ankles; are they relaxed? Good, now relax your calves, et cetera, et cetera. Nothing! All I could see was Deni's back to me on the *motor,* my arms wrapped around his waist.

Now my whole body was awake and alert and . . . whoa . . . the opposite of relaxed.

The band of girlettes tumbled onto the grass in a heap, playing and scrambling with my chalk. I squinted at them, shielding my eyes from the sun. Dad said I shouldn't wear my sunglasses here so people could see my eyes. "Only tourists wear sunglasses," he said on my first day. "Besides, eyes are the windows to the soul, Sienna."

True. So they saw into my blinded soul. I grinned to myself, and then suddenly a flash of red and white and gorgeous was standing between the sun and me.

"Hello," Deni said, all fresh and clean in his school uniform. His shirt flapped opened around the collar, and I couldn't help staring at his smooth skin, already glowing with morning sweat.

"Hello," I said back, my lips curling up. Then I realized the girls were watching me watch him, and I needed to fill in the silence. "Do you know where the goat is?" I blurted out. "The girls don't seem to know."

The goat? You think about him all night and then ask about a goat?

"The goat? The goat was eaten," he said.

I gasped. "By *who*? Who ate the goat?"

"Us." He stretched out his hand to include me and the girls. "Me. You. Us."

"We? *Me?* I ate the sad goat? *When* did I eat the sad goat?"

"Last night. You saw meat in the fried noodles? That was goat."

My stomach churned. "Oh." I felt weird staring up at him and so started to stand.

He offered me a hand. "Better than horse, no?" he teased.

We were eye to eye, and then the girls moved in between us, tugging on Deni, trying to get his attention. He spoke to them in their language, then playfully grabbed the chalk in one hand and hid it behind his back. The delighted girls pointed and guessed which hand.

"Good drawings," Deni said, glancing down at the

sidewalk art. "I like that one the best." He pointed to Elli's drawing. The orange stick girl with blue eyes and yellow zigzag hair. Me.

"But your skin does not look *that* orange in real life." He grinned.

"I'm wearing a peach shirt!" I protested. "And orange shoes." I pointed to my old Converse.

"Ahhh. I see."

I would have given a kidney to be back behind the outbuilding again. And I was pretty sure, from the way he was looking at me, that Deni felt the same way.

But the little girls were paying too close attention, so I shook off those kinds of thoughts and said, "I don't know if it helps them—the art—to get over their bad memories, but it's fun."

"It is nice of you to come and try to help us."

It was the first time he'd mentioned it. He hadn't asked why I was there with my dad and Team Hope. And I wouldn't have really known what to tell him if he had.

"I'm happy they like it."

"They like you," Deni said in a low voice. "You bring light with you where you go."

"So do you," I said. He smiled and started walking away. I fell into step beside him.

Kids were a dozen thick surrounding Deni and me now. All the Acehnese kids were wearing their school uniforms: red pleated skirts with a gentle flare at the hem for the girls and red cotton pants for the boys. White button-down shirts for both. The girls' heads and necks were covered with white *jilbabs*—only their tan faces stuck out. The boys were wearing traditional hats that I'd learned were called *song koks*.

Everyone seemed at ease except Deni.

"Same thing over and over again. We perform, the *pesantren* owner gets richer. Do we see any money? No. I got some money from a donor once. He gave me five hundred euros. You know what I did? I passed it out to the children. It is ours. Why should I give it to Bapak? He was very angry I did not give it to him. He is still angry about the five hundred euros. It is like nothing I do can please him."

"That must be really frustrating."

He glanced at me. "It is. It is almost too much."

I waited alone outside the door listening to Bapak's speech. He was obviously back. I hated the part when he segregated the kids by how their parents died. It was loud when the kids shuffled to stand and quiet when each group sat back down. Finally, I heard the loud beats of the Acehnese drum circle filling the air and I knew Deni was where he was supposed to be.

Above me, dark rain clouds gathered. A crack of thunder shook the sky. When heaven split open and rain began to fall, I tilted my chin back and let water dance across my face.

I closed my eyes.

Smelled wet dirt as it turned into mud.

Heard the heavy drops of rain plop, plop onto the ground.

Felt the tropical rain run down my cheeks, my neck, my chest.

Breathed in the vibrations of Deni's drum.

Boom. Boom. Boom.

I never wanted to forget.

Drum, mud, rain. Drum, mud, rain.

Moved my head to the music's hypnotic beat.

I wasn't sure exactly who I was here.

But for the moment, it felt good to be her.

THE INVITATION

After the morning ceremony, the rain ceased and the kids had to go to class.

Their schoolroom was mostly dried out, and it was back to work studying religion, English, math.

I wrote in my journal while they were busy. Took a nap. Went to group with Vera. This time another girl shared. Her story was a little more hopeful: she managed to get her little brother to safety, and they were both here. He was one of the soccer kids I played with.

"Sienna? Do you have anything you'd like to share?" Vera asked, after.

I was sitting cross-legged, picking at my shoelaces. "No."

"Maybe someday soon?" she asked.

I met her eyes. "Maybe," I said honestly. It seemed to help the girls. The sharing. I wondered if it might help me.

After group I chatted with the older girls for a little while. It wasn't as easy to talk to them as it was to the younger ones. Maybe because I felt guilty for hiding this secret. For hiding my relationship with Deni.

"That was an amazing story," I told the girl who shared. "What's your name?"

"Nada."

"I'm Sienna. That's so amazing that you saved your brother. I'm totally in awe," I said.

She smiled shyly. She wore a filmy lavender *jilbab* and round-rimmed glasses.

I asked if I could take her picture. She said yes and smiled when I clicked.

After another simple dinner of noodles (this time, thankfully, with no mystery meat), I joined Dad and the rest of the *pesantren* on the field for a soccer game.

Rain long gone, the day had grown scorching, as if the sun was making up for all that time behind the clouds. I couldn't believe the boys were running around playing soccer. Even near sunset, it was still broiling. The heat soaked into the grass under my palms.

I sat next to Dad holding a cold water bottle to my forehead, wishing we had a pool to jump in.

Deni was goalie, and he was good. I watched him leap into the air, sweat pouring down his face as he stopped the other team's ball over and over again. His black T-shirt stuck to his chest with sweat. He flashed me a quick wink after he deflected a ball with his forehead and his team cheered. I felt my digital camera in my pocket.

"How did your art therapy go this morning? And Vera's group this afternoon?" Dad asked.

"Huh?" I watched the soccer ball Deni just kicked spin around in the air.

"The chalk art with the little girls before the ceremony? The therapy?"

"Oh, sorry. Art was good."

"Good. The little girls seem receptive to the art? Vera said you gave her some great feedback the other day, by the way." He eyed me carefully. "She got a lot out of looking at their pictures."

"Did she?"

"Yes. She said you were very perceptive about using art to gauge PTSD."

I shrugged. "It just makes a lot of sense, using art to describe emotion, like a story or a song. I mean, it's all sort of the same."

Dad nodded. "Yeah, it is. Same tools, different mediums. How is the teen group?"

I shrugged again. "It's sad. The stories are really awful. And I don't really help; I don't know. It's okay."

"Well, I can talk to Vera, have her give you something more to do—"

"No," I cut him off. "It's fine. I take pictures when they let me. Vera needs some for her research project and asked me if I could."

He was smiling at me.

"What?" I wiggled around in the grass.

"So you're okay with going?"

"Yeah, it's fine."

He seemed way too happy for something that was not a big deal. "That's great, honey."

Yeah, okay. Anyway. We sat quietly for a few minutes.

Me watching Deni while pretending not to be watching Deni, which was kind of hard when your dad was a psychiatrist.

"Deni seems like a nice kid," Dad said, glancing at me sidelong.

Caught.

"Yeah, he is. I can't believe he can move like that in this weather," I said. "I'd be crawling across the grass. I mean, I haven't even done anything physical today and look at me." I lifted my arms to show him they were glistening with sweat.

"They're used to it. They don't know anything different."

"They would probably think El Angel Miguel was cold! Especially the foggy mornings."

"Probably. Speaking of home, you can call Bev and Spider with the international cell phone if you want."

Just then, Deni caught my eye. I was thinking his smile might melt me right into the muddy grass until Dad's words soaked me back up.

Dad pulled a cell phone out of his pocket. "So we should think of the timing. We don't want to call California in the middle of their night."

"*What?* No." I pushed the phone away. "That's okay. . . .

I'll be home soon. I'm sure he's . . . I mean . . . I'm sure they're both really busy."

I yanked up a handful of grass, suddenly feeling guilty. But for what?

I hadn't done anything wrong. It wasn't like Spider and I were together or anything. Or Deni and I, for that matter. I mean, really.

"Let me know if you change your mind," Dad said, looking at me a bit funny. He rambled on about time differences and what we were going to do tomorrow, but I couldn't concentrate on anything except Deni.

When the game ended, and the soccer crowd and Dad left, I hung out on the grass, absently studying my phrase book, waiting. When everyone was gone, Deni finally wandered over.

I handed him my bottle of water, which he drained in one long gulp.

"Good game," I said.

"*Terima kasih.*" He wiped sweat off his forehead with his sleeve. "Thanks for watching."

"Hey, Deni?"

"Yes?"

"Why were you making fun of me at the first greeting ceremony when I thanked you . . . you know, when I said *terima kasih* and you sort of laughed?"

His brows knitted. "Making fun? I didn't make fun. I thought it was the sweetest thing, that you learned our words of thank you and tried to use it. I was . . . also . . . very nervous. It's not every day a beautiful stranger appears at the *pesantren*."

"I was nervous too. But mostly excited."

"But that is the fun of it, no?" he said, the tone of voice giving the words a different meaning. "Speaking of fun. Would you like to go with me someplace tomorrow night?"

Like a real date?

"Where?" I asked, twirling a piece of hair around my finger.

"Someplace. Do not worry. I will not be so dirty when we go," he said.

His forearms glistened in the rosy twilight. I didn't care if he was dirty, clean or what. I'd go now if that was what he was offering.

I lowered my voice, looking around for spies. "How will we sneak out?"

He shrugged, like *details, details*. "You come to the gate before dinner; I take care of the rest."

"Okay," I said, and watched his dimple dip deeper into his creamy skin.

How was I supposed to say no to that smile?

"See you then," he said.

"See you," I replied.

When he was out of my sight, I fell back onto the

prickly grass, butterflies racing around in my stomach. I watched the silver clouds above me, full and ready to burst.

I knew exactly how they felt. Oh, man. I sighed. I was in so much trouble.

ANOTHER DAY

After a painfully tedious day of waiting and waiting and waiting some more, I told Dad I was tired and headachy. That I'd had a long day, what with the art and the teen therapy and the volleyball game on the grass in between. We were also working all day on setting up the family system and matching older kids with younger ones. I told Dad I had the perfect girl for our bunk, and he said she could try tonight.

"Oh yes. You must be tired." With Nada in the dorm, I would be off duty. I could rest. And most important, I didn't have to worry about getting home in time to tuck in Elli and the other girls. Dad kissed me on the forehead and I was free.

I slipped easily through the open crack of the white wooden gate. When Deni met me, I felt his eyes running over me, taking in my new and improved appearance.

He and the gatekeeper were puffing away on cigarettes; the Indonesian sunset—pink, yellow, orange—shone on their faces, and they chattered like old friends.

"Those things will kill you, you know," I said to Deni, shyness creeping into my voice.

"Yes," he said, inhaling. "But sometimes they can buy your freedom." Deni took one more long drag, exhaled slowly and then dropped the cigarette to the dirt, squashing it under his shoe like a bug.

Deni was dressed up too. Blue button-down shirt tucked into tan chinos, his thick wavy hair wet and combed. Even his partial goatee was shaved off, leaving nothing but smooth chin. His hands were shoved in his pockets in a meaningful way. How could putting your hands in your pockets look meaningful? But somehow he pulled it off.

I lifted my ankle-length skirt, careful not to let the eyelet bottom drag in the dirt. My hair was clean, shining, loose down my back. And that was no small effort. Washing and conditioning with Elli as my sidekick, pouring bucket after bucket of fresh water on my hair, then running the comb through it over and over, untangling the knots.

But now here I was. Here we were.

Me smelling like buttercups and Deni like soap and cigarettes and opportunity.

Deni said something to the gatekeeper, who threw his head back, laughing. Then Deni shot me a wink. "You look beautiful."

"So do you," I said.

We pushed our way through the crowded, busy city streets. Deni held on to my lower arm protectively, pulling me along with him as we darted across the streets. Shop owners stood in front of their booths trying to persuade us to buy their wares, just like in Borobudur. "Come here, angel, three American dollars for this real gold necklace."

Deni waved them away.

Everywhere there was chatter, yelling and music blaring.

"Here's a good place," he said, pulling me into an open-air restaurant. Tapestries and smoke and several TVs filled the spicy-smelling room.

After checking us out curiously, the hostess led us to a low table inches from the ground. We sat on fluffy orange pillows on the floor.

"*Makasih,*" Deni said to the waitress.

"What's that mean?" I asked, squirming to get comfortable.

"Thank you."

"Not *terima kasih*?"

"*Makasih* not as formal. More for tourists. Like you."

"See? You were laughing at me."

"No. I really wasn't," he said, his eyes shiny and earnest.

Loud singing and dancing blasted from the TV screen in the corner. Young Indonesians dressed in flashy clothes and wearing tons of makeup performed on a colorful stage. It looked like some sort of talent competition. "What is this program?" I asked.

"*Indonesian Idol.*"

I spit out some of the ice orange soda the waitress had

brought over and then wiped my mouth with my sleeve. "Sorry. Oh my God, are you serious? Like *American Idol*?"

Deni nodded without irony, because why would it be ironic for him? "Yes. She is a very good singer." Deni pointed at a light-skinned Indonesian girl wearing tons of purple eye shadow and cherry red lipstick. Wearing tight blue jeans and an even tighter shirt, she swung her hips to the tune. I mean, I was being totally daring wearing a short-sleeved shirt tonight and the girl on the show was dressed like, well, girls on *American Idol* back home.

"Have you seen this before?" I asked Deni. "There's no TV at the *pesantren,* right?"

"No, there's not. I only watch when I'm out."

Out? So he went out often? I wrinkled my nose, then realized how silly I was being.

Of course he did. Why would I think this time with me would be his first?

"Why isn't she wearing a *jilbab*?" I asked.

He shrugged. "On television some girls do not."

"That's okay?"

His eyes lit up. "Yes. But on television here they will never show a kiss. It would be vulgar. They show kisses on American television, I have heard."

I blushed. "Yeah, they do."

The dinner was fluffy coconut rice, *nasi uduk,* and *gudeg,* which Deni explained was jackfruit cooked for a long time so it looked like meat.

"You like?" Deni said, eyebrows raised. "It is mixed with *kuda*. You remember, horse." He cracked up at my open-mouthed expression. "I am making a joke," he said. "Only jackfruit, do not worry."

Deni scooped up his food like there was no tomorrow. The jackfruit was cooked in palm sugar, sweet, almost too sweet, and dark brown.

We ate quietly for a while, new contestants appearing on *Indonesian Idol*. He stared at me for a beat before asking, "Why did you come to the *pesantren*, Sienna? Do you not have studies?"

"It's summer vacation, so no school."

"Did you want to travel to Indonesia?"

"At first I didn't, but then I changed my mind." I licked palm sugar off my fingers.

"I am glad you came," he said softly.

"So am I. How are things going in the group with my dad? Is he helping you?" I asked, digging into a partially melted scoop of green ice cream.

Deni nodded. "I have a terrible nightmare night after night about my *ibu*."

"What happens? . . . I mean, if you don't mind sharing."

His face clouded over. "She is dressed in black for mourning. It's the day the sea came. She rises out of the ocean and reaches her arms out to me, trying to pull me under the sea with her to my death." He shook his head as if trying to remove the image from his brain. "It is horrible."

"That is horrible." And then I realized I hadn't had a nightmare in three nights.

Dreams are portholes into the subconscious, Sienna.

Was my subconscious getting better? My awake self sure was. That I felt.

"I wake up cold, wet, yelling," Deni said. "My friends, they wake me up. Your father is teaching me ways to get away from the dream."

"Is it working?" I asked.

He shrugged. "A little. It's hard to change such a thing."

"I know."

He cocked his head. "You know?"

"I have a horrible dream too . . . night after night . . . about my mother."

"Your *ibu*?"

I nodded. "And the ocean. Do you really want to hear this?"

"Yes. It is Another Day." He held my eyes. "But if you do not want to, do not tell me."

I wiped my hands on my skirt. "No, it's okay. It was a long time ago. I don't talk about it very much. That's all."

"She drowned?"

"Well, her plane disappeared. Over the ocean. They never found the plane."

His eyes waited for me to tell him more.

I took a deep breath. I never told that story. Ever.

"I was almost twelve years old. Mom and Dad were not

far from here. In Thailand. They were doing relief work at a camp where the people had been relocated after a typhoon. They were passing out malaria pills and stuff like that. Anyway, Dad was busy with his patients and Mom heard that kids in a town just over the mountain needed first aid supplies after a school collapsed. Dad said it was raining. A bad storm. She left in a single-engine plane and something happened—they don't know what—pilot error or engine failure; all we know is that she, well, she never came back—and she never showed up at the village. The kids were waiting for her. They were waiting and she never came."

Tears stung my eyes. I didn't want to cry. "They looked and looked. At first they thought the plane might have crashed in the jungle, but there was no evidence of that, so they just assumed it went down in the sea. That's the reason I don't surf or body board anymore. I have nightmares about her . . . me . . . drowning in the ocean."

Deni reached over and wrapped his fingers around mine. Right there in the restaurant. Right out in the open.

"And to you now the ocean is an unhappy place," he said, his eyes warm. "And so you dream of it that way."

I nodded, biting my lip. "Not that it compares to anything that happened to you—I mean, I can't imagine what you went through . . . I don't know how you do it, how you stay so sure of yourself . . . and having nightmares on top of it."

He looked deeply into my eyes. "We do not choose what happens to us. We can only choose what we do after. What we do now. We can only choose to keep going."

"Well, your family didn't have a choice. The wave came. You all ran. But my mother had a choice. She didn't have to go up in that plane in a storm, so why did she go?" I looked at Deni for an answer. My hand looked so safe wrapped in his. "And Dad won't talk to me about it. I used to ask all the time for more and more details, so I could find out what happened, so I could go find her, you know? But he just said, 'She's gone.' "

"Your mother must have wanted to help. That was a choice you made too, to come here. You chose to come here to help. Even though you might think it was dangerous."

I shook my head. "I don't know if that's the same thing. I mean, there was a storm and . . ."

"Maybe hers was not the choice you would have made. But you cannot go back and save her," Deni said.

I wiped the tears streaking down my cheek with the back of my hand.

Deni set some paper money on the table.

"We go," he said, gently rubbing my thumb.

Somehow, he got me out of the restaurant and back onto the busy street. When had it started to rain?

This time he wrapped his whole arm around me, pulling me close to him. We walked for a bit in the hot downpour, Deni's eyes darting around, looking for someplace to hide from the rain or a place to be alone.

We ducked into a dirty alley filled with empty chicken cages and fell into each other against a wall. Rain splashed down. A tin overhang barely shielded us from the storm. And the drops pinged onto the metal.

Deni wrapped his arms around my waist. His eyes asking me a question I knew the answer to. I pressed my chest to his, and his lips moved against mine.

"Deni," I whispered. And we clung to each other like we were drowning because, in a way, we were.

THREE YEARS AGO
THE DARE

I kissed Spider once.

We were playing truth or dare on Spider's rooftop outside his second-story window.

Bev was the one who dared us.

"Truth or dare?" she said.

"Dare," I said. Why'd she even bother to ask? I *always* chose dare.

Her eyes darkened with mischief. "I dare you to kiss Spider."

I shook my head quickly. "No way. Changed my mind. Truth!"

Her hands flew in the air. "You said dare, you have to do it."

"No, I don't."

Bev pointed at me, shaking her finger. "No take backs, Sea."

Spider scratched his sandy hair. He looked nervous. "Bev, come on. Dare her to jump into the ocean without a wet suit or something," he said.

It was dark. Middle-of-winter cold. I would freeze for sure.

But freezing or *kissing*?

I'd take my chances. "That's fine," I said, agreeing with Spider's idea. "Let's go."

Bev shook her head smugly. "Nope. A kiss. That's your dare."

I remembered looking at him. Brick red freckles sprinkled across his nose and cheeks. His blond bangs hanging over his eyes.

"Okay, fine." I leaned over and kissed Spider, quick on the cheek, like he was Dad sitting in his easy chair.

Bev wasn't pleased. "Kiss means ON THE LIPS. Try again."

"Bev, come on," I hissed frantically in her ear. "Don't make me kiss your brother."

I glanced over at Spider, who was turning all shades of lobster.

She rubbed her hands together. "Sorry. A dare's a dare. What are you, Sea, chicken?"

My eyes burned in the moonlight. "You're so mean sometimes."

Bev shrugged. She knew how awful this was. SHE hadn't kissed a boy yet either.

I wouldn't do this to *her*.

"Leave her alone, Bev. This is lame anyway," Spider said, picking at the roof tiles.

Off the hook. Then why did I feel so disappointed?

"It's okay." I shrugged, suddenly changing my mind. "I

have to, Spider. A dare's a dare. Just . . . just close your eyes," I prodded.

"If you insist," he said with a lopsided grin, his eyes closed.

I scooted forward slightly, skidding my butt over the slanted rooftop, careful I wouldn't slip off and tumble into the yard.

When I was close enough to feel his breath on my face, I sat on my knees and leaned in.

I'd never kissed anyone on the lips except Mom and Dad, and that was when I was a little kid. I took a deep breath, closed my eyes and puckered up like a girl in a lipstick ad.

A tingling softness spread over my mouth that tasted like salt, tasted like the sea. Was that kissing?

"Spider! Beverly!" The twins' mom's voice suddenly filled the rooftop. My eyes flew open and I spun around. She was staring at me.

"Sorry, we were just . . . playing a game," I said.

"Truth or dare." Spider leaned back a little, still flushed. I smiled at him and he smiled back. . . . It was like getting forced awake from a perfect dream.

But Mrs. Adams didn't look mad. She looked like she'd seen a ghost. "Sienna—sweetheart," she said slowly.

Her usual smiling face was sad, her lips quivering.

It was just a kiss. Was it that big of a deal? "I'm sorry,"

I said again. "Bev dared me! We won't ever do it again. Pinky swear."

Spider laughed as Bev denied my accusation.

"You need to come inside," Mrs. Adams said.

"Let's go back in, you guys," I said.

I scratched up my knees crawling back toward the open window.

Mrs. Adams had tears streaming down her face. Her hands were shaking. She was holding a red cordless phone that was beeping loudly, like someone on the other end of the line had hung up a while ago.

Why hadn't she hung up her end?

Beep. Beep. Beep. Beep. Beep. Beep.

I never forgot that sound.

"Sweetheart." Mrs. Adams touched my thin shoulder. "I'm so, so sorry. I don't know how to s-say this. Your grandmother just called—"

She hugged me like she was trying to protect me from her own words.

"You need to go straight home" was all she could manage to say.

SCARS

It was still raining when we snuck back through the white gate, but not as hard.

Deni let go of my hand when we got close to the dimly lit *pesantren* property.

My hand felt naked without his.

He turned and kissed a raindrop off my cheek. The half-moon reflected off the dark, grassy field.

"What happened to your leg, Deni?"

His shoulders hunched. "I walk crooked now. You noticed."

"No. I can barely notice. I just . . . well . . ."

What? Admit I stared at him all the time? Had been watching him since I first arrived?

He leaned back against the gatekeeper's post. Glanced up at the moon before he started talking, like telling the sky was easier than telling me. "It happened the day the wave came. I was escaping on my *motor;* people were grabbing at me, trying to cling on to my back as I drove. To get a ride. But I had no more room. A group of boys jumped on, fearing for the water, and the *motor* crashed. It landed on my leg. I looked behind me and the water was coming close. The boys ran and I pushed the *motor* off my leg and got back on. But my leg, here, see?" He lifted the bottom of his pants to show me a thick, deep blue scar clear even in the shadows. "This is what happened." He shrugged. "But I am still here."

"Did you go to a doctor? That scar looks deep . . . Maybe my dad could look at it? He's a psychiatrist, but he's also a medical doctor."

He waved off the thought. "There were thousands drowning. . . . My cut was nothing. It is still nothing compared." He scrunched his face as if trying to force the memory out of his mind forever.

I imagined Deni, blood gushing from his leg, fleeing the tsunami.

It was stupid, but I wished I could have been there to help him. I wished I could help him now.

"Deni." My fingers curled around his forearm. "You know I'm leaving in less than a week? I . . . don't want things to be weird for the rest of our stay. I mean, I want to be with you, but I don't want us to get into trouble." I gulped. "Especially you."

His eyes shut briefly as if he was trying to decide. Then his dark lashes fluttered open and he traced an invisible line down my cheek with his finger. "So we make sure we are not caught."

"When will I see you again?" I whispered, my face tilted up at him.

"I will find you," he said in my ear.

And then, Deni started to slip away.

"Deni, wait!" I called after him. I wouldn't let him go that easily. Not after all this.

He turned around quickly, as if he'd been hoping I wouldn't let him go.

He wrapped his arms around my waist. "Dawn is not for a while," he said, "and no one can see us in the dark."

I'm not on a plane. I'm standing on a beach of white sand, staring out at a black sea. Except for larger-than-life gulls screeching above me, I'm alone. And then I'm not.

A figure.

Dressed in black with a veil covering her face, she floats above the waves.

Calling out to me: Sienna.

I try to run, but my feet won't move. Cemented to the sand, I try to close my eyes, but they won't close.

The woman comes closer, skimming over the tops of the waves like she is flying. She stops. Hovering over the wet sand. Dead fish, cans, bottom-of-the-ocean debris cling to her torn black robe like barnacles. She reaches her arms out to me and the wind lifts the veil off her face. "Come, Sienna . . . come."

I choke on my scream when I see who it is: my mother. The skeleton of my mother. Trying to pull me into the sea.

"Deni!" I screamed, tears pouring down my face. "Help me!"

"Sienna, Sienna!" A child's voice.

I rolled over, orienting myself. Elli looked so scared, her hands on my arms, shaking me. "Sienna?"

My ears rang from my own scream. "I'm okay, sweetie. Sorry, I . . . had a bad dream."

Chills ran up my body. Shaking, I got off the bunk and helped Elli back to bed, soothing her and some of the other kids I had woken up with my night terror.

"I'm so sorry," I said, kissing her cheek good night. "*Terima kasih* for waking me."

She still looked disturbed but squeezed my hand and closed her eyes. After a long time staring at the half-moon out my window, I fell back into a fitful sleep.

Pink light floated through the room. Someone else was shaking me awake. Calling my name. "Sienna? Sienna?"

Not again.

"Wake up." His voice was no more than a whisper. "My father is looking for me."

I sat up. Rubbing my eyes, I asked, "What time is it?"

"Dawn," Deni said. "Come?"

The little girls were still asleep, but the call to prayer couldn't be too far off. Glancing back at Deni, early sun rays washing over his excited face, I wondered what was worth the risk of sneaking over to the girls' side in daylight.

"My father is alive!"

"What do you mean *your father*?" I whispered. "I thought your whole family was . . . killed in the tsunami."

His shook his head and spoke in a low voice. "My father was a fisherman and was at sea the day the wave came. He fished his whole life. He knows the ocean like he knows his heart. I never believed that the sea took him. And now there is proof!"

"Let me get dressed. I'll meet you by the wall near the river."

Quickly I snuck off my bunk, slipped on a yellow sundress and practically flew down the path to meet him. Deni's father was alive? The thought was incredible.

When I spotted him waiting for me, an orange-tipped cigarette dangling from his lips, he was looking off in the distance. I stopped short and watched him, feeling weird, like maybe I shouldn't interrupt. That whatever he was thinking about was important. But then he saw me, tossed the cigarette into the dirt and ground it to ashes.

"I am not like them, Sienna," he said, gesturing toward the street kids by the river. "I am not alone. Each week I wait to hear news, knowing if he is alive, he will come looking for me."

"So your father is really here at the *pesantren*? Where is he?"

Deni's face twitched. "No. He is not here. We have word from Aceh, my friend tells me, that someone is looking for a boy named Deni who came to a *pesantren* in Yogyakarta."

My excitement faded as I realized he didn't have concrete proof. "Oh. And you think this person is your father?"

Deni's eyes hardened. "I do not think. I *know*."

We sat quietly for a while watching the Fudge Popsicle Haze rise over the river. I tugged a piece of my hair, not knowing what to say, feeling bad for bursting his bubble, but it could be *anyone* looking. It could be *any* boy named Deni.

"But Deni, it's been six months—"

"Still," he cut me off, "they are finding survivors."

Why was I being so negative? It wasn't so strange that Deni thought his father might be alive. I read some of those amazing stories about relatives reconnecting after the tsunami.

But I knew why Deni believed.

Because it was easier.

Easier than grieving.

"Well, that would be amazing if it was him," I said.

He looked at me strangely, his eyes firm with conviction. "It *is* him, Sienna. You must believe."

I was being such a hypocrite.

For a long time after her accident I thought my mom was alive too.

I mean, here I was three years later, *still* clinging to some hope.

That instead of dying when her plane crashed into the sea or drowning like in my nightmares, Mom was marooned on an untouched Thai island. That she spent her days picking bright yellow bananas and drinking sweet coconut juice out of green shells. That she walked along white sand in the moonlight, her long hair flowing down her tanned back, sending shiny glass bottles of rolled-up letters to Dad, Oma and me. That she was waiting to be rescued.

That she was waiting for someone to find her and bring her home.

I didn't even cry at her memorial service.

There was no casket, no ashes. To me it wasn't a real funeral. I refused to believe she was gone.

It was that phrase. That official phrase that somehow kept me hoping:

No evidence of a plane crash.

No wreckage found.

No known survivors.

So what about the *unknown* ones?

I never got to grieve like Dad or Oma.

Dad might still wear his wedding band, he might still appease my hope, but he knew she was gone.

And I still hadn't accepted it. That maybe she was never coming back. And now it was too late for me. They were better because they'd grieved. I was worse. Before this trip, I was so stuck and afraid.

I didn't want Deni to end up like me.

I reached out and touched his hand. "I understand, Deni. Believe me, I really do. I"—I couldn't believe I was using this word—"*used* to think my mother was alive too. And I didn't even have a good enough reason to hope . . ."

Then the call to prayer cried out, and I sighed, frustrated, knowing our time was up.

"Meet me here after?" I asked.

"Okay," he said. I watched him dash off.

We both cut out halfway through breakfast and we were back by the wall.

I brought Elli with me for a distraction, not wanting to encourage talk-talk. She was sitting next to me, coloring, while Deni hovered close, talking quietly.

Then Tom walked up.

"Deni, there you are. The *pesantren* owner needs to speak with you."

Deni jumped up, wide-eyed. "About my father? Is there more word? Has he sent for me?"

When Tom glanced at me, I recognized that look.

It was the same look Spider's mom had on the rooftop. Whatever they were going to tell Deni, it wasn't good news.

Tom touched Deni's shoulder. "I better let him explain, son."

Deni looked at me, his eyes full of worry and questions.

"It will be okay, Deni," I said. I wanted to go with him, to hold his hand, to be whatever he wanted me to be, but how could I do that? And then Tom was looking at me like he was seeing me for the first time. Looking back and forth from me . . . to Deni . . . and back to me. Tom's instincts were unfortunately dead-on.

"Sienna? What are you two doing out here?"

I glanced at Deni from the corner of my eye. "Nothing . . . talking . . . and helping Elli with her art before group starts," I said, guilt creeping up my chest for using her as a cover.

His eyes narrowed. "After breakfast the *pesantren* owner called a special meeting to explain what's going on with Deni—didn't you hear him?"

I shook my head. Deni and I both left early; we hadn't heard.

"You know you can't be out here with him alone," Tom said.

I shrugged and picked some mud off the wall. "We weren't alone," I said, gesturing toward Elli. Tom raised his bushy eyebrows as if to warn me: *We'll be talking about this later.*

But Deni backed me up. "It is the truth, Dr. Tom," he said. "I was talking with Sienna about my father. That he is alive. That is all. Her father knows we are friends." He smiled at me after he said it.

Tom acknowledged him with an unconvinced nod. But then I felt a familiar icicle of dread plunge through my chest when I understood the root.

It wasn't from happiness Deni grinned; it was hope.

• • •

Elli and I waited on the porch of Bapak's office, listening to Deni and the owner argue loudly in their language. Elli drew stars, moons and planets on the concrete in lavenders and mint greens, the heat crawling over my back as the morning dragged on.

Deni had been in there a long time.

I couldn't make out much but heard Aceh mentioned several times. Deni's voice kept cracking and I wondered if he was crying.

"Stars," I said, pointing to Elli's drawing. "Stars," I said, pointing up at the blue sky.

She looked at me like I was being silly. "No stars," she said. "Sun."

"Ha, you're right. Smart girl," I said as the door finally flew open, slamming into the wall, and Deni stormed out of the building. He didn't see us. At least I didn't think he did. His face was angry, and whatever Bapak said couldn't have been good.

I started to stand, my legs numb from sitting for so long on the hard porch, but then the owner walked out too, staring after Deni, shaking his head. He glanced over at me and Elli with harsh charcoal eyes but didn't say anything. I started drawing with Elli again.

I wished he hadn't said whatever he said to wipe away Deni's hope.

"Elli," I whispered once Bapak was back inside, "take this stuff back to the room, please. I have to go find Deni."

She tilted her head, asking, *What?*

"The bunk," I said, scooping up the chalk into her hands. "Go."

I sprinted across the lawn to the trail. It was so humid I felt like I was running through soup. But Deni wasn't on the trail. He wasn't on the wall.

Where would he go?

The *motor*.

I ran toward the front gate. Sure enough, Deni was on the other side, revving it up, wearing his cracker helmet. His face was a mix of rage and disappointment. There was no extra helmet for me.

"Deni!" I cried from the other side of the closed gate. The gatekeeper was nowhere in sight. "What happened? What did he say?"

He turned to the sound of my voice. Looked at me but didn't answer. I leaned over the gate.

"Deni!" I yelled. "Please come back in. Or can we go somewhere? Tell me what happened."

He stared at me blankly, like he didn't recognize me. Or if he had, he didn't want to. He revved the engine again and then screeched off into the crowded city streets without me.

RUMORS

With nothing better to do, I accepted Dad's invitation to walk with him into town. Dad suggested a little shopping. Get some souvenirs for everyone back home. Guilt crept up my neck. I was a terrible friend, forgetting about them with everything else on my mind here. So I bought a coin purse for Bev embellished with a blue elephant dotted with orange and purple beads. I tucked three Indonesian coins inside. For Oma I looked through dozens of batiks, which Dad said are the traditional art of Indonesia, until I found the perfect one: a flowing wall hanging hand-painted in five shades of brown, with a bird free-floating in a flower garden of kaleidoscope shapes. Spider was the trickiest. But when I stumbled upon a small wooden sitar, I knew that was just the thing. I wrote all three postcards, thinking about the one Mom sent to me. Then I tucked them in with their presents and with Dad's help mailed them from the post office.

Dad took me to lunch at a restaurant that reminded me of the one I went to with Deni. At first the distraction was nice, but I couldn't keep my mind off of him, wondering where he was, who he was with. If he was going to be okay.

• • •

The rest of the day *pesantren* talk-talk filled the thick air:

"A person looking for a Deni but not at a *pesantren*."

"Someone saw Deni's father in Jakarta."

"Not Deni's *bapak*; it's his mother who lives."

"No one is looking for an older boy named Deni. It's a small boy they are looking for."

"Deni gets wild crazy like this sometimes. It's like when the wave came."

"He runs away when he is angry. He is very angry now."

"Bapak won't let him go. He won't help him find his father."

"I don't know if he will come back."

I flopped onto a patch of muddy grass, overwhelmed with talk-talk and guilt that this was somehow my fault, that I wished his hope away.

I needed to fix it.

I waited for him on our wall, but he didn't come back.

When the sun went down, Dad insisted I join Team Hope and the kids for dinner. They talked about this and that, but I could only stare at the empty place at the foot of the table where the other soccer boys were eating without him. I asked Dad if he knew what happened with the owner, if he'd heard anything.

"Someone from an NGO, a nongovernmental organization, in Banda Aceh called and left a message on the *pesantren*'s answering machine last night asking if a boy named Deni lived here. The problem is the person asking for Deni did not leave any forwarding information. No phone number or name. It wasn't a lot to go on, and I doubt the *pesantren* owner would have even mentioned it, but one of the older boys was working in the office and heard it and let Deni know anyway."

The call came while we were out. While he was with me in the alley in the rain.

"So that is something. It could be our Deni, right?" I asked.

"Doubtful," Vera chimed in between bites of sticky rice. "Indonesians don't use their last names, and there are many Denis. Before the owner is going to invest valuable resources in looking into it, he would need confirmation. The name of Deni's father at least . . . Deni, son of . . ."

"So are they going to start looking for the person who left the message?" I asked.

Vera looked at Dad, who looked back at me. "No one has that kind of manpower, honey. They are still head high in disaster relief up in Aceh. And everyone is tremendously busy here at the *pesantren*. The few adults they have working are up to their eyeballs in stuff to do already."

"Right, they aren't about to call every single NGO inquiring . . . ," Vera added, catching Dad's agreeing eye.

I bit my lip. "So no one will do anything to help Deni, then?"

Tom shrugged. "The person may call again, but Deni was insisting that Bapak pay for a bus ticket to travel up to Aceh so he could look for himself. There's just no way. Deni is a ward of the orphanage now—the owner adopted the surviving Aceh kids. If he pays for Deni to go searching based on a *rumor*, all the kids will want to go back home."

I sighed. "So he has to stay here? Even though his father may be alive? That's so unfair! He may not be an orphan at all. Dad, we can give him money, right? For a bus ticket?"

Dad scratched his chin. "It's not that simple, kiddo . . ."

I pushed my bowl of untouched rice away from me. "Why not? How much could it cost? You could go with him, Dad. You said you wanted to go to Aceh . . . or we could all go. Talk about something productive—helping Deni find his dad."

My mind raced with ideas.

Until I registered their faces.

"What? What's the matter with my idea?"

"We're leaving in a few days, Sienna. We still have a lot

to do here; we're just placing the older kids with the younger ones and so far the trial is successful. And we are making great progress in the afternoon therapy sessions—we can't just leave these kids without following through on what we started."

Vera added, "Your intentions are noble, but we can't just go jetting off to Aceh," to which Dad nodded, of course, in utter agreement with Señorita Skunk. "Not to mention the fact that it's completely out of our jurisdiction to go against Bapak's wishes."

I rolled my eyes.

"Hey, the *pesantren* may be poor," Dad said, "but the kids are enrolled in school here at least. It's best for Deni to stay and focus on his future. And sweetie," he said, lowering his voice, "I don't think it's a good idea for you to get so attached."

Vera nodded. Tom caught my eye and nodded too.

". . . or to encourage false hope," Vera said, pounding the last nail in her lameness coffin.

When I stood up, the table rattled. "I'm NOT giving him false hope." My heart burned with frustration. "I thought we were here to help. This is someone who needs us—*really* needs us—and you won't help him? Great. That's just great. Why the hell did we even come?"

Tears scorched behind my eyes as I ran out of the room.

"I warned you something was going on between the two of them," I heard Tom's deep voice say behind me.

"I was hoping you were wrong," answered my dad.

I spun around on my heels, forgetting where I was, forgetting it wasn't okay to make a scene. "Well, he wasn't!" I yelled at their startled faces.

FOUND

I fell into a turbulent sleep, filled with falling stars, exploding planets and drowning fishermen. I woke up in a cold sweat and squinted into the darkness, wondering if I'd screamed out in my sleep. The other girls were still, their long hair spilled over thin pillow tops. If I had yelled, it must not have been that loud.

But I couldn't go back to sleep. I needed to look for him.

The night was so warm I didn't need a sweater. I just slipped on my flip-flops and headed toward the wall.

Something slunk across the path, its yellow eyes shining like headlights in the dark, and I jumped. I cursed at the feral cat rubbing against my cotton pants. "Fabulous. Now a black cat's crossed my path," I muttered.

I checked the wall. No.

Maybe he made it back to his dorm, then? Maybe I'd see him in the morning.

I was starting to head back when a stroke, gentle as a feather, breezed across my shoulder blades. I whirled around.

"Deni—jeez. You scared me to death. Where have you been?"

He didn't say anything but instead ran his fingers down my arm, reached for my hand and whispered, "Must be quiet."

He pulled me toward the wall, but instead of sitting on it, he hopped over and headed down the grassy slope toward the river where the street kids hang. I followed him. His face wasn't angry anymore; it was determined. He squeezed my fingers tight.

Needing to fill up the silence, I babbled. "It's going to be okay, Deni. I mean . . . maybe the person will call back and leave their name . . . and the *pesantren* owner will change his mind and let you go? If he doesn't, we'll figure out something else. . . ."

He didn't say anything, just kept pulling me toward the river.

When we got to the place where the street kids fish for cans, he let go of my hand and gestured for me to sit.

"What's going on, Deni?" I whispered. "Where were you all day?"

He licked his bottom lip and my stomach leapt. I wondered if he'd kiss me again . . . or try to. Maybe under the circumstances that was a stupid thing to be thinking about, but still, I did.

"I was with friends," he said. "Looking for money."

"For what?"

"I'm going to Aceh."

"What? Dad said Bapak won't allow it. . . ."

He shrugged. "I care not what Bapak says. If he will not pay for me, I will find a way."

"Well, what if you go and can't find your father?" I

asked gently. "Will Bapak let you come back and finish school?"

A frown shadowed his face. "He says if I go, I leave for good. I give up my place here."

"That's not fair."

He clenched his fist. "The owner is not a fair man. This you know."

I nodded. "When will you leave?"

I leaned into him, feeling the heat of him.

"Tomorrow," he said quietly. "I go tomorrow." The soft of his mouth kissed my hairline. "I am sorry to leave you when only we have just begun to meet." His voice cracked with emotion.

My throat ached. I wasn't ready for him to leave either. I turned until my lips found his.

When we finally broke away, I traced the hard line of his jaw with my finger. "If you go," I said, "I'm coming with you."

"You cannot come. Aceh is too dangerous," Deni argued in the moonlight. "And the bus ride will be so long. You, *rambut kuning,* do not do so well in the heat."

"You've noticed that, huh? So we'll fly."

"Fly?"

"Yes, fly, on a plane. You need money, right? I have money. I have a credit card. It would take hours versus days on a bus. Please let me come with you—I'll help you look for your father and I'll fly back before it's time to go home. No problem."

I surprised myself with my confidence, but I meant it. I wasn't leaving until I helped him. I snuggled in closer.

And we were busted.

A flashlight blinded me first. I buried my face in Deni's neck to escape the glare.

"Sienna?"

Oh no.

"Deni? What are you two doing out here in the middle of the night?"

Deni didn't move away from me. He kept his arm tight around my shoulders. "Good night, Doctor," he said.

Dad ignored him and shined his flashlight straight out toward the river as if searching for an answer. It was the first time I noticed the group of street kids sleeping on ratty blankets.

"Don't shine the light on them," I told Dad, feeling protective. I leaned forward and pushed his flashlight down, creating a milky circle on the grass.

Dad frowned. "Do you have any idea how much trouble we could all get into if the owner caught you together? Not only would Deni be thrown out of school, but also our reputation as a group would be tarnished. What are you thinking, Sienna?"

"We aren't doing anything."

"This isn't summer camp at home. Deni isn't Spider— this is not allowed."

Deni isn't Spider. Why'd he have to say that?

"Doctor Andy," Deni said, "Sienna and I are friends."

Dad eyed Deni's arm still wrapped around me. "From the look of it, you are more than friends."

Deni didn't budge. "So? I am a man, Sienna is a woman."

"She is a fifteen-year-old girl. A teenager! Look, Deni, I like you, but you know the rules. No boys and girls alone without supervision. Ever. And Sienna, you know the rules as well. I'm really disappointed in you."

With "awkward" swarming around me, Deni stood up and walked toward the end of the wall to give us some privacy. In the shadows, I saw him reach into his pocket and pull out a pack of cigarettes. While Dad lectured me about personal responsibility, I watched Deni's smoke circle up in the moonlight and wished I could also just disappear into the sky.

Deni finished his cigarette and then came back toward us pointedly. "I'll walk you back to your room, Sienna. Your father is right. It is late."

"I will walk her," Dad said, stepping between Deni and me.

They stared at each other. I was guessing both of them were gauging how far they were going to press this. "Please," Deni said, after a tension-filled beat. "I am sorry to have caused you so much upset." He stretched out his hand to Dad, who took it halfheartedly. "I will go, then. Sienna, good night."

I watched his silhouette limp toward the dorms.

"Sit down," Dad said when Deni was out of earshot. The anger had left his voice and was replaced by concern. "Look, I know when you are away from home, things are different. It's easy to lose yourself in the experience, and that's part of the experience. But remember, kiddo, *this is real*. The relationships you make here are real. They'll affect your life now and once you're back home. And remember, we're on a plane home in less than a week."

"But Dad, I know it's all real. I'm not a little kid. I know what I'm doing."

And then I was suddenly livid. Who was Dad lecturing *me* about responsible relationship choices?

"And what about you, huh? You and Vera? Don't think I haven't noticed all your . . . *flirting*. You guys work together! How unprofessional is that?"

Mouth agape, Dad's face collapsed in the moonlight. Looks like someone else was caught too.

"Vera has nothing to do with this," he said after a long, heavy moment.

"I'm just saying," I snapped, "don't be a hypocrite."

"Honey, your feelings might be real, but realistically, what is the use of you getting so attached to someone you'll never see again?"

"What's the point of wearing your wedding ring if you aren't going to be loyal to your *wife*?"

I couldn't believe the words came out of my mouth, but there they were, like thorns piercing skin.

Dad's eyes flashed with new anger. "If you want to discuss your mother or Vera, we can do that at another time. Tonight we are discussing you and one of the orphans we came here to help."

A frustrated tear ran down my cheek. "I am helping them."

"I don't want to argue with you, Sienna," he said, his voice relaxing, "but I mean it about Deni. If you're not going to do it for yourself or for me, do it for *him*. Break things off before he gets too attached. Honey, listen, I understand you feel close to him, and judging from the way he looked at you, I'm pretty sure he thinks you're special too. But I've heard his stories, and I'm willing to bet you don't know everything about that boy. Believe me, kiddo, he's already lost way too much."

Deni and I are together in our alley kissing against the wall when we're ambushed. Dozens of police flashlights blind us. We're trapped, and now rocks are being thrown at us, leaving bruises the size of grapefruits. I grab Deni's hand and we tumble over a barbed-wire fence. We make it to the other side, cut and bleeding, but I don't feel pain. We run through city streets toward the sea- shore. They're at our heels. We know if they catch us, they'll kill us, or worse. Finally the ocean lies before us.

There are no stars in the sky.

There is no moon.

They draw closer and closer until we have no choice.

Clutching hands, we dive into the black sea, together.

Deni and I avoided each other like the plague all day. Dad watched over me so closely that I didn't even dare try to catch Deni's eye. I taught art, participated in teen group and ate my meals, where I made polite conversation with Team Hope.

Dad couldn't suspect anything more than he al- ready did.

Finally, Deni gestured to me outside the dining hall after dinner with a snap of his head toward the river. I nodded, knowing we'd meet there after dark.

Saying good night to Team Hope at dusk, I headed back to my room. When Dad hugged me and whispered in my ear that he was proud of me and my good decision, I winced with guilt but still didn't change my mind.

One of the street kids stood up in the moonlight and walked on top of the concrete wall next to the river, holding thin arms out to the side like he was crossing a balance beam.

"He will fall," Deni predicted.

I watched the boy. He was about thirteen years old, his face anxious determination. "Maybe not."

Deni pointed knowingly. "Watch."

Sure enough, the boy lost his balance halfway across and slipped. Grabbing hold of the concrete wall just before he fell feetfirst into the mucky river, he awkwardly scraped himself back over the wall.

"How did you know he wouldn't make it?" I asked.

"Some people don't learn from their mistakes. That boy is not smart. He tried the same thing last night. The wall is still too slippery, and he is too unbalanced. He tries every night. Every night he fails. He should give up trying."

He was telling me something. Something I should get. "Deni . . ."

He held his hand up, stopping my words. "You come here like an American angel hoping to rescue me. You know . . . I cannot be rescued."

And then I knew he was talking about me going with him to Aceh.

The scrawny street kid, defeated, picked up a handful of pebbles and chucked them into the water, dragging on his cigarette silently.

"He will get up and try again," Deni said.

I should try again.

"Deni," I said, a push in my voice. "Please listen to me. I want to take you and see where you lived, where all this happened. I'm not trying to rescue you. I'm trying to help you."

"You heard your father. I don't want any trouble for you."

"It's *my* decision. You have to take risks for people you . . . well, you care about."

Deni reached over and took my hand. The boys across the street huddled together. The boy who fell looked happier now that he'd joined his friends.

When I finally got up the nerve to look at Deni, his eyes told me more than his words. "I don't want you to get hurt," he said.

But the way he was looking at me also told me he understood that it was too late to say no. I wrapped my arms around him and buried my face in his neck.

"We go tomorrow, then?" I asked.

His lips breathed into my ear. "We go tomorrow."

We're naked except for my hair, which is wrapped in a lime green jilbab.

We're lying together in what I know is our home: a grass hut on the edge of an aquamarine sea.

Our bed is soft feathers and banana leaves.

He takes off my jilbab *and my hair falls out across his chest.*

He strokes my cheek and forehead and hair.

Everything smells like warm lavender: the tropical air, Deni's skin, even the banana leaves we lie on.

Suddenly we hear a lion roar and water pours through every crack in the hut and rises fast.

We are thrown together, tossing and spinning, trapped in a saltwater whirlpool. We search for breath. Finally, when I feel my body growing limp, a giant hand reaches down into the eye of the watery tornado.

She pulls us out.

She rescues us.

The plan was to pack and sneak out of the *pesantren* with Deni before anyone figured anything out.

So I announced over fried-rice lunch, "I'm off to town to take some pictures, so don't expect me at dinner, okay."

"Fine," Dad said in a voice gruffer than usual, "but don't forget you have Vera's group this afternoon."

"Well, it might take a while," I said. "Mind if I skip?"

Vera looked disappointed. "I was hoping you would share your story," she said. "And you've already skipped a session."

My stomach lurched. I had forgotten I'd said next time I might share. "Sorry."

"We can talk about it more tonight, about you sharing tomorrow," Vera said. "You're moving into my dorm; Nada is moving into your bed. She feels perfectly comfortable and wants to try it alone. The transition, like we talked about."

Into Vera's dorm?

Nada's taking my spot?

I guess I knew this was coming, but I felt bad. I'd no longer be there to see Elli and the girls wake up in the morning. I'd no longer tuck them into bed at night. Then I realized how ridiculous I was being. I was leaving anyway. I was already going to miss them.

I got ready to sputter out an argument. But then I stopped.

Maybe this *was* a good thing—now Elli and the girls wouldn't miss me tonight. But it could also be bad—if I was supposed to room with Vera, they would know I was gone earlier.

Under the table, I wiped my sweaty palms on my pants.

Dad avoided my eyes.

He was *really* pushing it with this Vera thing.

"Just move your stuff over whenever," Vera said cheerfully. "It will be fun. Like a slumber party!"

She did not just say that.

"I'll move it over right now," I said. "My stuff."

Everything except my backpack. That stayed with me.

It's not like I could haul a whole suitcase to Aceh anyway.

Dad looked relieved that I didn't make a scene, while Vera smiled like a cat who'd just gifted her owner with a fat mouse.

I saw them both through my camera lens: Vera with her skunk pulled back in a tight bun, Dad with his morning eyes and icky hair.

Click.

ADVENTURE

Just like he promised, that evening Deni was waiting for me on the other side of the gate, leaning against the *motor*, a woven bag slung loose over his shoulder. "You have not changed your mind?" he asked.

"Not a chance," I said. Without another thought, I hopped on the back of the *motor*, put my arms around his waist and leaned into his back just like before.

When he started the ignition, the engine rattled loudly in the hot air.

"Should we walk the *motor* until we are off the grounds?" I asked.

"They will not hear."

"I told Vera I had to wash my hair in the *mandi* and not to wait up for me," I said, which made him laugh. "She offered to come and help me. Thank God I talked her out of it."

But he wasn't listening anymore. He was looking up. "Rain is coming. We go." He looked at me hard. "Do not let go of me."

"I won't."

We took off down the dirt driveway and twisted onto the streets of Yogyakarta.

We'd only been riding a few minutes when it started to

rain—really rain—like a total downpour. The streets were slick with oily water and I was holding on to Deni for dear life.

"Is this too dangerous to drive in?" I yelled.

"It is only rain," he called back.

Twenty minutes later Deni pulled the *motor* into the chaotic loading zone at the airport. Buses and taxis zoomed around us, splashing water as they sped by. I was soaking wet but relieved we made it in one piece. Besides, I had other things on my mind, like: *Will my dad show up and drag us back to the orphanage?*

Deni left the *motor* at the curb and we walked under a shelter. "My friend will get the *motor*," he told me.

"Will it still be here when he arrives?" I asked, unconvinced.

He shrugged. "I hope so. Ready?" he asked.

I sucked in a deep breath. "I guess so."

We approached the ticket counter and I read the phrase directly from the transportation section in my book: *"Saya mau dua tiket ke Aceh dan satu tiket Aceh ke Yogya."*

I want two tickets to Aceh. And a one-way ticket from Aceh back to Yogya. For me. For when I flew back without Deni.

The man behind the counter started typing. Deni translated to me that the first leg of the flight for Aceh left in about an hour. We were lucky.

I showed the man behind the counter my passport and handed over my credit card. The man looked at us funny, maybe because of our ages? But the credit card was in my name and matched the name on my passport.

That's all I needed.

I paid for both tickets, and soon Deni won the agent over with his good humor. As he handed us our boarding passes, I figured we'd spend tonight traveling, one night in Aceh, and then I'd return to Yogya in time to fly home to America. Simple.

"What are those?" Deni asked as we passed luggage carousels.

"For luggage, suitcases and bags. If you pack a lot of luggage, they store them in the bottom of the plane."

"What would someone need that much luggage for?"

I smiled. "Well, a lot of people pack a lot of stuff for trips. Our bags are small; we'll just carry them onto the plane."

Deni followed my lead through checkpoints, past security guards/soldiers dressed in camouflage, holding machine guns, and to the gate, where we waited to board the plane.

I couldn't believe it was only a week ago that Dad was holding my hand through the airport, which seemed so ridiculous now. Why had I needed to hold Dad's hand?

I scanned the airport, expecting to see Dad or Tom or Vera scouring the terminal for us, but they weren't there.

"Are you okay?" Deni asked, leading me toward some chairs to sit once we'd found our gate.

"I'm fine . . . just a little nervous."

"Me too," he said, tugging on the strap of his bag.

"Really? Well, don't worry. It'll be fine."

We sat quietly for a second. It wasn't too late. I could say I made a mistake. Nothing had happened yet. The *motor* was still outside. I hadn't actually left for Aceh, so they wouldn't be too mad, right?

But then what about Deni?

I tapped my foot on the tile floor.

He already had his plane ticket. He could fly up to Aceh alone.

But then we'd have to say good-bye here at the airport. Right then.

No. Couldn't do that.

But what if something went wrong up there and nobody knew how to get in touch with Dad? What if I got lost and he couldn't find me?

Breathe. Breathe.

Deni looked over at me. "You feeling better now?"

"You know when you decide to cross the street how you can't chicken out halfway and run back to the curb?" I asked. "How you have to keep moving forward so traffic will know what you're doing? So you don't get squashed like a bug? I guess that's what I'm worried about. Chickening out halfway there and not ending up on the other side of the road in one piece."

He studied my face. "You, Sienna, will always land in one piece," he said thoughtfully.

"I hope so, Deni," I said, resting my head on his shoulder.

The plane was rickety and old. I tried to forget Tom's casual comments about Indonesian in-country flights not meeting FAA standards and enjoyed Deni's expression as the bucket of bolts vibrated into the night sky. Watching him reminded me of Spider when he caught his very first wave. Exhilarated.

Once we were safely in the air, Deni said, "At home, planes are only for the very rich. We would ride buses to travel to the next village."

"At home, I didn't fly much either."

To think this was my greatest fear less than two weeks ago.

This time, I tried to ignore the danger and rolled with the sensation, like on a wave, like on the *motor*.

"Before the tsunami I never left Aceh," he said, staring out the window. "I wonder what it is like now. How much has changed in the time I have been away."

"Well, they've been doing a lot of work. I bet it's better now."

He looked doubtful. "How can you fix something that has been destroyed?"

I wanted to hold his hand but didn't want to risk being inappropriate and have someone question our traveling together.

A flight attendant came by and handed us each a small plastic cup of water and two sweet rolls. I wasn't sure if the water was purified, so, disappointed, I pushed it aside.

"And everything is free?" Deni asked me, grateful for the extra roll, which he tucked into his bag.

"Well, you have to pay for the plane ticket first," I said.

"Thank you, Sienna," he said.

"You're welcome," I said, leaning into him.

Switching off the light above our heads, I grabbed a blanket and laid it across our laps. Everyone else on the plane was nodding off, so I reached under the blanket and let my fingers find his.

When we switched planes in Medan, I wasn't the only white person on board.

The small plane to Aceh was full of health care workers, engineers and contractors, basically volunteers from all over the world. A mix of languages filled the cabin: French, Japanese and English.

While I was shoving my bag under the seat in front of me, Deni started chatting with some Australians across the aisle. "We're with the World Doctors organization and volunteered after the tsunami, and we've returned twice since," a woman with a pixie cut said. The man sitting next to her was a handsome rugged type with an easy laugh and a scar on his cheek. He reminded me of Indiana Jones, the way my dad looked before Mom disappeared.

"Sienna's father is also a doctor," Deni said, gesturing to me.

"Really? Where is he sitting?" I noticed her brown wraparound skirt and her tailored white button-up shirt. She seemed very with it and organized.

I felt my face flush. "Actually, he's not . . ."

Deni jumped in. "He still has much work. He is meeting

her later." He raised his eyebrows at me. It wasn't *entirely* untrue.

The woman reached out her hand. "I'm Amelia. This is my husband, Mac. Nice to meet you, Sienna." I noticed the tiny jade stones in her earlobes shine.

"Eh, Deni, are you coming back to Aceh to stay, mate?" Mac asked, leaning forward.

"I hope to," he said.

Amelia looked at me kindly but with questions in her eyes. "And you two are traveling alone?"

"We are not alone," Deni said confidently. "We are with each other."

Amelia's brown eyes widened, but before she could ask more questions, the flight attendant's heavy cart rolled down the aisle between us. I asked for a Sprite; Deni got a Coke.

"Thank you," we said. I gulped down the Sprite. Free cold drinks. No more uncomfortable answers to tricky questions.

As the World Doctors continued chatting with Deni, I leaned back and tried to sleep.

Deni drummed his drink tray with his thumbs as he talked. "At my friends' house we have certain customs. You know of them from your book?"

"Customs like what?" I asked with a yawn.

"Okay." Deni stopped drumming. "You have not been

to a dinner at a family home yet. Remember I told you about the tea?"

I nodded.

"We are staying with my friends' family. There will be many formalities—they will offer to sit on the floor, and we will be served tea after much talk about life. They will ask you many questions. They speak some English. A couple things I tell you so you don't offend. When they offer you tea, wait until they offer it to you twice before you take a drink. Or they will think you are dying of the thirst and keep pouring you more and more drinks. Also with the food . . ."

"Wait until it's been offered twice?"

"Clever girl." Deni winked. "Yes. Otherwise . . ."

I held my finger in the air. "They will think I am starving and will overfeed me?"

"You are too smart. This you already know."

I nudged him with my elbow, wishing we were all by ourselves on this plane. "I'm just a quick learner."

"And I am a great teacher," he joked. "When you sit on the mat, sit cross-legged with your feet pointed into you. Never point your toes at another person. It will greatly offend."

"At home pointing fingers is considered rude, but pointing toes? I didn't even know pointing your toes at someone was something that could ever happen. Why?"

Deni shrugged. "I don't remember. Just do not do it.

Food is the same as at the *pesantren* except of course better. You eat the same. Ah, and the hot tea is very, very hot and very, very spicy."

"How spicy? How hot?"

He ran his fingers through his thick hair and raised his eyebrows. "Very, very."

"We're almost to Aceh," Mac said across the aisle.

Deni leaned over me and peered out the window. He looked nervous and sad and excited all at once. I couldn't even imagine how he felt, the strange anticipation over seeing his home after being away for six months. I was nervous too, and also excited, and also sad. Maybe looking down at his home, he felt the way I did when I first looked at the ocean after hearing about Mom.

How could something I loved betray me like this?

But Deni didn't want to look away. He leaned farther, trying to soak it all in.

We switched places so he could see better, and Deni pointed out a flat landmass. The morning sun highlighted a spot where the ocean met the shore.

"It looks so different from up here," he said. "That was all a rain forest. That is where the tsunami ripped out all the trees and life. See? The white part between the ocean and land that is not jungle? Everything was torn out. Everything there is gone."

From the air, the strip of land Deni was talking about

looked like God painted a thick white stripe across the earth.

"I can't believe the sea went three miles onto the shore," I said quietly.

He tugged on his goatee, which was beginning to grow again. "The water rose across the whole of Aceh, it seemed."

The air smelled thick as we walked down the metal stairway attached to the plane. Thick and sweet like perfumed mud. The airport was not much more than an airstrip in the middle of a field of rice paddies.

"Is that the airport?" I asked curiously, holding on to the rail. A small, open-air terminal was all there was.

"Yes," Deni said, behind me. "It is like a tiny version of Yogyakarta airport, no?"

At the bottom of the stairs drivers held up signs: Red Cross. Doctors Without Borders. World Health Organization. World Vision. World Doctors.

"That's you guys, right?" I asked Amelia.

"Yep!" she said, waving enthusiastically to a young blond man holding their sign. "That's Ethan. He's an American fresh out of residency, volunteering in our health clinic for the summer."

"Cool," I said, smiling at the eager blue-eyed doctor waving the sign. Ethan reminded me of pictures of Dad taken while he was in the Peace Corps in Africa, before he met Mom, before they had me. Why did everyone keep reminding me of Dad? I swallowed away a twinge of guilt, knowing it was morning back at the *pesantren* too. He probably already knew I was gone, and if he didn't yet, he would soon.

"You kids need a lift somewhere?" Mac said.

"Um. Maybe. Deni? Do we need a ride?"

Deni shook his head. "Thank you, but I will call my friends. They will come. Sienna? We go?"

Amelia stopped me. "Sienna, would you mind if I talked to you for a second?"

I glanced at Deni.

"I will meet you in the front, then. I will call my friends inside," Deni said. "Nice to meet you." He waved to Amelia and Mac.

"It was great meeting you too, Deni. Best of luck here." Amelia lifted her tan leather purse higher on her shoulder. "Your friend seems very sweet," she said once Deni was out of earshot.

"He is," I said, watching him go.

"You met him at the orphanage?"

I nodded. "Yes."

"He must have been through a lot. . . . It seems like you two are very close."

I fidgeted with my backpack. "Well, you know how it is when you meet someone and it's like you already know them? That's how it was with me and Deni." I shrugged as if that explained the rest.

"But you are going home soon? Back to America?" she prodded.

I wondered why she was being so nosy.

"Yes. But . . ." I wasn't thinking about that just yet.

To stop her from asking me anything else, I blurted out, "We're going to be . . . looking around the different NGOs. . . . Maybe we'll run into you later?"

"That would be lovely. Where are you staying?"

"With Deni's friends."

"You know there's not much here for . . . tourists. Since the tsunami, things are better—they recently signed a peace treaty for the civil war, but there is still a lot of political unrest."

I didn't say anything.

Her eyes narrowed. "I know you are with your friend, but before your father joins you, if you run into trouble, come see us. We're at the World Doctors headquarters in the tent in the old town center. Here's my card."

If we run into trouble . . .

Amelia's perceptive. She figured out right away that we didn't know quite what we were doing. As we walked through the airport toward the street, I filled her in on what we'd been doing at the *pesantren.* Her eyes lit up when I mentioned my dad's name.

"Your father is the trauma psychiatrist Andrew Jones? I so hope I get a chance to meet him! You probably already know this, but your dad's globally renowned for his cross-cultural PTSD work. I can't wait to read about the work he did at the orphanage."

Wow, these doctors from Australia knew about Dad and Team Hope? I knew he did important work, but I had no idea he was actually *famous* in his field.

"Thanks," I said proudly. "He's a good guy."

Her eyes crinkled, not unkindly, but loaded with suspicion. "I'm just surprised he let you come up here alone. Especially someone who is so aware of the environmental dangers of a disaster site like this." Amelia tilted her head, waiting for my response.

"I'll see my dad soon," I said with more confidence than I felt. "And like Deni said, I'm not alone, we're together."

After promising again that I'd get in touch if I needed her and waving good-bye to Amelia and Mac, I spotted Deni standing at the curb, sort of bouncing on the balls of his feet like an excited kid. I jumped back as an old banged-up white Land Rover raced around the corner and screeched to a halt, shooting dirt clods into the humid air.

A boy about Deni's age with a bright smile and longish hair jumped out of the driver's seat and practically tackled Deni, talking a mile a minute in what I assumed was Acehnese. Then a girl, dressed in white pants and a pink silky *jilbab*, got out more slowly but took Deni's other hand in her own just as eagerly. His friends made me think of Spider and Bev—the three of us together. And Deni looked so happy.

"Sienna!" He waved me over. "Come! I want you to meet my friends. This is the American girl. This is Sienna."

The boy, wearing a San Diego Chargers jersey, shook my hand enthusiastically, and I couldn't help but crack up when he flashed me the hang-loose sign.

"Nice to meet you," I said, returning his surf gesture.

He laughed loudly and clapped. "You know them?" He puffed his navy blue shirt out. "Chargers?"

"I do." I nodded. "They're an American football team from California. Like me."

He smiled wider and slapped Deni's back like, *Way to go, buddy*.

"Sienna, this is Azmi. He's my friend from since we were little boys. This is Siti."

"Hello," said Siti, who was shorter than the boy but looked more mature. "Nice to meet you." Siti lowered her long eyelashes. Her brown skin was flawless against her pastel scarf.

I checked to see if Deni noticed how beautiful she was, but he was still smiling at me.

After we piled into the car, Azmi insisted on showing me around Aceh before we went to his parents' house. And it was a darn good thing that beast had four-wheel drive, because the road from the airport into Aceh was not in the best shape. The road was paved but also covered in mud. I wasn't sure if it was because of the tsunami or recent rainstorms and I didn't want to sound stupid by asking, so I didn't.

The countryside was gorgeous, though. Emerald green and lush and, like the drive to the temple, farmers wearing cone-shaped hats bent over fields of rice paddies. Everything seemed light, breezy and fine. So fine that I wondered how far away we were from the tsunami damage we saw from the plane. I was sure I'd find out soon enough.

Deni and his pals chatted away while Azmi drove and Siti rode shotgun. Deni and I were sitting together in back, but he leaned forward as far as he could to be near his friends.

We bumped along for a while, bouncing to some kind of Indonesian dance mix on the radio.

Then we arrived at the beginning.

"Oh my God, *what happened here?*"

On both sides of the muddy road the gutters were lined with parked vehicles.

Not cars, but completely mangled, crash-test-derby, utterly destroyed things that might at one time have been cars. They were rusted and twisted, and I couldn't tell headlight from taillight. They lined up one after the other and seemed to snake on forever.

"They ran out of space for the broken autos," Deni explained. "The line goes all the way to the ocean."

"Wow. How far are we from the ocean?"

"Still far."

As he drove, Azmi shot me the hang-loose sign in the rearview mirror, which seemed so weird now that we were in the midst of all this devastation. But they lived here. They saw this every day. It was me who wasn't used to it.

Deni leaned back in his seat and told me the story. "They had no tractors, so they brought trained elephants down from the mountain. What a sight it was watching the men ride the beasts and watching the animals' strong backs pulling the cars out of the water one by one."

"How did they do that? Were they attached to a harness or something?"

"Yes, they pulled the cars with ropes and nets, pulled them from the sea that was now our town. It was a big job. A job I wish I would have had." Deni stopped talking and looked out the window.

A few minutes later I pointed out a mound of mud and dirt on the right-hand side of the road. A sign with the numbers **26/12/04** was written in black marker. It was nailed to a piece of wood.

"That's the date of the tsunami," I said. "What is that pile of dirt?"

Deni's face hardened. "It is where the dead lie," he said, his voice heavy.

Oh my God, it was a mass grave.

"Are there more?" I asked.

Deni nodded solemnly. "Yes. That is why they call this the City of Ghosts."

Azmi turned the music up even louder as if to drown out our conversation. Deni and his friends were quiet, moving their heads to the beat.

The hot air hitting my face had an electric buzz to it. Everything was so intense. I felt like I was riding through some other dimension. The music helped.

We bounced along on the semi-paved road until it became so rocky and bumpy that it was nearly unmanageable. Azmi, however, was loving the stick shift and laughed as he cranked the engine up and down the steep ravines.

"The wave did all this damage?" I asked over the music.

"The water was more powerful than you can imagine," Deni answered.

Deni clarified what I was looking at as we drove along, but instead of its usual softness there was an edge in his voice, and I didn't blame him for being angry. I remembered how I acted after my mom disappeared.

"This empty land used to be villages and huts and markets," Deni said. "Before, you did not have a view of the ocean from here. Many buildings were in the way. The ocean took everything out to sea like a giant suction."

"Look at that boat!" I said, pointing to a smaller version of Noah's Ark flipped completely upside down in a watery sandbank.

"There were so many boats stuck in the sand after the

water went back to the sea," Deni explained. "That one was too big; even the elephants couldn't move it."

Azmi said something in his language.

"Azmi and Siti's father was a fisherman too. He still is. He was one of the lucky ones." His fist clenched tightly as he met my eye. "Lucky like my father."

We stopped when we could see the shoreline clearly.

I looked out at the glassy sea. I couldn't imagine those calm waves rising up the way they did. My heart pounded and I was so relieved when Azmi turned the Rover around at the harbor. We passed more and more debris: logs, twisted pieces of metal, chopped-in-half fishing boats smashed into the sand, more metal, more wood, more junk. "This is clean compared to before," Deni said quietly, his eyes flashing. "There were bodies everywhere. We had to cover our faces with scarves to hide our noses and mouths from the smells of the decay."

Just like the article I read back home. One of the pictures I saw of the workers could have been Deni. I didn't dare mention it.

He stopped talking for a second, remembering. "Me and Azmi worked here. . . . We carried bodies in from the shore. We did it for days and days, all day long, sometimes long into the night. They were everywhere. Here. There." He pointed out the other window. "Everywhere were rotting bodies. Women were mourning and screaming and . . . most of the bodies could not be . . . *apa*?"

My voice cracked. "Identified?"

"Yes." He nodded, his jaw clenched. "Swollen from the water, they were big and *apa*? Puffed?" He winced like he could still see the brutal images. "And cut up. They took pictures of the bodies and hung them up to be identified before they could be buried in the graves that you see. It was not good."

I couldn't stop picturing the hundreds of bodies piled on top of one another, wrapped only in blankets and covered by a mound of dirt. Deni and Azmi, just boys, dragging the decaying bodies around the shore. How could anyone recover from that?

"I'm so sorry, Deni," I said as he stared straight ahead, a mask of vile memories shrouding his face. And even though I was dying to wrap my arms around him, I didn't dare. I didn't know what he'd told his friends about us, who they thought I was to him, and of course, again, it wouldn't be appropriate.

He faced me. "Why are you sorry? You did nothing wrong."

"I'm sorry you had to go through all of this. I wish I could have been here to help you."

He stared into my eyes hard. "I want you to understand. I left my home because I did not want to see. They said, 'You will have a new life. You can get your education.' I thought here I had nothing. But I was wrong. This is still my home even if something terrible happened here. If you do not want me to talk about these things, I will not, but please do not be sorry for me."

I nodded. I hated it when people felt sorry for me too.

Deni said something to Azmi, who turned the music up even louder. Deni stared out the window, remembering a horror I could barely imagine.

"You see this mosque?" Azmi asked me, stopping the car again a few minutes later. "My family was trapped on the roof watching the water rise around us. On that roof is how my family survived." A white mosque stood alone in a littered field of trash and garbage and metal. It was the only real building for as far as the eye could see. A strip of white canvas tents were lined up across the street.

"Is that a . . . refugee camp?" I asked.

Deni nodded. "Azmi and Siti's family lived there for many months."

Deni stepped out of the SUV, his voice filled with emotion. "This is the mosque I told you about. After the storm, it was the only thing left. Not even a tsunami could tear it down."

I remembered the story. "It was a miracle it survived the water."

His eyes never left the mosque as he spoke to me. I could tell he wanted to be alone but didn't want to be rude and leave me alone.

"You go on ahead, I'll catch up," I said.

Meeting my eyes for a second, he nodded, and I watched him stagger up the concrete steps and disappear into the building, as if this was the end of a long, long journey.

I stood against the car and stretched in the beating sun.

The mosque had an ornate copper roof and open windows that were bulb-shaped like the carvings in the doors at the *pesantren*.

I wiped some sweat off my forehead and fluffed my T-shirt. It was even hotter here than in Yogyakarta, and without the breeze from the car windows I felt almost faint. I walked halfway up the steps, following Azmi and Siti to get a closer look at the exterior while being mindful of giving Deni privacy.

The arches carved out of the walls cast shadows on the now-dry floor and I imagined the flood of water rushing through, desperate families dashing for the rooftop.

And then I saw Deni.

He was kneeling on an orange prayer rug, bending forward rhythmically. I'd never seen him do his prayers before.

"I'm going also to pray," Siti told me. I watched as she took a black skirt out of a barrel and wrapped it around her waist, concealing her white pants. She wrapped a second scarf on her already-covered head.

After she was dressed, she took a brightly colored prayer mat out of a big barrel in front of the mosque and glanced at me shyly. "You come?"

I glanced inside. Deni was still praying. I felt like I was intruding enough just by watching him.

"No, thanks, Siti. But thank you for asking."

She smiled and joined Deni inside. I watched to see if

she laid her carpet next to him, knowing I'd be jealous if she did. But she didn't, and I was glad.

Azmi lingered behind and followed me around the side of the building.

INDONESIA MENANGIS was spray-painted on the white chipped paint. "What does that mean?" I asked, shielding my eyes from the sun's bright glare.

His beaming smile faded. "Cry," he said. "Indonesia cry," he translated before deciding to join the others inside.

While they prayed, I wandered around the marshy land, hyper-careful of where I stepped.

It was so hard to believe this was the place where so many died.

I felt weird walking there, but I was curious and I didn't want to wait in the car. I slopped through the mud over to what must have been the foundation of a house. Concrete blocks laid in a rectangular shape, with rusted metal pipes sticking out. Everything was covered with sand and muck.

I walked around the inside, imagining the people who had lived there.

Were they home the day the sea came?

A rusty pot handle was sticking out of the dirt. Were they cooking when they heard the roar? Did they run out the door and toward the mosque or toward the mountain? Did they have a teenage boy who escaped by *motor*?

• • •

I watched him tuck the prayer rug back into the barrel and walk down the steps toward me. His eyes were red, and I could tell he'd been crying. I touched his arm. I couldn't help it, and for the moment I didn't care who saw. He took a deep, long breath and looked up at the sky.

"Are you okay?" I asked.

"I don't know," he said. "Are you?"

I thought about all the images I'd seen that day: the mass graves, the beat-up cars, the destroyed homes. I thought about Dad back at the *pesantren,* awake now and certainly worried about me. I thought about how everything was a million times worse for Deni.

"Yeah," I said, squeezing his hand. "I'm okay."

At Azmi and Siti's house, we were asked to sit on a large bamboo mat that covered most of the small living and dining space.

"Come, come, come, come. Please, sit, sit, sit, sit," said their *ibu,* who was wearing wide round glasses and a peach silk scarf on her head. She was soft and round in all the places a mother should be. Their *bapak* was short, with Azmi's beaming smile. Dressed in dried-mud-covered pants, he smelled like fresh fish when he took my hand and placed it to his heart.

"Where your father? Your mother?" Ibu asked me immediately, taking her turn with my hand in her rough warm one.

I glanced at Deni, who nodded. "My father is joining me soon," I said.

Frowning, Bapak turned to Deni and asked him directly, "You bring American girl here alone? *Without her father?*"

"He's coming," Deni insisted in the same firm voice, glancing over at me like, *We better stick to this story.* I nodded quickly.

"Okay." Bapak grinned with open arms. "Tonight you stay here. You are our family tonight. Deni, Azmi tells us you are coming home, that you sent letter from Yogyakarta!

We are happy! Please. Sit. Eat." He gestured toward the mat where tea and plates were set up, waiting.

"I'm happy too, Bapak," he said. "I have missed my friends."

Ibu held tight to Deni's arm. "Much has changed in Aceh. Much is better, no?" she asked.

Deni nodded. "Much has changed, but much is still the same."

Ibu poured steaming tea into our cups. At a trillion degrees with a gazillion percent humidity, sweat was dripping down my back. I would have done about *anything* for a bottle of ice orange.

Ibu and Bapak were smiling at me.

"Drink, drink," they said, pointing at the steaming cup in my hand.

Deni eyed me. I felt rude not drinking but remembered his warning: *Wait until the second offer.*

"Drink, please, drink," Ibu repeated with more urgency. That was two.

All eyes were on me as I took a sip of what? Jalapeño sugar water? The scalding liquid burned my throat. I choked down the spicy tea and set the cup back onto the saucer.

"Delicious," I said. Deni was right: it was very, very *hot* tea.

"Hungry?" asked Siti, who had been in the kitchen since we arrived. She set bowls of smooth curries, fried fish and funny-shaped fruits onto the center of the mat. Everything looked delicious. We hadn't eaten since the snack on the plane. I tucked my feet even farther under my butt to make sure I wasn't pointing my toes at anyone. Deni winked at me. So far, so good.

Ibu disappeared into the kitchen and returned with covered aluminum round bowls, like the ones in Thai restaurants, filled with fluffy jasmine rice.

"Thank you so much." I hoped they couldn't hear my stomach growl. "This looks delicious."

"Eat, eat," Ibu said, gesturing toward the food.

Wait.

"Eat, please, eat," she said again.

"Thank you," I said.

Everyone was staring at me. Deni leaned over and whispered, "Guests eat first."

So I dished up some rice with the serving spoon and covered it with seafood curry. Individual bowls of water sat in front of us to rinse our fingers off between helpings.

"Brothers and sisters in America?" Ibu asked me after we'd all dished up.

I shook my head. "No. I wish I did, though."

"Siti's sisters and mother were taken by the wave," Bapak explained. "She is our family now."

"I thought Siti and Azmi were brother and sister?" I asked Deni.

"No," he said. "Cousins."

Azmi explained that their house was built by Habitat for Humanity. A cute wooden structure with a porch, their home was small but clean and seemingly well built. They were one of the lucky families, Azmi explained. Many still lived in the tent camps.

"Did you live in the tent camps after too?" I asked Deni.

Deni shrugged. "Tents were for families."

And Deni was alone. His whole family was gone.

"Our tent was full," Azmi said. "Or he would have been with us."

My heart broke for him. He lost his whole family, and he wasn't even allowed to stay with friends? No wonder he left.

I wondered when he was going to ask Bapak and Ibu about his father.

"Where did you stay?" I asked carefully.

"A different place each night. Mostly I slept on the highest ground I could find, on a dry blanket if I could find one. Tents were a luxury after the storm."

He read my face and stopped talking. I knew no matter what, he didn't want me to feel sorry for him. I looked down at my tea, pretending it was the steam misting up my eyes.

"There was not much time for sleep," Azmi said, "with so much work to be done."

Deni nodded in agreement, but his brow furrowed and I blinked.

I cringed, flashing on the mass graves. Deni and Azmi hauling bodies out of the muck.

And Deni with no place to go home to after.

Perhaps to change the conversation to something lighter, Azmi said, "Many celebrities were here after the tsunami. I forget their names, but they were from a strange religion to do with science?"

"Scientology?" I guessed.

"Yes! They set up booth and tried to convert Muslims to their way of thinking. One of the famous American movie stars was here!"

Deni laughed for the first time all day. "They were surprised when they were asked to leave Aceh."

I rubbed my head, embarrassed. How obnoxious. No wonder Dad insisted: *We are here to help with their PTSD, not to comment about religion, customs or anything else. Would we want Indonesians coming to El Angel Miguel and criticizing how we live? Always be respectful.*

Then Deni said, "So many Westerners offered to adopt tsunami orphans that the Indonesian government declared no non-Muslims could adopt the children."

Bapak added, "It was very important, especially after disaster, to keep our culture for the children."

"That makes sense," I said.

And then Azmi asked randomly, "You know Arnold

Schwarzenegger?" He dipped his fingers in the water bowl and then pantomimed someone shooting a machine gun.

I laughed. "Well, I don't know him personally, but I've seen some of his old movies."

After dinner, we took a walk, Deni, Siti, Azmi and me. I was completely aware of Deni's hand swinging closely to mine as we walked. When we passed a tall, smooth tree with hairy twigs and huge yellow and orange flowers, Deni stopped short. I stayed with him as Azmi and Siti kept walking.

"It is a *jeumpa* tree. *Jeumpa* flowers." He picked a flower and held it close for me to smell. "You remember the song the little girls sing at the *pesantren*?" Deni asked quietly, his eyes lighting up. "It is the song of their homeland. See?" Deni stroked the smooth bark of the tree. "The song is about this flower. It only grows here. In Aceh."

I breathed in the sugary scent, taking a mental picture of this moment, this place. I paused on Deni's face, memorizing the way he was looking at me for when we weren't together anymore.

He moved a lock of my hair and tucked the flower behind my ear.

BARGAINING

I'd seen some movies where they depict refugee camps, but nothing like this.

After the *jeumpa* tree, we reached a field dotted with hundreds of canvas tents. They were set up on a flat piece of land that must have been dozens of acres.

I couldn't believe six months after the tsunami, people were still living in tents.

Deni, Siti and Azmi pointed out a bunch of construction sites beyond the camp, telling me stories as tractors moved mud and trucks rolled down the road carrying long pieces of wood. Hammering and sawing buzzed in the distance.

"It looks so different," Deni said, looking around in amazement. "So changed since I left for Yogyakarta. The reconstruction hadn't begun." As we walked, canvas tents were on either side of us, many small ones and a few larger ones. Children were playing outside and then running back inside the tents.

A goat walked by attached to a rope. A skinny boy led the way.

A chicken squawked, and I noticed coops near several of the larger canvas tents. A closer look told me doves were inside.

"Some birds have beautiful singing voices and enter

competitions," Deni told me. "My *ibu* kept doves when I was a boy. She would buy cassette tapes of famous doves singing and play them for our pets so they could learn to copy the beautiful voices.

"We have a folk story that says, 'A man is only considered a man if he has a house, a wife, a horse, a *keris*—a dagger—and a singing dove in a cage.'" He pointed down the street. "There used to be a bird market a way down the road. I wonder if it is still there."

A thought hit me as I checked out the long row of dirty cages and noisy birds: *Bird flu.* One of Bev's warnings and here I was maybe in the heart of it. I asked Deni about the outbreak. He nodded worriedly. "We will stay away from the bird market if you wish."

"Sounds good," I said.

His arms swung casually by his sides, but his face drew tense. "What's wrong?" I asked.

"I think we should start asking in the tents for my father," he said quietly.

"Should Azmi and Siti help too?" I said, my voice low.

"They will look and ask too, but still they say they have not heard that my father is alive."

"Well. We're not giving up yet," I said. "What should I do?"

"You ask, 'Rahmad—father of Deni.'" His voice cracked when he said it. My hands sweated nervously for him. This was huge.

"Okay," I said. "The NGO tents start over there . . ."

"NGO?"

"Nongovernment agencies—it's what World Doctors is."

The first tent was big and bright yellow. Deni opened the canvas door flap and entered. I followed him in.

A woman, dressed in a powder blue sari and black pants, was sitting behind a small counter. She smiled warmly at us, and Deni asked her something in I assumed Acehnese. People were lined up on the floor, but instead of sitting in chairs, they were resting on bended knees. A woman nursed a young baby, a man held a cloth on his bleeding hand, a couple of kids looked woozy, like they might throw up—their mother was fussing over them. This was obviously a medical tent.

Then a woman came in that I instantly recognized. "Hiya, Sienna, hello, Deni. How are you doing?"

"Amelia," I said, feeling at ease. She asked too many questions, but maybe she could help us.

"What brings you here?" she asked.

I glanced over at Deni, who was still talking to the woman behind the desk. She was digging through papers while Deni looked on anxiously.

"Deni's looking for his father. . . . Well . . . he's asking around to see if anyone has heard from him."

"His father? Does he have reason to believe his father is alive?"

I nodded. "That's the reason we came," I whispered,

smelling her vanilla perfume. "Someone is looking for him here. . . . Don't say anything to him, please. . . . I don't think he wants to talk about it. I mean, unless he asks you about it first."

"I haven't heard anyone asking for a Deni, but I'll keep my ears open, and I won't say a word."

"Thanks."

"While you're here, would you like to have a look around? Your father will be arriving soon, no?"

My face flushed. "Oh yes. Really soon," I lied. "Deni? I'm going with Amelia, you want to come?"

"I will catch up," he said.

I hated leaving him, but I was curious about the NGOs that I'd heard so much about from Dad. So I followed Amelia to the green tent next door, a feeding tent, which was not much more than a line of people waiting for food. A few people worked behind a long table—scooping cups of porridge out of huge tin pots into bowls. One woman handed out one hard-boiled egg to each person in line; another man handed out one biscuit each.

"We try and get fresh fish, fruit and vegetables when we can," Amelia said. "Today was a bad day," she added to explain the simple dinner. I thought about the delicious meal we had back at Azmi's and felt guilty.

Back outside, a Land Rover, just like Azmi's, screamed by, blaring a siren.

"That's the ambulance," Amelia said. "They're bringing

in a new patient. I've got to dash—please stop by later if you get a chance, and good luck finding Deni's dad." She waved over her shoulder as she ducked back into the medical tent.

A few minutes later Deni met up with me, Azmi and Siti outside. "The Land Rovers are ambulances?" I asked.

"Yes," Deni said. "They were donated after."

"Were we driving in an ambulance all day?"

"Ibu works for the clinic sometimes," Azmi said. "I asked if we could use it. It's very exciting Deni returned. People who left Aceh do not return."

A heavy silence fell before I asked Deni, "Did that lady know anything about your father?"

"No." He shook his head, frustrated. "After all that, no."

I looked down at the row of tents. If we went together, it would take too long.

"Let's split up. Me and Siti can take the right side of the street, you and Azmi the left. Okay?"

"*Terima kasih,*" he said, using my version, his eyes shining with hope.

I had my script ready to go.

"Rhamad—father of Deni?" I asked at the next tent. The woman dug through papers, just like in the medical tent, and shook her head no. No luck at the second tent either, or the third, fourth, fifth. After a dozen or so, Siti and I met back up with the boys. The setting sun cast a shadow across Deni's face. I could tell he'd had no luck either.

"We should go toward home soon," he said regretfully.

I wanted so badly to try and make him feel better. "Don't give up yet. There are still two more to try," I said.

The four of us walked together through the crowds of people, past chickens and bicycles, in the dusky heat toward a bright orange tent that read REPRODUCTIVE HEALTH.

The boys went across the way into the Red Cross tent, and Siti decided to wait outside. I ducked under the yellow tent's simple flap. I squeezed my fists tight.

Come on, be the one.

A few girls walked in after me, one carrying a toddler on her hip. They joined a line of women and teenage girls kneeling along the canvas. The tent was set up much like the medical tent. A sleepy-looking woman was sitting behind a card table.

I waited my turn in line. When she asked me if I needed help, I said, "I'm looking, well, my friend is looking for his father . . . Rahmad, father of Deni, does that sound familiar?"

She blinked, suddenly wide awake. "Rahmad? Father of Deni?"

"You know him? My friend Deni . . . he's been living at an orphanage in Yogyakarta. Someone called him, from an NGO here, we just don't know which one. . . ."

Her head tilted to the side as she looked me over. "You're American?"

I nodded. "Yes."

She leaned closer. "How old is your friend?"

"Seventeen," I said.

Her lips closed tightly before she permitted them to open again. "Come back tomorrow."

"So? Do you know something about him?"

Her eyes flashed wildly, but she said in a calm voice, "Tomorrow, you return."

I didn't know what to tell Deni. The woman didn't tell me anything, but it was obvious she knew *something*. I decided it was better not to get Deni's hopes up based on a strange woman's odd behavior. I'd just go back tomorrow like she said.

It was late by the time we walked the long way back to Siti and Azmi's house, and everything was dark and still. I felt Azmi's and Siti's curious eyes on us as we walked home in the dark and again now in the front room. Siti excused herself, and then Azmi and Deni spoke intensely in their language that I didn't understand.

I stood there awkwardly while they talked, staring at two thin mats that replaced the bamboo tea spread on the floor, the yellow moon glowing outside the open window.

Azmi finally left the room, shooting me his standard hang loose.

I raised my eyebrows at Deni. "What was that all about?" I asked.

"He's wondering about you. About us."

"And what did you tell him?"

Raking his fingers through his hair, he shrugged.

"So that's it? I'm a shrug to you?" I teased.

"Yes," he teased back. "That is all."

The room was steamy hot. "Who is sleeping here?" I asked, gesturing toward the bamboo mats.

"You," he said. "And Siti."

"Where will you sleep?" I asked him, biting my lip.

"With Azmi," he said, but didn't break my gaze. "In the other room."

I was suddenly very aware that this was our last night together.

"Don't go to sleep yet," I whispered.

He lowered his dark eyelashes. "You have special plans for us?"

I couldn't help but smile back. After the day we'd had, we could use a nice night.

"Maybe . . ."

"Ibu and Bapak. They are here. Siti will return after her prayers. And Azmi will be waiting for me." He looked at me questioningly but moved closer, our chests nearly touching in the shadowed room.

"Then we don't have much time," I whispered. I threw my arms around his neck. He pulled me in close. I wanted the whole night together. I wanted everything. But this was what I had: one moment, and I wasn't going to waste it.

"I don't want to leave you," I said.

"Then stay." His voice in my ear was hushed but intense. "You don't have to go."

"I can't. . . . My dad is probably worried sick. I have to go back."

I listened for footsteps as he pulled back a bit. He cupped my face in his hands.

"Then I'll fly to America. I'll help rebuild my home and I will save money. Sienna, I promise. I will find you."

I ran my hands down his arms, laced my fingers through his. Invited his face to mine.

His hands roamed down my back, clutching me to him. Hard. Desperate. I reached under his damp T-shirt, covered his heart with my hand. His lips found mine and didn't stop and didn't stop and didn't stop until we heard a clanging in the other room and knew our time was running out.

I kissed his scar, his neck, his ear. "Find me," I whispered back.

Roosters and the call to prayer woke me at dawn.

My neck was sore. Siti snored quietly beside me. I wanted so badly to turn her into Deni. Most of the night I lay awake in a hot sweat, thinking of him. Remembering his promise: *I will find you.*

I never allowed myself to think that we could really be together.

And now, like Deni, I had hope.

Hope for someday.

No one else was awake yet, so, yawning, I stumbled to the porch. The sun beat down so hard it already felt like noon.

I thought of the logistics of us meeting up again.

How long would it take to save the money to come to America? Months? Years? Years was not good.

Maybe I could persuade Team Hope to come here again. Back to Aceh. There was still so much work to be done. Maybe we could fly back next summer? Or we could write at least? I rubbed my temples, feeling an odd mix of joy and misery. Joy that I would see him again, but misery imagining life in the meantime without him.

I waited outside while the family rolled out their mats, preparing to do their morning prayers. Deni sauntered out of Azmi's room with a knowing smile on his face that raised my whole body temperature. He caught my eye through the window and I blushed. I watched Deni rise and fall in prayer. I watched the sweat glisten off his chest. I watched his face scrunched with concentration.

And then I knew. No matter how long it took, it didn't matter. He was worth waiting for.

I listened as roosters crowed.

I leaned back against the wood slat wall.

Maybe Deni could do an exchange program? We could go to college together!

It didn't matter what we did. We could just be together.

When the call ended, I stood and glanced through the window again as he rose from his mat, opened the front door and greeted me formally. Then, closing the door halfway so no one could see, he ran his fingers down my forearm and explained in a low voice, "Ibu bought a special breakfast of Dutch treats for you yesterday. The chocolate bits are special desserts for Indonesians." He squeezed my hand. "I am happy to introduce you to my family."

I thought back to our first conversation when he explained traditions, that if a boy brought a girl into his home to meet his family, he wanted to marry her.

This was Deni's family now.

Breakfast was set up on a low table: steaming coffee, a

white loaf of bread with the crusts cut off and a bowl full of chocolate sprinkles like the ones we use to decorate cupcakes with at home.

"Thank you, Ibu," I said.

Spooning a bunch of sugar into the coffee, I accepted every refill offered until my hands were shaking.

Azmi and Bapak left to go fishing right after breakfast. "The fish do not bite as much as before the wave came. But we work hard and we'll sell at the market today," Bapak said. I didn't know if I'd have time to come back before I left for the airport that night, so it was sort of sad watching them go.

When Siti and her aunt disappeared into the kitchen, Deni touched my arm.

"How did you sleep?" he asked.

My toes curled. "Terrible." I smiled. "You?"

"The same."

As he leaned back against the wall, his veins stuck out from his arm. I glanced back toward the kitchen. For the moment, no one was watching us, so I twined my fingers into his. "Deni," I said quietly, "I hope we find him today."

"Me too," Deni said, squeezing my hand. "Me too."

Deni, Siti and I sat in a row on the hot seat of a three-wheeled bicycle called a *becak*. The driver, a teenage boy, sat behind us pedaling along at a slow, easy pace. We cruised through dried mud streets past yelling street vendors, *motors* and oxen carrying their wares. I asked Deni to take a picture of Siti and me posing with the driver, who struck a hang-loose pose just like Azmi.

Deni then asked Siti to take one of him and me together. He put his arm around my shoulders, squeezing me gently. Siti raised her eyebrows and clicked, but didn't say a word.

After the ride, we decided to split up again. I needed to head back to the orange reproductive tent to talk to the mysterious woman and Deni had a few more places that asked him to come back today as well.

We planned to meet up in an hour for a cold drink.

"Today is the day," he said to me with an optimistic wink. "We will find him."

"Fingers crossed," I said.

I slipped back through the slit of the tent. It was a different person at the counter, younger, just a couple of years older than me. She was wearing black cotton pants and a flowing white blouse. Her *jilbab* hung loosely around her head, some stray long hairs falling across her heart-shaped face.

"Can I help you?" she asked. She had wide brown eyes and a soft smile.

"Yes. I was here yesterday talking to a woman? Is she here?"

"Sorry, she is not here today. Only me."

My heart sank. "That's weird," I said, looking around. "She asked me to come back today. . . ."

Crap. Now what would I tell Deni? He'd have to follow this up on his own. After I was gone. My eyes burned just at the thought of it. I wouldn't be there the next day to help him.

My heart sped up with annoyance. "Will she be back tomorrow?"

"Yes. You are an American?" she asked me, her voice calm and even.

I nodded, tapping the floor with my shoe. I wasn't in the mood for small talk, but she seemed so nice, and it wasn't her fault her coworker was a flake. So I asked, "What about you? Are you a volunteer?"

"No." She shook her head. "I work here. I am from Aceh. I was here the day the wave came."

"You were? That must have been awful." I glanced toward the tent door. I really needed to talk to Deni.

But the girl kept going. "I fell off the back of a *motor* trying to escape the wave. I stayed far away in another village for months afterward. A family cared for me until my strength returned."

She laughed then—awkwardly, nervously, like the kids at the *pesantren* after they told their sad tales. "Thank God a nice family found you," I said.

"Yes. Now I am here." She spread both arms in the air.

"Fortunately most of my family survived, and this clinic also is my family now. So many lost their children in the tsunami. We are here to help women and children get healthy again."

I glanced around at toddlers playing together in a corner, women deep in conversation.

"It seems like a neat place. Well, I'm sorry, I don't mean to be rude, but I have to go. Please tell the other woman who works here that my friend—Deni is his name—will be back tomorrow to ask her if she knows anything about his father. I won't, well, I won't be here anymore." My voice cracked. "But hopefully, she'll be able to help him."

"Deni?" the girl asked.

He was probably already waiting for me. "Yes," I confirmed with a nod, and headed toward the slit in the tent. "Please tell her Deni will be back tomorrow."

I ran as fast as the heat would allow toward the meeting place.

Siti was sitting alone, her head in her hands.

"Are you okay?" I asked.

She didn't answer.

I sat down next to her, wiping my forehead with the back of my shirt. "It's roasting today. I'll get us some drinks." But she still didn't answer, and then she started rocking back and forth, sobbing. "Siti? What's wrong?

Are you sick?" I asked. It was so hot. "Come on, let's find Deni and we'll take you back home."

"No," she said, but it was more like a wail than a word.

"What is it?"

She raised her head, tears pouring down her face. "The wall."

"What wall?"

She pointed out a decrepit wooden building. A gnawing sick feeling grew in my chest. It must be something really bad to make Siti so upset. Squeezing through the thick crowd of people, I noticed the wall was covered with Polaroid snapshots.

As I got closer, I realized they were pictures of faces.

Hundreds of faces. I gasped. The pictures were of dead people, grisly, horrible pictures of hundreds of corpses. The worst pictures I'd ever seen in my life: close-ups of bloated, cut, puffy faces, most with their eyes closed.

"What is this?" I managed to croak out.

"The wall of the dead," Siti said quietly from behind me.

The pictures were so horrifying I had to look away.

"Where is Deni?" I demanded.

"Deni is gone."

"What happened?"

She pointed to a picture on the bottom row of a middle-aged man with chiseled features and a short beard. He looked just like Deni.

"Deni's *bapak*," she whispered.

"Deni just saw this wall?"

"Yes!"

"Did you know about this?" I accused her. "Did you know he was dead?"

"I did not know!" Siti cried. "We never saw the picture!"

"Siti," I said in my firmest voice, "I need to find him. Where did he go?"

I ran in the direction Siti pointed.

Away from town. Away from the picture.

Toward the sea.

A friend of our family lives in Manhattan, close to what used to be the World Trade Center. She said after 9/11, after the buildings fell from the sky, there were photographs of people who worked there. Missing people. With notes and phone numbers and contact information for strangers to read. She cried every day when she passed the walls, imagining the people hanging those pictures and writing those notes. Hoping someone would call with information about their loved ones.

I couldn't believe this was happening to Deni.

Catching sight of his back ducking around the corner of a tent, I yelled, "Deni!"

But he couldn't hear me. There were too many people. Too much noise.

"Deni, wait!"

He reappeared on the main path, walking fast, practically running, away from the wall, away from me. I didn't know where he was going, I only knew that what he believed was true—wasn't. And then he disappeared, and there was no way I could catch him.

His father was dead.

And there was nothing I could do now to help him.

I was halfway down the crowded, gummy road when someone grabbed my arm.

"Sienna? What happened, sweetheart? What's wrong?"

It was Amelia. She was wearing a World Doctors T-shirt, and her short hair was sticking up in front with sweat.

"I . . . he . . ." I burst into tears, and though I tried to squirm away, Amelia firmly guided me into her clinic through a makeshift curtain into a private room.

"Tell me what happened," she said.

I sat on an exam table. Suddenly I couldn't keep anything in. I told her everything.

"I need help, Amelia," I said. "I don't know what to do about Deni. . . . I have a plane to catch and I can't leave him, but I also can't . . . Oh God, everything is such a mess."

She stroked my arms and my hair and talked to me in a soothing voice. I choked back tears until they turned into hiccups. The way she spoke to me, touching me, reminded me so much of my mom.

"Do you"—hiccup—"have any kids?" Hiccup.

She shook her head. "Not yet. But we hope to. When we finish this trip, we're going to try."

"Good. Because you'd be a great one. A mom, I mean."

"Thanks, honey."

"My parents used to work together . . . like you do. They just went out for two weeks a year after they had me. They didn't want to stay away long. . . ." My voice choked up again as I thought of them together, remembering us as a family.

Amelia touched me under the chin. Her nails were short but nicely manicured, the way Mom kept hers. "I bet they wanted to rush home to see such a sweet girl as you."

I held on to her hand. "This is going to sound kind of weird. But can I have your address? Or e-mail address in Australia? Maybe when I get back home, we can keep in touch?"

"Oh, honey," she said softly. "I'd love that."

Her Acehnese assistant came in and told Amelia she had an important phone call.

While she was gone, I tried to pull myself together, but I had no idea what to do next.

"Sienna," Amelia said, reentering the room and wiping

my eyes with the sleeve of her blouse. "I need to tell you something. Something very important. That was the Reproductive Health Clinic. You two were right about someone looking for Deni." She tilted her head and said softly, "But it wasn't his father."

LIFE

I was still sitting on the exam table when Amelia brought her in moments later.

Amelia touched my arm. "Sienna. This is Rema."

Same wide eyes. Same soft smile. It was the girl I was just talking to.

"Hello," she said. "I am sorry to bother you, but I have a question. I told you the story of running from the wave? I was with a boy. On his *motor*. I fell off as the water came," she said. Then she lowered her voice to almost a whisper. "May I ask you, what does your friend Deni look like?"

When she said his name, I felt sick the same way I did when Spider's mom came out on that rooftop telling me I had to go home right away. Like whatever words came next were going to change everything. "Deni? Um. He has dark wavy hair," I started slowly. "He's about this tall," I said, leveling my hand above my head. "He has a little beard, a half of a goatee." Her head tilted in question, so I clarified. "You know the word *goatee*? It's like this." I pulled on my chin to describe Deni's facial hair.

Her eyes flashed with recognition.

"But lots of boys look like that," I said defensively.

"Does he drive a *motor*?" she asked.

Yes, but so does everyone. "He used a friend's when we were in Yogyakarta," I said.

"His father's name?" she prodded.

I wanted to run out of the room. "Rhamad. It was Rhamad. Deni just found out that . . ."

"His father is dead," Rema confirmed with a sad nod. "The picture is on the wall."

She knew? "Deni didn't know," I said, narrowing my eyes. "If it's the same Deni . . ."

"I just found out myself. I didn't know where he was. I could not tell him."

It was the same Deni.

But what does she want with him? Goose bumps rose on my arms, and Rema's eyes were wide. She clutched her white blouse too hard, crunching the silk material up into a ball. "You're . . . Amelia says you are traveling together. You are . . ." She frowned. "Deni's girlfriend?"

My mouth was dry. After last night. After everything we'd been through, there was only one way to answer. "Yes."

Rema looked at me with tortured, watery eyes, like I'd just stabbed her in the heart. "We were engaged to marry," she said. "Before the tsunami."

Deni was *engaged*?

Amelia held on to my arm to keep me from tipping over.

Rema waited for a reaction. I tried to catch my breath and failed.

"He heard someone was looking for him; that's why we—that's why he came back. He was sure it was his father." I faced Rema. "It was *you*?"

She nodded. "Yes. I stayed for many months with the family that found me. I was very weak. When I returned finally to Aceh, only two weeks ago, Deni's family home was destroyed, his family lost to the sea. I could not find many of Deni's friends, and at first, I didn't try to find him. But then someone said a group of kids were taken to a *pesantren* in Yogyakarta or Jakarta. They didn't know which one. I was hopeful Deni may have been one of the lucky ones. He was so good on that *motor*. But there are so many schools it was hardly worth the effort to try, and after losing everything, I wanted him to have a good life. To study and succeed.

"But then I couldn't bear it anymore. I could not let him think I was dead. I missed him. I loved him. So I spoke to the refugee camps and all the relief organizations here, told them, if he came back, where to find me. I took my job and I waited to hear news—and then, once I learned of his father, I looked harder. I started calling all the *pesantrens* in Jakarta and Yogyakarta, hoping, looking."

I bit my lip hard. "He wouldn't have left unless he thought you—he must have thought you were dead."

She nodded. "Everyone thought I was dead. I thought he may have been dead too."

"Did Azmi and Siti know you were alive?"

Her eyes filled with tears. "Azmi and Siti. I am so happy they are okay. I have only recently been strong enough to work. I have not seen many of our old friends. But then I was speaking to my coworker and she told me Amelia was speaking about meeting an American girl who was traveling with a boy. A boy named Deni. Please. I need to see him. I need to see Deni."

The three of us rumbled down the potholed road until we came to an even worse road. I couldn't believe I was sitting next to Deni's fiancée or ex-fiancée or whatever she was. Is. I ground my knuckles into my temples.

"How do you know where he is?" Rema asked me curiously.

I will find you . . .

"I just know," I said.

Amelia stopped the car but left the engine and the air conditioner running.

We sat inside for a few minutes, parked about a hundred yards from the mosque. I didn't know for sure if he was inside, but if I ever knew him at all, then that was where he would be.

Rema looked really nervous and was wringing her hands. "I hope this does not cause a problem for you, Sienna. You have been so kind."

I forced out the words. "He thinks you're dead. He knows his father is dead. Just go. It's okay, really."

I'm not going to say it was easy watching Rema get out of the car.

In fact, it was really, really hard, and I felt guilty for hating her, for wishing it was me going into that mosque to comfort him. But I could never give him the gift she was about to.

I wasn't the girl he needed to see.

"Good luck," I said to her as she stepped out.

I watched Rema walk toward the mosque.

Amelia gently laid her hand on top of mine. "Sweetie, I know this is the worst timing on the planet, but it's already four p.m. If you're going to make it to the airport, we have to leave now."

No.

"I can't leave him without saying good-bye. Whatever happens between . . . them, I still need to say good-bye."

I didn't want to spy, but I had to know if she found him. I walked up the stairs and peeked through the cutout windows. They were standing on a prayer mat, in the center of the room, Deni and Rema, framed in the arch of their mosque. He was shaking his head, talking in their language, clutching her arm. The light from the windows reflected on the floor. Rema looked down at her bare feet and Deni reached out, lifted her chin.

I felt sick.

I couldn't watch for another second. But I couldn't tear myself away.

Amelia finally led me back down the stairs.

"I'm going to the ocean," I said.

I wanted to be alone.

She nodded. "I'll be in the car, waiting," she said. "It's going to be okay, sweetie," she called after me.

I stepped over sand and rocks and muck and mud. I stepped over sad and broken creepy things like a beat-up tennis shoe, a muddy piece of cloth, half of a plate and a headless doll.

I stepped farther and farther away from Deni.

The air was humid and broiling but smelled like the ocean smelled at home.

What did Deni say when he saw her?

Did he think he was seeing a ghost, like Dad did that first morning at the *pesantren* when he thought I looked like Mom?

Deni, I can't even imagine.

As horrible as this was for me, your worst day just became your best.

ACCEPTANCE

I sat alone on the pebbly shore.

I was going to miss my plane.

I didn't even have my backpack with me—it was still at Azmi's. I just had my camera and the clothes on my back. No Deni. No parents. No way home. Nothing except the blue-brown water lapping against the rocks. Flying creatures buzzed around my head. Too late, I slapped them away.

The air smelled like spices and rot.

It smelled like regret.

We never should have come to Aceh.

He would have been happier not knowing about his father. He could have lived forever with hope.

What was so good about the truth anyway? It just made everyone miserable.

Angry tears stung my eyes.

And then I noticed something in the water.

I had to stand up to know for sure. But humps, dark humps, were rising up and down in the low waves close to the shore.

No. It couldn't be.

Sea turtles.

There were two of them, swimming side by side. Just like the ones on the front of Mom's postcard from Thailand.

Huge ancient turtles floated along as if this place wasn't damaged at all. They looked exactly as Mom described in her last words home to me.

The Indian Ocean.

Chills ran up and down my spine.

This is the place I hoped for a miracle.

Where my mom would magically appear, explaining that she'd been knocked unconscious for three years. Like Rema, she'd been living with kindly strangers who nursed her back to health, and now *poof,* here she was.

But that miracle wasn't mine today.

That miracle was Deni's.

One of the turtles looked at me with wise brown eyes, and I dared to say something stupid. "Mom," I asked quietly. "Are you here?"

I watched the turtles some more, remembering when I first met Deni at the *pesantren,* the drum circle, kissing in the alley in the rain.

"Mom? You can hear me, can't you?" I said out loud.

Never mind. I'm being ridiculous.

Then the bigger turtle spun around and peeked its head up like it was listening to me.

"Hello." I knew I must sound like an idiot, but I didn't care. Deni was with Rema. I'd already lost. "Mom," I started again. "I'm in trouble."

Except for the hum of the waves, everything was still.

I listened. Listened for her voice in the waves.

Weirder things have happened, and if her spirit really was here with me, with her crazy mixed-up teenage daughter, I needed to ask her for help.

"How am I supposed to say good-bye to Deni?"

I shut my eyes. Imagined her reply.

When you see him, you'll know the right things to say. And if for some reason you don't get the chance, trust he knows how you feel.

Trust he knows how you feel.

I opened my eyes again.

"Thanks, Mom," I said as the turtles disappeared beneath the turquoise sea.

GOOD-BYE

Deni had a bittersweet smile on his face as he walked toward the ocean alone.

I hoped the tears in my eyes stayed where they were.

We didn't say anything at first. There were just no words as we walked together over the rocks and debris along the shallow shoreline.

I knew this was the last time we'd be alone together. He was back home. And now he belonged to another girl.

Small fishing boats bobbed around not too far out.

My heart caught in my throat.

Nothing was worse than good-bye.

"Sienna?" Deni said finally, quietly, breaking the silence between us.

He looked at me the way he always had. We were back to being Deni and me.

"I'm so sorry about your father," I said, sniffling. The tears in my eyes were beginning to fall.

He rubbed his chin, nodding. "So am I. But I'm not sorry I had hope."

"You were right to believe."

He touched my forearm gently. "I didn't tell you about Rema before—it was too hard to talk about." He glanced out at the ocean as if seeing it happen again. "We were trying to escape the wave. People were everywhere. Tugging on us, trying to get on the *motor* too. Remember when I told you the boys tried to jump on the *motor*? We crashed. My leg was bleeding. I pushed the *motor* off of me and she was gone. I never saw her again after the crash. She must have been picked up by the crowd. I revved the engine, tried to go back to find her, but the water was coming—rushing to me. I . . . couldn't turn around. This giant wall was coming and she was nowhere." His face broke. "I had to leave her behind."

I couldn't believe he'd been living with all this guilt. No wonder. "It wasn't your fault. . . ."

A shadow of pain crossed Deni's face. "She says she lay alone in a village . . . I looked for her for two weeks! No one had seen her. I saw that wave come. Bodies were everywhere; there was no way she could have lived and then . . . she lives . . ."

He squeezed my arm. "It *was* my fault she was alone. I should not have left."

"It's okay, Deni," I said, laying my hand on his. "You didn't know. It's a miracle you found her. That she found you."

"I would never have known she was alive if we hadn't come." He broke my gaze, looking back at the sea. He didn't let go of my arm. "But now I have made you a promise too. And I don't want to break my promise." His face crumpled. "I don't know what to do."

I took both his hands in mine. They were big, warm, soft and familiar.

But his eyes looked like they did when he was telling me about his nightmare that night in the rain. I remembered Dad's words: *He's already lost way too much, Sienna. Do it for him.*

It made me sick to say the words.

"You have to forget about me. You have to stay here with Rema."

His eyes flashed, angry, like he wanted to swat away my words. "How am I supposed to forget about you?"

The crashing waves filled in the blanks.

I sat on the sharp rocks, pulling him down next to me. No one was here, no one could see. I put my arms around his neck, kissed his face.

"I'm so sorry," he said, rubbing his eyes.

"I am too."

He hugged me, pulling me closer to him. We hung on to each other like that.

"I wish you have a happy life back in America," he said, his voice cracking. "A magical life. I have my *ole-ole* to remember." He pulled the fake statue from the temple out of his pocket. The one I gave him.

I nodded, swallowing back tears.

He tried to smile. "You like *motor* now, no?" He raised his eyebrows. "What do they call them in America?"

"Vespas," my voice squeaked out.

"Vespa," he repeated. "Buy one. You are rich American." He grinned. "You can remember us."

I saw us on the moped. Me clutching on to his waist, my face buried in the sweat of his back.

"You can remember me."

His fingers wiped the tears across my cheek. "And you make me a promise," he said, his eyes red and moist. "You promise to always hang on tight."

I could barely form the words. "I . . . promise."

We were quiet for a moment, watching the waves soak the shore. He let go of me and reached into his pocket. Handed me a neatly folded piece of paper. "For you. Forgive me the bad English. Please do not read it until later."

"When did you write this?"

He licked his bottom lip, his burnt caramel eyes soft. "Last night while I watched you sleep."

My tear slipped onto the paper. I grasped the note in my palm, afraid to let it go.

"I want you to have a happy life too, with . . ." God, this was hard. "With . . . Rema. Finding each other after all this time is remarkable." I squeezed his hand. "Like the mosque still standing after the storm. It means something bigger than us. Bigger than we can understand."

"I understand," Deni said tenderly. "It was the same thing that brought you to me. Brought your father to the *pesantren.* Helped to chase away our nightmares. It's all the same thing."

"My mother," I said, because this was my chance, my only chance to tell him. "I told you her plane crashed in this ocean." I said it quietly and slowly. "The Indian Ocean. It was three years ago, off the coast of Thailand, which would mean really close to the epicenter of the quake. It means her plane crashed somewhere out there—" I pointed out at the endless sea.

"Before she . . . before she died"—I cleared my throat—"she mailed me home this postcard of two sea turtles swimming off the shore. It was the last thing I have from her, and while you were up there with . . . I saw them. I mean, maybe not the same ones, but two sea turtles just like she described. It was like she was trying to say something to me." I frowned. "I know it sounds weird . . ."

We probably shouldn't have because of Rema, but because he was Deni and I was me, we did it anyway. I buried my face in the small of his neck, touching my lips to his salty skin.

Deni whispered into my hair, "Your mother loves you. She is everywhere protecting you. She is here with us now. Your mother, my mother, my father, my sisters. They do not disappear when they die. They leave us their strength."

A giant wave crashed over a log adrift at sea. The log bobbed around, twisting with the motion of it, but it didn't sink. It stayed afloat. I scanned the top of the frothy water, hoping to point out the floating humps to Deni. But the sea turtles were gone.

"Saya akan rinda Anda," I said. I will miss you.

His eyes filled with tears, and I could barely stand it.

I wanted to tell him that you can meet someone and they can change your life forever, even if you have only known him for a short while, that when you leave, you're a different person than before you met him . . . and I understand that because of meeting Deni.

I wanted to tell him that, all of that, but I knew he couldn't say it back.

"Saya akan rinda Anda," he whispered. "I will miss you too, Sienna. And *terima kasih*, for everything."

"I thought that's only what tourists say." I dared to look into his eyes.

"It's what you say. So I will always use it. I will always love it."

He touched my hand to his forehead and then he touched his own heart.

We held hands like we would never let go.

We held hands until the log floated all the way out to sea.

THE HAZE

I sat alone at the Aceh airport holding Deni's unread note in my hand.

I felt so utterly alone that I unzipped my backpack and searched for Spider's shell.

I made myself a deal: if it was broken, if it was shattered, my life was officially over.

But it wasn't. It was perfect.

So I set it back in and opened up my journal. Took out my postcard from Mom. I was rereading it over and over again when I heard my name and looked up.

Running through the airport, face flushed, beard longer, eyes wildly looking around, Dad spotted me. "Sienna Hope Jones!" he yelled out, his hug nearly crushing me. He was crying, I was crying (well, I was already crying, then I was crying even harder). I must have looked so weird standing there bawling, Deni's note in one hand, Mom's postcard in the other.

"Are you okay?" he demanded. I got the feeling if I said no, I'd be in even bigger trouble.

"No. Yes. I don't know."

"You aren't hurt? Sick?" he said, checking me over. "Nothing's broken?"

Do hearts count? "I'm okay, Dad."

He rubbed his forehead. "I would have come sooner,

but there was a huge storm, my plane was delayed; it was a nightmare. I just kept imagining the worst. Don't you EVER leave me again without my permission, do you understand me?"

When I nodded, he hugged me again. Then he dug into his pocket and handed me a tissue. "When Nada gave me the note you left on your old bunk—everything came back—your mom's crash. You're just like her, you know. I should have known you'd come alone."

"You think I'm like Mom?"

"You've always been like her. You've just . . . been subdued for so long, I stopped worrying as much. I let down my guard, and then this happens. . . ." He looked off into the terminal, like he was explaining it to someone other than me.

He squeezed my hands tighter and stared me down. "Sweetie. I can't lose you both."

Then he glanced down at the open journal balancing on my backpack. At the two sea turtles. At the glassy blue ocean.

"What is that?" His face froze with recognition.

I handed it to him.

My heart pounded as he read it, eyes as glassy as the sea in the picture.

"Where did you get this?" he asked me.

"After you came home."

"Why didn't you ever tell me?"

I shrugged. "I don't know. I guess I wanted to have something special just from her."

"And this is part of the reason you've been holding on to all that hope?" Dad asked.

I shrugged again. "I guess."

His fingertip ran down her writing like he was seeing her again.

I felt terrible. Terrible for scaring him and terrible for keeping the card a secret. Terrible for reopening all the hurt.

But I had to ask him the question that had been weighing on me for so long.

"I want you to tell me what happened to Mom."

He kept staring at the card.

"I was at the Indian Ocean, Dad."

"Yes," he said quietly.

I took a deep breath. "I don't understand why you let her go that day. Didn't you know it was dangerous? It was raining? Why didn't you stop her?"

"I tried."

"What do you mean you tried?" This was news to me.

"Honey, I haven't wanted to share this with you because I was afraid you'd blame her. And you shouldn't. That's the last thing I want."

"Just tell me. What happened? Dad, I can handle it."

"There was a storm that day in Thailand and it was getting worse. The roofs were flipping off the makeshift huts, the supplies were getting wet and ruined. It was a mess. Then we received this SOS call over the radio. Your mom answered the call. There was a school with a collapsed roof, kids were hurt. She insisted we go help them. The pilot of the small plane refused. He said in the storm there was no way. It would be too dangerous. I told her we'd wait out the storm. We'd go after it passed. She said the kids couldn't wait. . . ."

"Dad. What happened?"

"We got in an argument—she could be very stubborn. I insisted she stay—she said she was going. That she had to go. But I didn't believe her. She was headstrong, but logical. I didn't think she'd risk it. I was busy helping the villagers when I heard the engine. I ran after the plane but it was too late. She took off into the storm."

"Oh my God."

"I know."

We were quiet for a while.

"How did she persuade the pilot to go?" I asked finally.

"She had a pilot's license. She just took off."

"Mom was flying the plane?"

"Yes." Dad rubbed his face. "She was convinced she could help those kids. She was an okay pilot, but anyone in a storm like that . . ."

I didn't want to hate Mom. She only wanted to help.

Still, I couldn't stop the burning anger welling in my chest. That was too risky. She risked too much.

"That's why," Dad said, his voice breaking, "the only thing we could assume is that she went down on one of the many islands or in the sea. She was too inexperienced. The storm was too rough. Are you okay, Sienna?"

I swallowed. "Yeah, I am. I'd rather know the truth, Dad. And I promise you're not going to lose me. I had to help Deni. Good things happened for him because I came. Really. But I won't do it again. If I want to do something like that again, I'll make sure it's okay with you. I swear."

I was not going to end up like Mom.

He studied me, then let out a long, low sigh. "I'm so glad to hear that. Speaking of Deni, where is he? Because he's due for a nice long chat."

I filled Dad in on all of it. On the mass graves and Azmi and Siti. On Amelia and then the story of Rema.

He listened, mouth agape, slowly shaking his head. "Unbelievable," he said.

"So he's home," I said. "Deni's finally home."

We met back up with Vera and Tom in Yogyakarta. Dad made me explain to the *pesantren* owner what had happened with Deni. Made me apologize for sneaking off. I was sorry. He could never know how sorry.

I gave Elli most of the stuff from my suitcase, promised to write, promised to send her more markers. I said good-bye to Nada and girls from the teen group. Talk-talk was at an all-time high. I didn't care, though.

Mostly I was just numb.

All in all, Dad said, the family system was a successful trial, they helped the kids learn how to better deal with their PTSD symptoms, and, no thanks to me, we might be invited back another time. But like all these projects, they were baby steps. There was no cure-all in two weeks. Two weeks was not going to take away that much pain.

But at least it was a start.

I could barely stand being at the *pesantren* without Deni, and then we finally boarded our plane for home.

"Do you wanna watch something?" Tom said, handing me his headphones after the Fasten Seat Belt sign went off. "Indonesian game shows. Could be fun."

Dad and Vera were sitting together, watching the same movie, laughing at the same jokes. For once it didn't make me totally ill. At least one of us was happy.

"Maybe later," I told Tom.

I excused myself to use the bathroom, where I finally opened Deni's letter.

For my Rambut Kuning:
The words to the song about my home. Terima kasih, Deni.
The jeumpa flower is a famous flower in Aceh. It is

fragrant and very beautiful. Its color is white and yellow and mixed with red; layered with petals, each one is very beautiful. When the moon is shining and the wind is blowing, petal by petal will fall. The flower is so fragrant when we perchance to smell it, the jeumpa flower is so beautiful.

When the bride and groom sit on their throne and the jeumpa flower decorates her hair, the fragrance will be as heavenly as musk. Ladies of Aceh always yearn for the fragrance of the jeumpa flower. In the light of the full moon, the night wind will blow and the petals of the jeumpa flower will fall. Ladies of Aceh are content when they remember the fragrance of the jeumpa flower.

I will find you. Deni

He wrote the note before he knew about Rema.

My tears fell on his words, smearing the ink, until I had to hold the paper away from my eyes to keep from ruining it.

He wrote that when he thought I was the girl who could maybe one day become his bride.

How am I supposed to forget you?

I woke up to the flight attendant's voice. "We've started our descent into San Francisco International Airport. Please make sure your seat belts are fastened and your trays are in the full upright position. Thank you for flying Air Ethelia."

It was funny how little I cared about the landing. Or the flight at all.

My seat belt was on, and I just figured we'd land okay.

You will always land in one piece, Deni had told me when we were in the airport waiting for our flight to Aceh.

The whole flight I'd been replaying Deni's words in my head.

Maybe Deni was right.

I imagined Mom waiting for us at the airport.

Her thick blond hair tied in a loose bun. She'd be wearing faded blue jeans and a tank top. Her arms long, thin and tan from hours working in the garden. She'd run up to us, her eyes dancing, and swoop me into a hug. *How was your trip, Sea?* she'd say. *Tell me everything.* And then whisper, *Especially the juicy parts.*

And I would.

I'd tell her everything.

I'd tell her about Deni and me climbing the ancient temple of Borobudur, the smell of the warm sweat of his back, the pulse of my heart as I wrapped my arms around him. How I leaned into the turns on the *motor* just like she taught me on my pink body board when I was a kid.

I'd tell her the sad parts too, the wall of death, the headless doll. I'd tell her about bringing Rema to Deni and leaving them together.

The clouds outside my window were turning cotton candy pink again. It was sunset in California.

On the way to Indo, the colors were leading me somewhere, to the street kids, to the other orphans at the *pesantren*. To Elli.

To Amelia, Azmi and Siti. To Dad and Mom. To Deni.

I held my warm palm against the ice-cold window, remembering.

The Orange Popsicle Haze lighting my way back home.

Oma and Bev were waiting for us at the airport with a handmade sign that read, *TEAM HOPE and TEEN RUN-AWAY SIENNA JONES.*

"Very funny, guys," I said, buried in a group hug until Bev shrugged me off.

"Wait. Do you have any infectious disease, missy?" she asked.

"I was exposed to the bird flu," I deadpanned.

"Seriously?"

I shrugged. "I was around lots of caged birds. And they don't want to put them to sleep there, even the sick ones. They're pets, especially the doves." I remembered Deni's story about his mom and her pet songbirds.

I couldn't believe I was back in California.

Oma laughed and hugged me again while Bev examined me closely for foaming of the mouth or oozing sores.

"Bev, I'm kidding. I don't have the bird flu. But it's true about the birds."

"Well, you're lucky. I was about to put you in quarantine!" She nailed me playfully with her sharp elbow. "And if you're wondering where my brother is, he gave up waiting for you and went surfing in Mexico."

Gave up waiting for me? Spider was waiting for me? "Whatever," I said.

They asked about the flight, the food, our adventure. I told them if we were in Indo, we'd be having this conversation over spicy hot tea.

"Ready to go, kiddo?" Dad asked me. "We could stop for pizza on the way home."

"No, thanks," I said. There was only one place I wanted to be, and I needed to go there alone.

I heard the music first, the strumming of the sitar.

On this side of the world there were no spices in the air, not that kind anyway, but it was a sitar all the same. When he saw me, he stood up. "Why, if it isn't Sienna Jones," he said in a fake cowboy drawl, dangling the wooden instrument from one hand.

I couldn't help but grin. "In the flesh," I said, adopting the same tone.

As he stood on Sunny Cove's towering cliff, Spider's back was against the moonlit sea.

He hugged me, and it was totally awkward for a second, but in one of those funny ways, so we both laughed.

"I thought you were in Mexico?" I asked, by way of small talk.

"I was. Just got home a couple hours ago."

"Me too. I mean, I just got home too."

"I know," he said. He played a few more notes on the sitar and then set it down.

"This is cool," he said, looking at the sitar.

"You like?"

"For sure. No one in the history of twelve-year-old musicians has ever butchered 'Stairway to Heaven' worse than me," he said, referring to his old guitar.

"I figured on the sitar, you could pummel it even worse," I joked, surprised how easy it was to be with him again. Remembering after such a miserable past few days how nice it felt to smile.

"I have no doubt," Spider said.

"I'm glad you like it. Haggling with street vendors and then mailing something from Indo is no small task. I had to drag Dad with me to help." I remembered that day going into town, finding the perfect thing to send back to Spider.

He avoided my eyes, looking at the sitar instead. "So how was your trip?"

I wasn't sure how much he'd heard, so I shrugged. "Good. Bad. Crazy."

He eyed me closely. "You look different."

I *felt* different.

"Jet lag?" I guessed casually.

He shook his head, his sandy blond hair moving in the sea breeze.

"That's not it. Something else."

"So, am I taller? Shorter? Wiser?" I teased. It was nice to see him. I had planned on coming down here, crying, moping alone.

"Wiser." He nodded. "Certainly. Taller?" He shook his head. "Still way shorter than Spidey-Man."

We were standing really close to each other. It seemed so weird, after being with Deni, being so close to Spider again.

"So . . . how was Mexico?" I thought about that whacked-out irony. Spider was out chasing waves while Deni and his friends were dealing with the trauma of running away from them.

"Okay. I hit the road right after you left. Too boring here without you."

"Really?" I smiled, disbelieving.

Spider scratched his head and shifted his weight from one foot to the other. "But you weren't bored, right? In Indo?" His eyes narrowed slightly. "I heard you ran off with some guy."

I bit my lip. "That's not really the whole story."

"What *is* the whole story?" Spider raised his eyebrows.

"Um."

"You don't want to tell me, do you?"

"It's not that I don't. . . . I just feel weird telling you. About another guy, I mean."

He moved closer to me. The ocean breeze was cold, and I shivered.

He wasn't smiling anymore. "Why do you feel weird?"

"Because," I said, flushing in the chill. "You know."

"I know what?"

"I don't know. Because of us. I mean, it's not like that with us. I mean, we're just friends, but still I feel weird."

Now he was rubbing my arms. "Want my sweatshirt?"

He didn't wait for an answer before pulling off his hoodie, exposing his tan stomach. I tugged his T-shirt down before the whole thing went over his head, my fingers accidentally touching his skin.

"Here," he said, sliding the sweatshirt over my head.

"Thanks."

He held on to my arms again, this time tucked snugly in his sandy sweatshirt. He bit his lip and then let me go. "Before you run off again, I have something for you." Picking up a small comics-wrapped package from a crack between the rocks, he grinned. "Your birthday present—it wasn't ready before you left. Sorry 'bout that."

"A birthday present? Wait a minute, did you know I'd show up here tonight?"

He smiled shyly. "Well, Bev told me what time your plane would land and I just thought, 'If I've ever known her at all, the first thing she'll do is walk to the cove.'"

I will find you. Maybe Deni and Spider weren't so different after all.

"So open it." Inside, sitting in perfect lotus position, was a tiny clay Buddha holding a flat tray. "It's a candle-holder . . . for your room."

I couldn't believe it. "You made this for me? It's so . . . perfect."

He waved off my compliment, but I could tell he was pleased. "I'm sorry it wasn't ready on your real birthday. I had to wait in line for the kiln, which was totally annoying, and blah, blah, art geek talk."

"I didn't even know you were into sculpting. It's really cool," I said.

"Hmm. Well, maybe you should stick around," he said. "Who knows what else you might find out?"

"You know, I went to an ancient Buddhist temple in Indo. It was so amazing. I took a ton of pictures. There were these stone Buddhas that you could only see through these tiny cutouts in the wall." I held up my fingers in the shape of a diamond to give him a visual. "It was one of my best days there, so this gift is just so . . ."

Apa? I heard Deni's voice in my head, searching for the right word.

"Perfect?" Spider helped me remember.

"Yeah." I nodded.

"I didn't know you were going to a temple." He shrugged. "I just thought you'd like it."

Neither did I.

"It's really sweet. Thank you so much." I held the candleholder to my chest like I was cradling a Buddha baby. "I have something to show you too." I pulled the shell Spider had given me out of my sweatpants pocket. The wind whipped my hair around my face. I was suddenly so hot, and the cool air felt refreshing.

"You still have that?" he asked, surprised.

"Can you believe it? It survived the whole trip—and so did I, so I think you were right on about the luck." I set the sand dollar in his palm and he examined it.

Waves lapped against the cliff. In the distance the lighthouse curled on its slow, translucent rounds. I chewed on the skin next to my nail. *Don't lose it,* I thought. *Just because you're home, don't chicken out. Tell him the truth.* "Hey, Spider?"

He looked at me gently. "Yeah?"

"I'm sorry I was so weird before I left. I'm sorry for a lot of things, but mostly . . . I'm sorry because I didn't let you know me anymore. After my mom died, I should have let you help me."

"That's okay. . . . That was a long time ago."

"No. It . . . That was dumb. I just didn't get how dumb it was until I was in Indo. I was afraid if you knew how scared I was of everything, you wouldn't like me anymore . . . and I just . . . couldn't deal with losing someone else."

"But that's not what I thought at all. I knew you were

scared, and you had every reason to be. If that had been me? I can't even imagine. I thought you were so brave."

"You did?"

He stepped closer. "Yes."

"But then . . . why did you always ignore me?"

"I didn't ignore you. I just gave up . . . trying. And it was stupid. I shouldn't have given up on you. And hanging out with you before you left just reminded me how awesome you are, how I've never known anyone else like you."

"Like me?"

He pulled me into him. "Sea, give me a break. It's always been you."

Spider and me. Spider and Sea.

Then it suddenly dawned on me why we couldn't be us before, why it was so much easier to be with Deni, not just because we shared something, but because he didn't know the old me, what I was like before.

And Spider. Well, he knew it all.

Even the stuff I tried so hard to forget.

In the quiet we both watched the waves. Sneaking looks at each other.

Then finally I whispered to him, "Spider?"

He looked at me. "Yeah?"

"I saw it, you know."

"Saw what?"

"The Orange Popsicle Haze—from the plane window at

dawn and in Indo, except it was more like the Fudge Popsicle Haze over there, the air was so polluted. . . ."

Spider raised his eyebrows. "Told you it was real."

"You made me a believer."

We looked at each other for a second, almost daring the other to chicken out and look away. Neither of us did.

"So I'm going out at dawn, if you'd like to come along," I said nonchalantly.

"Going out *where* at dawn?"

I pointed out at the ocean—the moonlight reflecting on the frothy waves.

"Out? Out surfing? *You're going surfing?*" His eyes narrowed suspiciously. "You didn't surf with that dude in Indo, did you? I'm a mellow guy, but that might piss me off just a little bit."

I laughed. "Deni didn't even know how to swim."

"Really? I thought Indonesians were really into surfing."

"I think that's mostly in Bali. He told me no one swims for recreation up in Aceh. The sea is strictly for fishing and boating." Then I stopped.

Spider's face got all serious. "Someday you'll tell me about it, right?"

"I'll tell you, Spider. But not today. And maybe not even real soon, okay?"

"Okay, but pinky swear you'll tell me?" He held out his tanned pinky finger, so different from Deni's, but the way he was looking at me in the moonlight was the same.

"Pinky swear," I promised as our fingers twisted in the cool ocean air. "So are we on? For tomorrow?" I asked hopefully.

Spider taunted me. "Six thirty?"

I grinned. "What are you, wimpy? Make it six. I'll be up. Jet lag."

He nodded happily. "You're on."

He leaned down, our fingers still twisted in the air.

He whispered in my ear, "Hey, Sea."

"Yeah?"

I turned and he kissed me.

Not once, but twice. Right on the lips.

He tasted like salt. He tasted like the sea.

He pulled me close. "Hey, Spider," I whispered as we pulled apart, our fingers curled together. "It's good to be back."

Back to me.

ACKNOWLEDGMENTS

Writing and revising this book felt like an epic journey. Not as epic as Sienna's but close. I have so many people to thank. First off, I'd like to thank my wonderful agent, Sara Crowe, who fell in love with this story and then found it the perfect home. Thanks for believing in me.

To my incredibly hardworking editor, Stacey Barney, who invited us into her home and then swiftly destroyed us, only to help glue us back together in a much stronger way. Thanks for your dedication.

To the art department at Putnam: you are cover gods.

I believe we are really the accumulation of those we've met along the way. And I've been blessed with truly amazing people in my life. From Santa Cruz to New York to Palo Alto and all the stops in between.

Special thanks goes out to my real-life critique group, Debbie Duncan, Christy Hale, Kirk Glaser, Kevin Kiser, SuAnn Kiser and Cynthia Chin-Lee. My online communities: the 2009 Debutantes and the Tenners. My life-journal friends and readers who've been with me from the very beginning, Jennifer Laughran for jazzing up my query, the Summer of Seven for always listening and making me laugh, the Gothic Girls for puppet mayhem, and the Teen Lit Bloggers for the Waiting on Wednesdays, especially my intern extraordinaire, Mitali Dave.

To the talented alumni of H & D's Children's Theatre who have grown from soulful kids to lovely adults, perhaps you'll see flickers of yourselves on the pages of this book. Thanks for bringing magic into our lives and reminding me how awesome teenagers can be. Hey, now we can bring *Lalaina's Rose* to Broadway.

To my childhood family: my parents, John and Deborah, for instilling an early love of reading, letting me pick out as many books as I wanted from the Scholastic Book Fair and never suggesting I get a "real major." I'm so happy I've made you proud. To my beautiful sisters, Bridget and Gretchen, for being my first and favorite readers.

To Grammy, a fellow writer, who turns ninety June 10, the day this novel is released. We'll celebrate the birthdays together.

To my in-laws, Mark and Ann, for unconditionally loving me and treating me like your daughter from the beginning.

To my creative-writing teachers and colleagues at both UC Santa Cruz and The New School.

To my English and drama teachers, who taught me not all of the school part of high school is boring.

To my early readers who read cold in one sitting, my stepmom Vicki (who is nothing like Vera), Molly and Rica. Thanks for two early enthusiastic thumbs-up.

Special thanks to some of my favorite authors who gave me early advice and encouragement, most notably

Nancy Farmer, John Green, Coe Booth and Laura Ruby. You have left extraordinary footsteps for me to try and follow. Thanks for paying it forward to a newbie like me.

To Rahmat and Sky Lee, for fielding my questions about horse sate and everything else.

To Usuludin, for outriding a tsunami and for sharing your story. Your bravery and your strength breathed life into Deni. *Terima kasih*, my friend.

To my beautiful children. You are the most charming creatures on the planet. You are beloved and make me want to be a better person. I'm sorry Mommy is so "boring typing on the computer." I'm finished! Now we can have a dance party.

And finally, to my incredible husband, Daryn, who is my best friend and my love muffin. Thank you for writing entertaining and heartbreaking journals. For fielding all my questions and for inspiring this story. Thanks for doing your best to make this world a better place for our children and for people everywhere.

And to you. Thank you for reading my book. I hope you liked it.